Mary Ann Poll

America's Lady of Supernatural Thrillers

GORGON

An Alaska Iconoclast Thriller

Since 1978

PO Box 221974 Anchorage, Alaska 99522-1974
books@publicationconsultants.com
www.publicationconsultants.com

ISBN 978-1-59433-419-1
eBook ISBN 978-1-59433-420-7
Library of Congress Catalog Card Number: 2013950639

Manufactured in the United States of America.

Dedication

To John. My best friend and most staunch
supporter. I love you more than I can say.

Acknowledgements

I am grateful to have this opportunity to offer my thanks to those that have helped make *Gorgon* possible.

For the third time, I thank my friends at Kyllonen's RV Park in Anchor Point, Alaska. Specifically, thank you Susan and Chevonne for providing a sanctuary for this writer. *Gorgon* would have not been completed without it.

Dr. Dwayne Poll—your opinion is the one I value most. Thank you for making the time to read an extremely rough draft and see the diamond in the coal. And, thank you for the ideas for the front cover. It worked!

My copyeditor Marthy Johnson. I shiver to think what *Gorgon* would have been without your guidance and direction.

Margaret Mulvehill—my great friend who rearranged her schedule and took care of our three cantankerous canines so I could get to Anchor Point and finish *Gorgon*.

James Keri of the Alaska Native Language Center and Alan Boraas of the Kenai Peninsula College who are the editors of *"A Dena'ina Legacy, K'TL'EGH'I SUKDU, The Collected Writings of Peter Kalifornsky*. Without this complete collection, the rich heritage of Alaska would be missing from the Ingress.

Wikipedia, that amazing online encyclopedia.

The staff of the Eagle River branch of the Anchorage Municipal Library. Their knowledge made it possible to find the reference books I needed without spending my life in the library.

Kayla Hunt—for sharing your insights and talent. You are truly a gem! (www.kaylahuntbooks.com)

Carol Douthat—my talented photographer friend. Our talks over coffee broke the writer's block. Not to mention added the levity I needed to press on with a smile.

Contents

Prologue
Unintentional Consequences

Orange flames danced off chestnut-colored eyes and cast warm hues onto the weathered wood walls of the lodge. An aged man turned to three adolescents who sat cross-legged around the sand pit. "There are those who do not understand. It is said I will bring them knowledge. What is done with this knowledge will determine the fate of our land."

The oldest youth jerked his chin to the elder's right. "Why does this stranger sit beside you at our ceremony?"

The older man narrowed his eyes and bent forward. "Do you question me?"

The child's face paled, and he dropped his head. "I do not."

The leader leaned back. "This man, whose name is Solac, came to our land with the white explorers on the big ships. His boat was destroyed in the big waters. I do not know why, but he lives when he should have died. Since that time, Solac has visited our villages. He is known by all the Denali. I call him my friend." Elder Shan's face broke into a warm smile. "I not only call him friend. He is my brother."

"With respect, father of our village, why has your friend come to us now?"

"He has a message you must hear. Solac came to our land looking for a way to protect his village. He used our land to hide something and told no one. Now the white men who seek our animals and money from their hides are coming here in great numbers. When Solac saw this, he knew the secret could be uncovered and it would destroy us—and them. He came to me for counsel."

Young eyes widened with fear. "Secrets are bad! This man should be put out of our village!"

"You have learned our traditions. I am pleased. Sometimes, we do not share all of our knowledge—a wise man and a leader of a village must know when to remain silent and when to speak. It is a lie if we do not share the truth when asked or when it will cause great harm. Today, my friend will tell the truth. He is about to share a story that will affect those yet to be born. It is a tale that you are not to teach to anyone but the ones who come after you to guard our history. Now you know why I called you here and why I instructed you to be silent after you hear his words. Do you still agree?"

The young man bobbed his head.

"Solac came to me when his heart could no longer bear this heavy burden. What he has done affects all of our peoples—from the great waters of Tikahtnu to Denali."

The oldest boy, the one who acted as their leader, focused on the elder's gentle brown eyes. "We do not understand."

"You will. You are here because you are the ones chosen by our village to keep our people's history."

The young man straightened his back. "I will do my best."

Elder Shan smiled. "I know you will." He looked at the ground and sighed. "In the days when those from the country where the sun sets crossed the sea to our land, in the days before the white man paid for our home, in the days before our land was known as cursed, there was peace here. It was a sanctuary which fed and protected our people."

"I understand."

The kind eyes flashed. "You have no understanding, but you will."

The youth looked at the crackling fire.

"This place we call home continues to provide for us. But you know the trees and grass are no longer abundant in our land because something made the peaceful spirits leave. Our people could not find a reason. Without a cause, we could not find a way to bring the blessings back to our land. Now I know why we will never know peace again—*one* man changed this land."

Young eyes narrowed in a mixture of hate and fear. "How could one man hold so much power?"

"Every man has the power to destroy—every man and every woman. What we do is like throwing a stone in Tikahtnu. It only creates a ripple to our eyes. The ripple causes the tiny fish to be tossed into another place in the Big River where it is no longer safe, and it is eaten." The elder contemplated the yellow flames of the fire. He turned back to his eager audience.

"The story is of a lost jar, a vessel of great envy but not because of its worth for trade or food. It is a jar which causes the spirit to hunger and crave to possess it. What lives inside is so evil, all who freed it were slaughtered. This pot was both a prison and a fortress that could not be destroyed. Many tried and many perished.

"As you know, young ones, I was born to show our people why the land is suffering. Now my work is finished in this world. Your life, from this day forward, is to remember our history until it is your time to pass from this land to the land we cannot see."

"You are not passing. You are not even sick!"

The old man smiled. "I am passing. I have been told to make ready, my grandson."

The youth lowered his head and studied the ginger-colored dirt floor. "The spirits are wrong. You are not sick."

The old man's eyes misted over. He reached for the boy's hand. "It is not our decision, grandson, when we leave this earth. Our time is ordained by the Great One. My time is coming."

The youth nodded.

"I am sorry to interrupt," Solac said. "My time is short."

Elder Shan nodded. "Yes. Please begin."

"I am from the land called Russia. I did not come here to explore, as those I traveled with did. I came to save my village."

"You saved your village and did not think? You ruined ours!" the youth spat at him.

11

"I have. That is why I have come to your grandfather," he nodded to the elder, "and to those he chose to hear my story. Maybe with this knowledge your land can be restored."

"You put the curse on us. You take it off!"

The man lowered his head. "I tried. I cannot."

"Fierce One, let Solac tell his story. It is our way. Then we judge."

"Yes, Grandfather." The young man leaned forward, picked a rock out of the dirt, and carved lines in the packed earth.

"I do not know when this evil was born—if evil *is* born. But I believe it existed before our world. I do not know why I became part of its story, but I remember the day I did."

"How are we to believe you?"

"Why would I lie and risk ending my friendship with your people?"

The young one met the stranger's gaze. "What you say is good. I will listen."

"Then I begin." Solac took a deep breath.

It was midday and our marketplace was full. A ghost came up out of the well in the center of the town. Its limbs hung useless, the lower arms connected to the upper by strings of muscle and bone. Blood streamed from its nose, eyes, and the torn limbs. But this was not the most terrifying part. When it opened its blackened and bloody mouth, it bellowed like a moose calf taken by wolves. All who heard the wail froze in their places.

The ghost said, 'your town is to be destroyed. Listen and take heed so you may be spared. In life, I was a young man from a tiny place north of your precious town. I was known for my bravery and loyalty, and I did not hesitate when asked to do dangerous things to protect my people. When a being not of this world came to destroy my town, I was eager to take on the challenge and vanquish it. This adversary came in a beautiful and unique jar—a rare treasure. All who saw it craved to possess it. This thing trapped us in its beauty and annihilated my village, one man at a time. Only a few of us did not fall under the spell.'

"A strong one. Much like you, my son of my son." The warmth of pride in the old man's voice brought tears to the youth's eyes.

The younger man dropped his head, slapped the tears way, and then straightened his back. "Please continue," he said.

> *The spirit spoke again. It said, 'the people of my town gathered wood and took it to the edge of the ocean many miles away. They even brought chairs and tables from their homes so they could make a fire big enough to be seen from the village. When all was ready, I took the vessel to the ice-cold shores of the water, accompanied only by one other. He would witness the pot's destruction. I lit the towering woodpile and waited for the fire to peak. I threw the golden object into the mighty flames.'*

"If the pot was destroyed why are we here?"

Solac looked the young man in the eye. "I did not say he destroyed it. I said he threw it into the fire. Here is what this spirit said,"

> *'The jar landed in the center of the bonfire. I made my way to the path that led to the village. Hands of red fire with fingers tinged in yellow and palms of blue raced from the bonfire and seized hold of me. It pulled me into the fire and devoured my flesh. The townsfolk did not know this because it swallowed up the witness, too.*

> *'When the fire burned out and the villagers could no longer see its smoke, the leaders came. The jar stood upright in the middle of the ashes, alabaster-white in the bright sunlight. There was no sign of me or the witness—not even a tooth. They took the vessel back to the village. The rage of being thrown in the fire caused the evil spirit to reveal its power. It opened its mouth and sounded a melody none could resist. Even those who had been held clean succumbed to its power. This thing now makes its way to your town. You have been warned!'*

"The ghost left and we never saw it again."

Elder Shan chose a thin piece of spruce from a pile of dry logs, yanked off a smaller limb, and then dropped the wood onto the fire. He drew a small circle on the floor in front of him and then a thin line and a larger circle. The swish of the dirt and the crackle of the fire were the only sounds in the small hut.

"So what happened to the jar?" The lead youth asked.

The stranger sighed. "Here is the tale as I know it."

'The people of my town were vigilant. Months turned into years. The destroyer did not come. Almost everyone decided the ghost was a demon and came to make us afraid.

'One day a small urn was discovered by one of the townspeople when on a hunt. He brought it to the village council. None understood this pot to be the same one the spirit spoke of. We should have known something was wrong when the overseer, usually a generous man, laid sole claim to the urn.

The stranger leaned toward the youth. "You see, this jar creates its own light; it is made of a magical stone. Jewels of red, the color of the berries we gather in the fall, are fused with the jar. I could not see where the stones started and the gems stopped. Sometimes the jewels became the deep blue color of Tikhatnu during a storm. Whoever looked upon it was filled with joy and wonder. The villagers believed it was the Great One and started bringing food and drink to the jar." Solac's eyes took on a far-away look.

As happens to any who make a thing great, the villagers became terrified of losing their most valued possession. The overseer was not a strong warrior and was seen as weak. So a blood fight broke out when my people could not agree on who was strong enough to protect the urn. The fight left many injured and the overseer close to death. The near-death of the beloved leader stopped the battle.

The people went to the jar and prayed for help. When they agreed that each member of the town would keep the vessel one night and the jar would journey this way throughout the town, the jar's jewels glowed bright red, then deep blue. The people believed their god had answered.

All was calm during the first rotation. But as it is with any evil thing, it waits until the time is right to strike. And it struck!

At the second rotation, a healthy young man died. He was found a night later when the urn was to go to another man's home. The arms and legs were stretched out of the joints and as white as the moon. It took a strong man to break his dead fingers and release the jar.

"How could he hold it so and be dead?"

"A question for the shaman," Elder Shan said. He turned to his friend. "Continue."

The town searched the village for one who had been possessed of a demon. They accused an old man of the killing and locked him up. On the same night another died. The townspeople screamed for its leaders to kill the old man. They argued he was a warlock and cast a death-spell from his prison. To keep peace, the innocent one was beheaded.

The slaughter did not stop. My town, which had been so peaceful, was cursed! None wanted to admit the common factor in the carnage was the vessel.

Count Varlaam Alexander, who oversaw many villages in my homeland, was a righteous man of God. When he received news of the magical jar and the troubles which rained down on my village, he told the overseer to bring the vessel to him.

Varlaam studied the jar and decided it was a lost icon of the early church. He seated it in a place of honor behind the altar in his chapel. Count Alexander looked on in astonishment when the thing first vibrated, then wobbled. The alabaster lid transformed into an indigo blue right before it catapulted from the urn. A smoky fog snaked skyward. The mist dissolved, revealing a beautiful woman, clothed only in a gauze robe.

The count put his hands on the altar and shouted, 'What are you?'

The entity said nothing. It lunged at him. When it struck the altar it recoiled as if it had been burned. The beautiful features contorted in pain, and tears flowed from its eyes. 'I am a soul trapped by evil. Please set me free.'

The count stepped closer to the altar. 'How?'

The apparition offered him her hand. 'Take it.'

Varlaam kept his arms at his side.

'Why are you hesitating? Is it not a man's duty to save a soul in need of help? Come.' The woman extended her hand again.

'A human soul! If you are flesh, I will help. In the name of my Christ, I command you to show yourself!'

The entity roared and lunged again. A mummified head snapped through the beautiful woman, then dissolved into an ominous fog.

'You are not human.'

'I was human. Until your God changed me to what you see.'

'Then you are an abomination in His eyes—and mine.'

'It no longer matters what your precious God thinks. He will not stop me from taking everyone in this village. They are mine.'

'They are not.'

'Oh, but they are. They have turned their backs on your God to worship me.'

The count made the sign of the cross and said, 'I have sinned, my God. I ignored these people because in weakness and fear for my own life I did not stand up for Your truth. Forgive me.' He raised his head. 'In the name of the Most High, tell me how I can rid my village of you.'

A blood-eyed skull snapped through and back into the gray vapor. The mist darkened, spiraled into an angry tornado, and twirled in place above the jar. 'I demand a willing sacrifice. Then I might leave your province, church dweller.'

Varlaam Alexander sighed and lifted his head. 'First, you must promise to return to your jar so I can remove you and it from this house of God.'

The air around the tornado snapped and popped, then went silent. 'Agreed.'

The fog condensed until it was a small black cylinder. The jar's lid flew to the side and hung midair. The vapor disappeared into the elaborate jar.

The count studied the urn as he tried to make sense of the vision he had witnessed. He shook himself. 'Nicholas, come.'

A sleepy-eyed adolescent appeared at the top of the chapel's rough-hewn stairs. 'Count Alexander? Why are you here at so late an hour?'

'Evil has entered this house of God. Stand watch and do not go near that,' Varlaam pointed at the jar, 'no matter what it begins to do.' The count rushed to the back of the church and out into the night.

Nicholas turned his attention to the pot. 'What is wrong with him? This is just a pot.' The jar rattled, levitated, and dropped back to the table. Eyes wide, Nicholas nodded and whispered, 'Yes, sir. I won't take my eyes from it!'

Nicholas jumped when Count Alexander burst through the heavy chapel door. The count held the golden belt of the priest, used only in the most holy days of the church year. He bound the jar in the glittering fabric.

'Father God, protect your servant Nicholas and me, a sinful man.' He turned to the youth. 'Gather four bibles, and follow me.'

Nicholas stepped toward the door behind the altar and stopped. He did not take his eyes off the jar.

'Now, Nicholas!'

Nicholas jumped and skittered toward the vestibule.

Varlaam nodded when he saw the bibles. He took hold of a candle snuffer, looped it through the gold binding, and hoisted the snuffer high into the air. 'Get behind me.' The count barked at Nicholas.

The tiny procession stepped onto an eerily silent street. The vessel swayed side to side in rhythm with the count's footsteps. Its deep red jewels turned a blood-red in the light of the full moon.

As they left the town behind, the forest rose up and closed in around them. Even the night animals were silent—just as if a predator was stalking them. The light thud of their footsteps resonated in the silence.

Count Alexander hesitated at the town's boundary—a dilapidated wood and rope bridge. He started forward. The gentle tumble of the stream grew into an angry roar. Frigid water pounded the bottom of the weak overpass and sprayed Nicholas and Varlaam. The howl of the water increased with each footfall and made it impossible to speak in a normal tone. Nicholas covered one ear for respite from the screaming waters.

The count looked over his shoulder and yelled, 'Faster, Nicholas. We must get across before the bridge gives way.'

Nicholas nodded and broke into a trot. The bridge swayed side to side and threatened to send the men into the stream's frigid water. Varlaam slipped and tumbled toward the rope rail. He threw out his free hand, took hold of a wood post, and pushed himself back to his feet. Once on the other side, Count Alexander stopped and looked at the stream. A soothing gurgle and trickles of water belied the raging river it had been moments before.

They trudged deeper into the forest just as dawn broke through the dark night. The sun was low in the sky by the time they came to a jagged opening to a mountain cave. 'Here is where we stop.'

'Why are we here?' Nicholas's voice shook with fear. 'It is cursed!'

'Where better? It is the one place no one dares enter. Here I can make the sacrifice I have promised to this creature so it will leave your town in peace.'

Nicholas turned frightened eyes to the count.

The count smiled and patted the young man's arm. 'No, no, young one. Not you. I will go in by myself. Guard the entrance. If I do not return, do not come to find me. Whatever happens, it will be God's will. If I do not survive, you must return to the village and tell the story.'

'I will not let you face the devil by yourself.'

'I am not alone. God is with me. Put the bibles under my arm.' Alexander crooked his elbow and Nicholas placed them where he was told. The count disappeared into the cave.

A shaky breath escaped Solac's lips. He lifted stone-gray eyes to Elder Shan.

"Why have you stopped?" the youth leader demanded.

"Because the next part of this story came to young Nicholas in a vision. It has been treated as the ravings of a crazy man. Since no one can refute it, I feel obligated to tell you. It may help you understand why your land is cursed. Here is what Nicholas said,"

After the count entered the cave of curses, he set the jar on a ledge surrounded by pointed rocks growing down from cavern's roof. The drips from each dagger-shaped outcropping echoed several times when they snapped to the floor. I could smell the water and mud. Alexander placed a bible in front, behind, and to each side of the jar. He left the golden belt in place. Then he prayed.

'As Your Son once prayed, O God, I pray You take this cup from me. But if You will not, then take me home to be with You and Jesus when I am spent. Your will, not mine be done.' His back to the jar, Varlaam knelt, closed his eyes, and waited. He was so deep in prayer he did not hear the jar vibrate. He didn't see the inky-blue light it emitted. He did not witness the golden

belt burst into flames and dissolve, or the rock on which the jar rested quake just enough for the bibles to slide to the floor. No, he didn't see or hear any of this.

The lid separated from its base. The black mist snaked out of the vessel and enveloped the count. By God's mercy I don't think he felt the pain of death. But he might have heard the words of the spirit before he fell unconscious. 'Foolish, foolish being,' the thing gurgled as it swallowed the last of Count Alexander's life-blood. Then it opened its mouth and sang a seductive melody.

The vision faded when Nicholas heard the melody. He thought the count was calling for help. He ran toward the cave, but a large earthquake knocked him to the ground. When the quake passed, boulders and rocks covered the entrance. He banged the blockage with his fists. 'Count Alexander!' Nicholas screamed. He scurried up the rocks wedged in the cave's doorway and spotted a small hole. He threw himself flat against the hard earth and squinted into the darkness. The mutilated and lifeless body of Count Alexander was directly beneath him. Nicholas watched a trail of ebony mist slither into the urn before he ran for town.

Some of the townspeople followed Nicholas to the site and climbed the small hill. They confirmed the count's death to the rest of the town. It was reported to the authorities of the land the count had died in a cave-in during an earthquake.

Saloc shook his head. "This is where most think the story ended. But like all who have an insatiable craving, the people of the town longed for the jar's return. Many said it was calling to them. Some of the town's men made a plan to clear the rockslide and retrieve the urn.

"If several God-fearing men in town had not come together to pray for God to intervene, I believe the jar would have been recovered and the village destroyed. These brave souls agreed the vessel would be taken to an uninhabited place so that none could be tempted by this destruction again. But this is my opinion. I will let the story speak for itself."

On a moonless night, this small band of brave men, which included young Nicholas, set out for the cave. Along the way they talked about the murders. Somehow, they realized the killings happened only in darkness and this thing hated light. They timed the removal of the last rocks in the daylight hours. Light flooded the cave.

Nicholas hurried to the jar and slid the Holy Bible under its base. He wrapped both in a burlap sack, stuffed them into a chest, and slammed the top. 'I will take this evil thing far away from our land,' he said. 'I will travel across the great water to a place where no people live and bury it there.'

Nicolas's hatred of the spirit kept him to his word. When he heard of the Russians' exploration of the ocean we now know is between Russia and your land, Nicholas made his way to a place called Okhotsk. The explorers' ships set sail from there. Like many from my land, Nicholas believed the unexplored lands were only inhabited by animals. He found favor with a man named Waxell, who was second only to the great explorer Bering on the ship named the St. Peter. Waxell made the way for young Nicholas to join the crew.

Two ships, the St. Paul and the St. Peter, sailed from Russia in the summer of the year my people call 1741. Because these vessels were named after the great leaders of his faith, Nicholas saw this as a sign from God.

The ships traveled many days and then were separated. The one he was on, St. Peter, was alone for many more days without sighting land. The captain decided to head back to Russia. The many months at sea had taken its toll. The crew was falling ill; some had already died.

When Nicholas received word they were returning to Russia, terror gripped his heart. He had not disposed of the urn. Now, it would be returning to his land. Visions of Count Alexander's mangled body assaulted his mind.

'Better I die then return this abomination to my home.' Nicholas snagged a rope, tied the box around his waist, and prepared to jump overboard.

He made his way to the bow of the St Peter. He picked up the pace when he saw several explorers heading toward him. He caught enough bits and pieces of the conversation to realize they were planning for an excursion.

'How can you go on a trip to explore in the water?' Nicholas asked.

'Where've you been? Sighted land hours ago.' They laughed at the young ship hand.

New hope filled Nicholas. He quickly formulated a plan. 'I've always wanted to explore. Is there any way I could come too?'

The explorer called Afon said, 'Now, why would we bring a scruffy kid? You'd be a rock around our necks.'

Nicholas straightened his back and looked the older man in the eye. 'I have been on this ship for months. I am strong. I can help carry your bags and instruments. You will have more strength to explore if I do this.'

Afon grinned. 'You have courage.'

'I just want to see the world, too.'

'This isn't a party, scruff. It's dangerous. You could get eaten. Even worse, you could fall off a cliff and not be found. You would die a slow and painful death from hunger and thirst.'

'Doesn't scare me.'

Afon focused on Nicholas for the first time. 'I'll talk to the others.'

A thin smile touched Nicholas's mouth. He stood straight as an arrow while they explorers talked among themselves.

'Well, it wasn't easy, but they agreed. If you didn't remind me so much of myself at your age, I wouldn't have argued for you. Don't let me down,' Afon said.

'God willing, I won't.'

'Then it is settled. Be here before daybreak. We won't wait.'

Nicholas made his bed by the explorers' rowboat. For the first time since he sailed from Russia, he slept. His eyes popped open at the sound of footsteps heading to the small boat.

'Hey, we have a rat—someone get the hook!' one of the explorers barked.

Nicholas skittered to the corner, hugging the chest.

Afon lowered the hook and let out a sharp laugh. 'Wait, it's just the scruff who wants to be an explorer. Must have slept in the boat all night so he didn't get left.' Afon jerked his chin at Nicholas. 'Make yourself useful, and let's get this boat to the water.'

When the boat reached shore, Nicholas jumped out and almost dragged it to the sand single-handed. He helped the other men bring their supplies to the island. While they readied for the exploration, he excused himself, citing a need for privacy.

He hurried into the woods, believing he would come upon the right place to conceal the cursed burden and be back with the explorers before they missed him. But Nicholas wandered too far looking for the perfect hiding spot. He lost track of the time. When he reached a meadow, the angle of the sun made his heart jump. He looked around; nothing was familiar. The sounds of screeching birds and chattering squirrels were all he could hear. Even those sounds weren't familiar.

'What am I to do?' Nicholas plopped down under a large spruce, opened the box, and stared at the jar. It began to glow. The deep indigo-blue made him forget where he was. He only wanted to stare at the color—forever. He slammed the lid.

Leaves rustled to his left. His eyes flew to a stand of trees. A man leapt from behind some alders. For the second time in a day, Nicholas felt like a trapped animal and skittered backward. A dark-skinned man walked forward, spear held up toward the sky.

'Please don't hurt me,' Nicholas squeaked.

The Native stopped and tilted his head to the left. He ran forward. Terror seized Nicholas, and he fainted.

When he awoke, Nicholas was in an earthen hut, lying several feet from a crackling fire under an animal skin. Several strange men sat at the door. Nicholas sprang to his feet. His eyes darted around the room until they came to rest on the wooden box, still beside him. He crumpled to the floor.

You see, Nicholas had fainted from illness more than fear. The scurvy was going through the ship, and it caught up with him. Those Natives took him from Kad'yak and to their home to heal him. He did gain enough strength to eat and live among the people.

As you can imagine, they could not talk to each other—he speaking Russian. He began drawing pictures. They responded to him, eyes sparkling with humor at his attempts to talk very loud while drawing. Somehow, though, they taught him some of their words. They became his friends. None asked Nicholas about the box. They accepted it as his prize because they were an honest people.

Nicholas insisted on participating in the next hunt. His new friends shook their heads at his stubbornness. You see, he breathed hard when he walked through the forest by the village. They knew he was not strong enough to hunt and told him no. He begged them until they agreed.

On the way to the hunting grounds, his friends told Nicholas of their legends. Nicholas was at peace listening to their tales while walking through the deep forests and beside the Big Water. He almost forgot the box. He was happy for the first time in years.

But then his friends told him the legend of a cursed place. When they passed a dark, treed gully he was told, 'do not go in there.'

'Why?'

'It is cursed. It belongs to the evil ones. Do not go in there or you will become one of them.'

'I will not go in,' he answered. His heart leapt. 'This is the place!'

he thought. 'It is already cursed. No one will come near, and this thing will not harm anyone else.'

Nicholas sneaked back to the cavern. He kept to his word and did not go in. At the head of the ravine, he found what he had been searching for—a mammoth tree stood partially hidden by saplings and brush. It had a split in its center the size of the jar. He yanked the box open, shoved the jar through the hollow, and stuffed dead leaves and sticks into the opening.

'In the name of Jesus may this tree become a prison for the evil spirit in this jar. Thank you God for bringing me here. Thank you.' Nicholas made the sign of the cross, turned, and ran from the tree. The creak of wood brought him to a stop. He looked back.

His eyes grew wide. The leaves and sticks snaked together and formed tight bars over the hole. The tree shook. Its leaves withered and died until the only thing left was a gnarled trunk with a topknot of green. Nicholas witnessed the shriek of rage when the being realized it could not leave its prison. But he did not hear the curse the spirit yelled at him. Nor did he hear the response and the curse issued by a demon high in the command of Satan. One who had claimed this gorge as his home and whose home had been vandalized. The scurvy returned, and Nicholas died a few feet from the ravine.

"This tree stands at the entrance to a gorge close to Tikhatnu. It is the ravine you know as cursed."

"You have done a horrible thing by not telling my grandfather and his people sooner. But if the place was already cursed, why do you tell us now? The people will not go near it. I know this place and the taboo, and I am young. What is done is done."

"The story is not quite over."

"How could it get any worse?"

"The people of Nicholas's village were enraged when they discovered their beloved object had been taken away. Most of the townspeople listened to the men of God and, although angry, accepted the truth and reasoning for the vessel's disappearance. It should have ended there. It did not.

"Some of them still burned with the hunger the evil spirit had put in them. A group of these men made it their life's work to find the urn. Several set out to the south. They created a story to tell to other villages as they traveled—a priceless religious object had been stolen and they wanted it returned. This enlisted many to help them by spreading the word of a priceless object that, if found, would make any who owned it rich.

"When the Russians explored your land, this story came with them. The explorers from the *St. Peter* knew of it. I believe they were looking for this thing and all the while it was under their noses with a young deckhand.

"So I tell you this story as a warning. This evil waits for someone to set it free. Its hatred has festered and grown stronger over the years. It has grown jealous of the demons it hears playing around it and flying between the physical and invisible realms, taking souls and bodies it hungers to have. As evil can and does, it is waiting. It became a part of a tree guarding the entrance to the inconsequential, by human understanding, piece of land you call cursed. Its rage and hunger grow daily. God help anyone who releases it.

"My story is done. Again, forgive me. May God have mercy on us all." Solac stood up.

"Wait! How do you know this, and why should my people believe you?"

"I am Nicholas. I am the one who brought this curse to your land." The man called Solac dissolved into a white mist and vanished.

Chapter 1
A Cry For Help

Kat Tovslosky squinted into the bright sunshine outside the windows of Jo's Bakery. She smiled when she saw the crowd of strangers on Main Street. Some were window shopping; others had settled on benches outside the Ravens Cove Library to take in the late-summer warmth. "It continues to be a record breaking visitor season."

"Hmmm." Bart Andersen's eyes never left the 8½-by-11 sheet of paper in front of him.

"So, tell me how it feels." Kat cupped her cheeks in her hands and looked expectantly at her cousin.

"How what feels?" Bart asked.

"How does it feel to be called Mayor Anderson?"

"I liked police chief or sheriff better."

"I know. Too much desk and council time, huh?"

"The paperwork is tedious. More, I would rather Tommy Orthell still be among the living."

Kat dropped her eyes and studied the light chocolate liquid in her cup. She shivered at the memory of Mayor Orthell's corpse. Purple and black oozed from his eye sockets. She recalled the torn throat and empty, bloody hole in his chest. Kat willed herself to the present.

"It wasn't your fault," she whispered.

"My head says it wasn't; my heart says it was."

"You didn't call down the demon Iconoclast and his legion. Nor did you create the Kumrande. Those cloven-footed, yellow-eyed

29

monsters are the ones who killed…" Kat's phone vibrated then began playing her favorite tune—Pacabel's "Canon in D." Kat pointed at Bart. "Don't go anywhere. I'm not finished. Hello!"

The late-afternoon light glinted off Kat's emerald-green eyes, turning them the color of spring birch leaves. "I'll be there as soon as I can."

"Be where?" Bart asked.

Kat put her cell phone on the table. "Well, I'm going to Anchorage."

"Why the sudden need to visit the big city?"

Kat chewed her bottom lip and took a deep breath. "You remember Mandy Thomas?"

Bart's head popped up, and his eyes narrowed. "How could I forget?"

Kat grimaced. "Stupid question. Anyway, seems she's gotten herself into a bit of trouble."

"I'm not surprised. The shocker is you think it's your job to get her out of whatever mess she's gotten into this time." Bart dropped his eyes back to the meeting notes.

"I know. But she doesn't have anyone up there. She sounded so hopeless." Kat stared into the light-brown liquid as if it were tea leaves, looking for an easy way to say what came next. "She wants to come back to the Cove."

Bart's head shot up. "Oh, that is not what I want to hear. I do not need her kind of trouble here!"

"You mean you don't want her causing a problem for you with Nyna Raeson, right?" Kat leaned forward and searched Bart's eyes. "You don't have feelings for Mandy—do you?"

"No! It's her need to make trouble. She can be outright vicious."

"True." Kat remembered Mandy telling the schoolkids her dad owned a ranch in Montana. When little Joe Kiln said she was a liar, Mandy told the teacher he had hit her. Little Joe ended up with swats from the principal and a few days at home. Years later, Mandy admitted it had all been a big fib and laughed at how gullible the teacher had been.

"So why are you going to help her?"

"She's implicated in a murder."

Bart buried his forehead in his heads. "Good Lord, if she didn't have bad luck she'd have none at all."

"I want to help her."

"I know how close you two were, but she turned from mischievous to bad somewhere along the line. I don't like you going into her territory by yourself."

"Why? Do you think the charges are true?"

"I don't know."

"I can't believe she's turned from a rebellious kid into a killer."

"Anyone is capable of murder in the right circumstance."

"She needs help. She's one of us!"

"She *was* one of us. She left."

"So do a lot of people. They're still from Ravens Cove."

"This is different."

"Why?"

"You could be walking into major trouble—even danger."

"When are you going to let go of this overprotective thing you've had since we were babies?"

"Never." Bart's wide-toothed grin made Kat giggle.

"Seriously. Anchorage isn't but four hours from here. I can call if I need help. I've made the trip many times—by myself I might add."

"I'd feel better if Melbourne was still here—and going with you."

"He's not. I wish he were." The pain of loneliness descended like a black cloud. Kat flashed Bart a wistful smile.

"When's he back from LA?"

"He's there 'indefinitely' is all I can get out of him. Seems Chief Binnings is trying to get Ken's head back into the Bureau and thinks LA is just what the doctor ordered."

"How does Ken feel?"

"When I can get him to talk about it, he's none too pleased. Seems he likes Alaska more than he knew."

"Seems he found what he was looking for in Alaska—specifically in Ravens Cove." Bart toasted Kat with his white ceramic coffee cup.

"Well, not enough to take the position of police chief in the Cove," Kat whispered.

"You know there's more to it. He'd have to leave the FBI, and it has been his life. He needs time to make a decision. The job's open if he wants it."

"How long are you going to be able to fill both roles?"

"As long as our little town stays little—and quiet."

Nyna strode to the table, placed her hand on Bart's muscular shoulder, and squeezed. "Why so glum?"

"Double duty is beginning to cut into my personal life." Bart slid to the chair by the window.

"You bet it is. It's a good thing I'm an independent, not to mention patient, person."

Nyna didn't miss the eye contact and silent exchange between the two cousins. "What'd I miss?"

Bart sighed. "Guess I'd better let you know before you find out from someone else." He turned to Nyna. "There's this—I think—You see—"

Kat threw her hands in the air and let them fall to the table. "I've got this one, cous." She leaned across the table. "What Bart wants to tell you is I'm going to Anchorage."

Nyna sat down. "Not so bad."

"And I'm going to bring Mandy Thomas back to Ravens Cove."

Nyna moved away from Bart. "Not so good."

Bart took hold of Nyna's slender hand and pulled it to his mouth. "You know it's over, Nyna."

"But does *she* know it?" Nyna's smiling lips drooped into a pout.

"We haven't spoken in years. And it doesn't matter what she thinks." Bart pulled Nyna to him and kissed her cheek. "Like it or not, you're stuck with this big ole lug." He squeezed her hand and let go.

"Can't you see he's head-over-heels for you? Besides, Mandy never stays in one place too long. She's a gypsy."

Nyna smiled. "True. And I'm a fighter." She turned to Bart. "Just try to go back to her."

"Not in a million years."

Nyna planted a light kiss on Bart's cheek and turned to Kat. "When's Ken coming back?"

"Don't know." Kat looked at the wallclock behind Jo's deli counter. "Oh, shoot! I need to get home, feed BC, and give Ken a call before it gets any later."

Kat breezed out the door of Jo's Bakery and zigzagged her way through the crowd. She stopped at a window lined with vintage jewelry, Kat tugged on the shop's teal-blue door.

"Hello. Welcome to The Bell Jar." A slender, forty-something woman came out from behind a glass kiosk filled with gold rings. Diamonds, rubies, and emeralds glinted from their settings. Perfume bottles in a rainbow of colors flanked the trinkets. A bone china vase was centered amongst the jewels and bottles. The cabinet lights bathed the paper-thin glass in a warm glow.

"Hi, I'm Kat Tovslosky. Just thought I'd stop in and welcome you to Ravens Cove."

"Thanks. This is a friendly town. I'm Annie Scofland." She held out a delicate white hand to Kat. Kat took it and returned the firm handshake.

A sharp bark and the tick-tick of nails on hardwood announced the arrival of a medium-sized brown and white dog. It stopped at Annie's left leg and stared at Kat.

"Who's this?" Kat asked.

"Don't know. She showed up today and insisted on being my bodyguard." Annie chuckled. "Didn't know I needed one in this place."

"She's a beauty." The little dog wagged its full tail and yipped.

"She acts like she understands every word."

"I think she might. A bright one for sure."

"So how's business?"

"Well, not much local business to speak of, but the tourists sure like the shop. So, I'd say good."

Kat looked at the old milk cans and a wagon wheel perched on low shelves along one wall. An early 1900s Singer sewing machine, complete with dark oak cabinet, was centered below. Kat walked over to the glass kiosk and pointed at an alabaster chest embellished with cranberry-colored jewels.

"Those jewels look like they are part of the stone—like someone fused them." Kat concentrated on the gemstones. They shimmered and deepened into a rich indigo. *How beautiful!* Kat closed her eyes. When she looked at the box again, the jewels were red. "Did you see..."

Annie pointed at Kat's finger. "What an amazing ring. Looks to be at least 100 years old. May I take a closer look?"

"Sure." Kat held out her hand.

Annie caught hold of the eyeglasses dangling from a royal blue chord on her neck. She took Kat's left ring finger and moved it back and forth. The small diamond glinted with each movement.

"Very nice."

"Thanks. It was my grandmother's and her mother's before her."

"Are congratulations in order, or are you wearing it for the beautiful piece it is?"

"I am engaged."

Annie concentrated on the ring. "Not to be rude, but if you ever want to sell it, I'd be interested." She raised her eyes to Kat's.

"It's been in the family a while, and it will stay in the family."

Annie's face lit in a quick, warm smile. "Always a saleswoman."

"Understand."

"Bring him by and introduce him. Maybe there's something in the shop you'd both like."

"I'll tell him when he gets back to town." Kat looked at her watch. "Gotta run. Nice meeting you."

Kat checked the time again. *Oh, man, it's late. Sorry, BC, you'll just have to wait.* Kat jogged up the street to the police station. The old brass bell chimed her entrance. She hurried to the desk she occupied part-time as the sheriff's secretary—when there was a sheriff. *Police chief.* She reminded herself. *There are no sheriffs in Southcentral Alaska—or anywhere else in Alaska.*

"I'll miss Bart's title," she mused aloud. Bart Andersen had always been called sheriff by the townspeople. The title fit both him and the small town that so reminded Kat of the Old West in the Lower 48. Kat sighed and slid into her chair. She picked up the phone.

"Hey beautiful." The warm tone of Ken Melbourne's voice caressed Kat's lonely core.

"I miss you so much."

"I miss you, too."

"Do you know when you're coming back?"

"Still don't."

"Well, I got an offer to buy my ring today."

"Saying you want to break up?"

"No. Just saying I'm not sure we'll ever get to a wedding at this rate. You're never here long enough."

"You know I have to do this right now, Kat."

"I don't. But I believe you think you do."

"I've got a phone conference with Binnings tomorrow. I'll see if I can pin him down on a return time."

Kat shook her head. *I've heard this before, and nothing has changed.*

"Hey, are you there?"

I'm here. I guess I can't ask for much more." Kat forced her tone to be warm and hopeful.

"I promise I won't be here forever. You may not believe it, but I don't enjoy being apart.

"I know," Kat whispered.

"I'll call with an update tomorrow."

"Tomorrow then… oh, I forgot. I'm leaving for Anchorage so I'll call you."

"Another grocery run?"

"No. Longtime friend is in some trouble."

"What kind?"

"Not sure." Kat grimaced at telling the small fib.

"Call me as soon as you find out."

Kat took a deep breath. "Between you and Bart a woman could come to believe she is totally incapable of living life. This is a friend, not an evil entity. Life before Iconoclast was normal. I'm going to venture a guess here and say it's normal again."

Ken chuckled. "Maybe. Still, call me when you get there. I might be able to help."

"Will do. I love you." Kat pushed the call-release button and held the phone in her hand just a bit longer—she hadn't told Ken how much she missed his touch and how lonely she was. She reached for the keypad then placed the phone in the cradle.

"Get a grip, lovesick girl." She wrote a quick note to Bart saying she'd reimburse the city for the personal call.

Kat stepped towards the door, completely unaware of the ebony vapor rising up through the floor boards. It came to full height and cast a deep shadow over the doorway to the jail cell. A threatening smile formed on the featureless mist and revealed razor-sharp teeth. A thin, translucent arm raced out of the fog and through her torso.

Icy chills coursed through Kat's body. She shivered. "Guess I'm more concerned about this trip to Anchorage than I thought."She yanked the door open and stepped onto Main. She pulled the cell phone from her fleece jacket and dialed.

"What's up, KittyKat?"

"Mandy Thomas called. I'm going to Anchorage. Can you take care of BC?"

"There's a name I haven't heard for a while. She in trouble again?" There was no mistaking the accusatory tone in Wendy Hareling's voice.

"Seems so."

"Glad she called you instead of me. I'll take BC. Just don't be upset if he's with Doc Douglas when you get back. He is not the friendliest animal."

"Just be nice to him, and he'll be nice to you."

"Right. When you leaving?"

"Depends."

"On…?"

"Can I borrow your car, too? I'm afraid Bart's old truck might end up broken down between here and somewhere I can't get cell service." The question hung unanswered for what felt like an eternity.

"When are you going to get a car of your own? Don't you get tired of asking for a car or hitching a ride with someone?"

"As a matter of fact, I do," Kat said. "As soon as I have the cash, I'll beeline it to a car dealer. Until then, I really need to borrow your car."

"Alright. But only because you are my best friend in the world— and on one condition."

"Which is... ?"

"You'll have it back no later than one week from today."

"I don't know what I'm going to run into."

"Well, I know Mandy. She'll keep you there as long as she can if it suits her."

"You're right. Deal. Going home to pack."

———◆◆◆———

Kat drove through the cobalt-blue light of Southcentral Alaska's summer twilight. "I never tire of this," she whispered as she marveled at the high mountains and green trees lining the highway. She stopped at the Kenai River and let her eyes drink in the aqua-colored water rushing to its destination—the Cook Inlet. Dedicated fishermen and at least one fisherwoman dotted the banks of the river. *A true Kodak moment.* Kat smiled and turned back to the car.

She stopped again at Turnagain Pass and took a deep breath. The crisp mountain air refreshed her. The late-evening peace of the pass relaxed her. *On to the big city.* She felt a pang of excitement laced with anxiety.

The traffic and noise affronted her senses and sent her nervous system into high alert. Although she loved this city, she did not enjoy the fast-moving traffic. A semi whizzed past, shaking the small Subaru. Kat gripped the wheel until her knuckles screamed in protest. "I'll be home in a week, I promise you, Wendy. A twenty-something driver in a low-rider whipped in front of her, forcing her to hit the brakes, and almost caused a pileup on the New Seward Highway. He whisked onto the off-ramp. "Maybe sooner than a week."

Kat exited and stopped at an open-all-night *Denny's.* Other than a group of teenagers who sat is a horseshoe-shaped booth sharing a plate of french-fries, the place was empty. Kat lowered herself into a small booth.

"Welcome to Denny's. What can I get you?" A perky waitress with royal-blue hair grinned down at her. Kat ordered a cup of coffee and pulled out her cell phone. "I'm here. Where are you?"

"At my shop."

"At three in the morning?"

"Been having a visit with Mr. Anchorage policeman. Just finished up at their station, and thought I'd try to unwind a bit."

"You *are* under suspicion for something?"

"Told you I was. A guy's missing and, for some reason, I'm the prime suspect."

Kat thought, *Bart's right. If you didn't have bad luck you'd have none at all, Mandy my friend.* "How do I get there?" Kat scribbled the directions on a napkin. "I'll be at your shop in thirty minutes."

Kat paid and headed west. She pulled into a seedy-looking strip mall and stopped in front of a blinking red sign announcing, "Massage, anytime day or night."

"This can't be right." Kat picked up the napkin and squinted at her scribbles. She looked up and locked eyes with a petite woman glaring at her through the massage parlor's window. "Sorry," Kat mouthed, let her foot of the brake and inched forward.

She stopped at a door wedged into the corner of the mall when she saw Mandy waving from behind the glass. Mandy unlocked the door when Kat got out of the car. She ran to Kat and dragged her into a bear hug. "Thanks for coming. I don't know what I'd have done if you hadn't."

Kat pulled herself free and placed her hands on Mandy's shoulders. "Tell me the whole story."

"I'd rather show you. Come on." Mandy grasped Kat's elbow and hurried her through the shop. Old, tattered clothing and swirls of red, green, and black on a dark-blue background swished by. She had a chance to see a moose's black outline against a large full moon in the middle of the multi-colored quilt. She turned her head. A bent wood chair, then a tattered maroon recliner soared by on the opposite side of the room.

Kat planted her feet. "What exactly is your business?"

"I run a secondhand shop."

"Really?"

"It's been very lucrative."

"Really?" Kat said again.

Mandy nodded and leaned into a silver bar on an off-white steel door. "My car's out here." She held the door open and motioned Kat into a small alley. Opaque ribbons of fog swirled around Kat like a macabre dance partner. A sharp wind slapped her face and brought with it the smell of rain.

"Should have worn something a bit warmer," Kat said as she zipped her lightweight slicker. Today promised to be a day when nature was going to let people know Alaska was never to be suspected of being tame.

The building moaned when a gust assaulted the weathered boards in its eaves. Kat jogged to Mandy's rust-pocked red Honda Civic. "Same car?"

"The body will disintegrate before the engine fails. Love a Honda." The engine ground to life. Mandy wheeled onto the four-lane road and headed south. She made a quick left onto a smaller thorough-fare and a right onto a one-lane street. Older houses gave way to a picturesque park and then to newer, larger homes sitting in a circle of their own. The Cook Inlet and Mount Susitna were in their full glory from this location.

"Wow. I never knew Anchorage had these kinds of homes."

"It didn't have many until recently; there seems to be a boom occurring. Housing is going up in places I never knew existed."

The red Civic came to rest in front of a storm-gray, two-story home. A milk-white porch flanked the house on three sides. A complementary trim of snow-white glistened from the roof, giving the house a pristine but cold persona.

Kat arched her left eyebrow. "And we are here...why?"

"This is where the missing guy lives. I thought you could take a look. Maybe you can find something to get me off the hook."

Kat spun on her heel and jogged down the porch steps. "For the love of Pete, we're trespassing! You not only make yourself look guilty by coming here. Now, you're implicating me in this mess!"

Kat swung around, threw her hands in the air, and slapped them to her side. "Give me one good reason why I shouldn't go back to

Ravens Cove *right now* and leave you high and dry?" The temperature had dropped. Small puffs of smoke emphasized Kat's words. She threw up her hood and strode to the car.

"Because I'm innocent!" Mandy yelled after her.

"Not good enough."

Mandy trotted up to Kat and took her arm. "I saw something the night he disappeared, and the police can't confirm it. That's why I need you to take a look."

"Tell me what you saw and where."

Mandy pointed at the house. "It was here. I was visiting this guy."

"What's this guy's name? Why were you visiting him, and what did you see?"

"A little at a time, okay? Let's get out of the cold." Mandy rounded the car and disappeared into the driver's side.

The engine roared to life. Kat dropped into the passenger seat just as Mandy flipped the heater's fan to *high*. Kat leaned into the warmth. "So…?"

"His name is Grady Spawldine. He's my, um, accountant."

"So, why were you at his home? Doesn't he have an office?"

"Well, it's complicated."

Kat turned and faced Mandy. Emerald-green eyes fixed on Mandy's amber ones. "If you want my help, stop with the games, and come to the point. Tell me the truth. I'll tell you if I'll help."

Mandy thought for a moment and sighed. "Well, we were friends, too."

"Like 'let's play cards on Friday night' friends?"

"Not exactly."

Kat's frustration hit the boiling point. "I'm done here! Take me back to my car—*now!*"

"Okay! Okay! He and I had an, umm, arrangement."

"Go on."

"Well, he set me up in business and paid for a place to live. I kept him company when he needed it."

Kat's eyes grew wide as the weight of Mandy's words sank in. *"YOU'RE HIS MISTRESS?"*

"More like a reciprocal relationship that met both of our needs."

"Oh, Mandy. What were you thinking? You could have come home and never had to go through the humiliation—or any of this."

Mandy concentrated on the stormy waves of the Inlet. "I have never wanted anything more in my life than to be a success and not have to depend on other people. After the fallout with Bart, I didn't know what else to do but run, make a life far, far away and never look back."

"You didn't get very far, my friend."

"I know. I was headed for the Lower 48, but I needed to make some money. I took a job as a waitress where Grady was a regular. One thing led to another."

Kat turned and faced the expanse of the Cook Inlet. She stared at the angry water and mulled over her loyalty to her town and those in it she considered family—blood or not. She considered what she would have done if the tables were turned. "I'll help you."

Mandy threw herself across the center console and yanked Kat into a suffocating hug. "Thank you so much."

Kat pulled her arms free and held Mandy at arm's length. "I *will* help you but there are a few conditions."

Mandy flopped back into her seat and stared straight ahead. "What conditions?"

"First, you will promise never again be a man's mistress. You are worth far more."

"Yeah—whatever."

"I mean it!"

"Alright. Alright. What else?"

"You will *not* lie to the police."

"They'll think I did it! I can't—"

"You will *not* lie, no matter what you think they think."

Mandy's eyes narrowed. "Anything else, Miss High and Mighty?"

"As a matter of fact, there is. When this is over, you will return to Ravens Cove. At least for three months. You will find a job. You still have your cabin?"

"Yes."

"Good. You have a place to live. Last thing."

"What?"

"You will stay away from Bart."

Mandy stiffened and turned toward Kat. "Bart can make his own decisions."

"Usually. I'm going to help him here. You devastated him when you left the Cove. I thought he'd never recover. He's found himself a new love interest. He's happy. I don't want you showing up and ruining a good thing."

"I'll try to leave him alone."

"Not good enough. I'll find my own way back to my car." Kat grabbed the door handle and gave it a push.

"Okay! Okay! Agreed," Mandy whispered.

"Good." Kat power-walked up the sidewalk.

Mandy jumped out of the driver's side. "Let's take a peek in the windows."

"Why? Haven't the police searched the house?"

"Yes, but they could have missed something."

Kat sighed and stepped to the front door. She cupped her hands around her eyes and squinted into the etched-glass. She was greeted by a kaleidoscope of indefinable browns, tans, and whites. She pushed off the door. "Can't make anything out."

"I think I see something." Mandy stood in front of a long glass window a few feet from the door. She peeked in, weaved back and forth like a mesmerized cobra, then pointed into the window. "I do see something!"

Kat joined her. The gauze curtains transformed the room's contents into ethereal colors and shapes. Kat managed to identify dark wood bookcases and a matching desk. A black patent shoe was pinned between the entry door and its frame.

"I thought you said the police had checked this place."

"They did."

Kat ran to the front door and pounded. "Mr. Spawldine? Mr. Spawldine are you in there? Are you able to get to the door?" She darted down the steps and rounded the house.

"What are we doing?" Mandy ran up behind her, breathless from the jog.

"Looking for a way in." Kat scanned the large expanse of the house. "There!" She pointed at the open backdoor and took off.

"Wait up. What about the police?"

"We'll call them. But if he's hurt, he needs help now. Wellness check, as Bart would say." Kat shot Mandy a quick smile over her shoulder.

"What if the guy's dead and the killer's still here?"

Kat reached behind her back and pulled out the .22 caliber pistol she kept close. She held it toward the sky and pushed the door with her fingernail. Cool tones of gray polished granite and stainless steel stood out against a backdrop of nutmeg-colored cabinets.

"Looks like a kitchen out of *House Beautiful* doesn't it?" Mandy whispered.

"I'll say. Grandma Bricken would love this." Kat cocked the gun. She crept forward, pointing the firearm toward the ceiling. Mandy followed her into a narrow hallway. Kat signaled for Mandy to wait. She listened. The rhythmic *tick-tick* of a clock marked off the seconds.

Kat stepped into a colorless and formal foyer. The white walls and marble floors emphasized a charcoal pant leg and the tan sole of a shoe matching the one she'd seen from the porch. Kat raced to the man lying on the floor. His arms stretched toward the front door.

"Mr. Spawldine can you hear me?" Kat said. She looked into cloud-white eyes. She placed her thumb and forefinger around the man's left wrist. The ice-cold skin made her recoil as if she'd touched a plate of liquid nitrogen.

Kat shook her head and turned to Mandy. "Now we can call the police."

Chapter 2
Of Snakes and Statues

Pulsing blue and red lights splashed eerie prisms of color onto the off-white walls and the late Grady Spawldine. The rhythmic blinking reminded Kat of an erratic heart monitor.

"So you just happened to find him this way?" A disheveled detective directed the unveiled accusation at Mandy.

Kat pulled her eyes from the lightshow. "*We* happened to find him this way, Detective…?"

"Dayton." He put a pencil against a small spiral notebook. "Your name again?"

"Kat Tovslosky."

"Spell it."

Kat leaned over the notebook and halted between each character of her name. *Let's get this right the first time, shall we, Detective Dayton?* The detective looked up and caught Kat scanning the open pages. "Thanks." He flipped the log shut.

A quick gotcha smile lit Kat's features.

"And you're sure this is Grady Spawldine?" The detective asked Mandy.

"I'm sure!"

Kat studied the corpse. The top of Grady Spawldine's head was split in a jagged gash, exposing tissue and skull. A dried river of blood snaked from the wound. It pooled on the marble floor, then continued its death march and came to rest beneath the left shoulder. The man's arms still strained upward then out toward the front door. His whole body was tense, as if he could take off and run—if he weren't dead.

"Something's sticking out of his right hand." Kat pointed to a clenched fist. A small but perceptible snippet of white peeked from between the index and middle fingers.

"Doubtful. The ME checked..." Dayton glanced down at the corpse. "Well, I'll be." The detective stepped to the right side of the body. He crouched, used the eraser side of his pencil, and lifted the pinky finger. "Hey, Jonas, can you get this for me?"

A six-foot sandy-haired man looked at Dayton, then back to the man Dayton introduced as his partner, Carson Watermill.

"What'd you find?" Watermill and the ME joined Dayton.

"Don't know. Hope it's a clue to solving this mess."

"Me, too. I might get home for dinner."

"Good thing rigor has begun to subside." The ME opened the semi-rigid fingers. He handed a crumpled piece of paper to the detective.

Dayton tugged at the corners of the note until it was straightened into a wrinkled square. He dropped it into an evidence bag. "Do either of you know what this means?" He turned the writing toward Kat and Mandy.

"Not me," Mandy said.

Kat leaned toward the evidence bag. *The Book of Fallen Angels* jumped off the paper and slapped her mind's eye. Terror blasted her stomach, then raced to her arms and legs. *Steady, Kat, steady.*

"You know it?"

"I know part of it," Kat murmured. "I've never heard or seen that word," she pointed to Gorgon. "A document named *The Book of Fallen Angels* disappeared off the Ravens Cove evidence shelf. We assumed it had been misplaced."

Dayton rubbed his chin and studied the late Grady Spawldine with renewed interest. "Wonder why it got mentioned here."

"This guy looks to have died from a massive blow to the head. You find anything the killer could have used?" The ME asked Dayton.

"Not yet. But we haven't finished our walkthrough of the house." Dayton raised his notebook. "About the book—"

"You need to see this." A uniformed police officer stuck his head out the door of the room with the gauze curtains.

"There's something else—"

Dayton turned back to the ME. "What?"

"If the blow to the head didn't kill him, the loss of blood would have."

"You mean from the head wound, right?"

"That's the logical explanation, but the head wound didn't bleed enough to account for it. I'll let you know after the autopsy."

Dayton shook his head. "I look forward to reading the report." He turned to Watermill. "Don't think we're looking for your run-of-the-mill murderer."

"I'll start looking for any other unsolved murders with this MO as soon as I get to the station."

Dayton nodded. "Let's hope we haven't inherited someone else's mess."

The uniformed officer cleared his throat. "You need to see what we've found."

"For the love of my late Aunt Millie!" Dayton pointed his notebook at Mandy, then Kat. "Stay put. I have a few more questions." Dayton disappeared into the study. Kat walked to the window beside the front door, pulled out her cell phone, and dialed.

<hr />

Josiah sat in Grandma Bricken's sunbathed kitchen enjoying the melodies of the summer birds of Ravens Cove.

"More coffee?" Alese Bricken topped the large handmade pottery cup to the rim before he could answer.

"Thanks." Josiah took a long sip and smiled. "Still as good as the day I discovered a taste for it." Josiah reflected on his long sleep in Ravens Ravine after his face-to-face meeting and subsequent battle against the evil foe's commander—Iconoclast.

The phone in the hallway trilled. "Hello to you precious child," Grandma said.

"Hi, Gram. Can you find Bart? He's not in the office and not picking up his cell phone. Mandy's up to her eyeballs, and now the lost book seems to be involved."

"*The Book of Fallen Angels?*"

"Yes. Get Bart to call me? And soon. I'm afraid Mandy and I are both going to jail if we don't get this straightened out."

"Why would you end up in jail? What would make them—"

"Gotta go," Kat whispered. She punched *end* and put the phone in her pocket.

Dayton's eyes went from Kat's empty hand to her coat pocket. "Seems there's a hidden room in the house." He looked at Mandy. "You wouldn't know anything about a secret room, would you?"

"Of course not!" Mandy answered.

"You sure? There's lots of weird stuff back there. Not your normal collection for an accountant."

"I'm good at figuring out weird stuff," Kat offered.

"Doesn't look like part of the murder scene," Dayton said more to himself than to Kat. "Can't see how it would hurt. Just don't touch anything."

"Hold on, Pete! You don't want anyone talking about this," Watermill said.

Dayton turned. "They've already been privy to things most civilians aren't. Don't think it would hurt."

"If it goes sour, don't say I didn't warn you."

Dayton's mouth formed a stubborn line. "I'll take the chance." He motioned to Kat.

Mandy trotted toward the study. Dayton stopped in front of her. "You, on the other hand, need to stay put." He waved to Watermill. "Keep tabs on her, would you?"

Carson Watermill nodded and took Mandy's elbow. Mandy threw a pleading look over her shoulder before she disappeared into the narrow hallway.

"Don't say anything, Mandy." Kat stepped into the late Grady Spawldine's study. Warm-toned bookcases filled with accounting and tax books lined the wall behind a straight-legged table. An ebony globe of the world stood alone on one shelf. The walls were bare except for a college diploma and a few award certificates. One of the bookcases jutted into the room, revealing a low doorway.

"I'll go first." Dayton stepped in front of her and disappeared into the darkness.

A loud "Umph" escaped Kat.

"You okay?"

"Fine."

"Thought you'd been hit in the stomach," Detective Dayton said.

"Nothing so dramatic. Just ran my shoulder into the doorway." Kat scanned the cramped hideaway looking for anything that could explain what had slammed into her chest and shoved her—hard. She saw a silhouette from the corner of her eye. She whipped her head toward the shadow.

"You sure you're okay?" Concern laced Dayton's words.

"Of course. Just a little jumpy, I guess."

Kat's eyes rested on a yellow Tiffany-style banker's lamp which lit a turn-of-the-century student desk. Several papers littered its work surface. The muted light glinted off the eyes of a stuffed owl atop a 2-by-4 and cinderblock creation. The makeshift shelf sagged from the weight of its load.

"Man, this guy liked his books." Kat headed for the shelves.

"He liked more than books." Dayton pointed at a statue of a beautiful woman. The figurine sat by itself on a three-foot tall plant stand. It was scantily clothed. A snake wound around the body from its neck to its feet. Her hand held the snake's midsection in a gentle embrace. A brass plaque read "Lilith."

"Who is Lilith?"

"Hoped you could shed some light on it."

Kat shook her head. "Why would you think I'd know anything about a scantily clad statue and the name Lilith?"

"Well, while you were on your phone, so was I. Seems your town has had some odd occurrences—lots of deaths for a small town. When you knew about the book, well, it seemed you might know more than you're saying."

Kat gained a new respect for this detective she had thought was a bumbler. "You're very astute."

"When I need to be." He smiled at her and winked.

"You think the statue may have something to do with this murder?"

"It could."

Kat chewed her lower lip. "I don't know anything. I do know some people who might. Want me to give them a call?"

"I don't need to involve —"

Kat's phone rang. "Can I take this?"

"Why not?"

"Thanks—what? I can't hear you."

"I can't let you out of my sight for a minute, can I?" Bart yelled.

Kat held the phone away from her ear. "Calm down. I'm fine. Mandy, on the other hand… "

Bart willed his voice to a normal level. "Not funny. Grandma said *The Book of Fallen Angels* showed up there."

"Not the book. The title showed up on a piece of paper in a dead man's hand."

"I was hoping you'd found it. I haven't had any luck here. Maureen Orthell swears she didn't take it. Maureen's the only person I'd have believed would want it."

"The Book of Fallen Angels was in her husband's family for a century. I can see where you'd think the book would give her something to hang onto."

"Exactly what I thought. She denies it, and I can't prove any different."

"I'll tell the detective here. Would you ask Josiah if he has ever heard of anyone called Lilith?"

"Lilith, you say? Hold on."

"In what context did you see the name, Katrina?" Josiah insisted on using Kat's formal name.

"It's a nameplate on a statue of an almost naked woman wrapped in a snake—a pet snake by the looks of it."

"Oh, it's probably a statue of the demon Lilith," Josiah said in a matter-of-fact tone.

"Why do you and that word always go together?" Kat rubbed her forehead in an effort to clear her mind.

"God's calling would be my only answer."

"I'd have to agree. What do you know about this dem—," Kat smiled at the detective, "dame?"

"Well, an old tale identifies her as Adam's first wife who ran away when Adam wanted her to be beneath him. She went far away, eluding God's angels sent to bring her back, and consorted with demons."

"Nice lady. So, why would someone have a statue of her?" Kat asked.

"My only guess is a type of worship. Though I've not heard of it before now."

"How about Gorgon? Have you ever heard it?"

"The word sounds familiar, but I do not know why. I'm sorry I can't help."

"I know more than I did before we talked. Thanks, Josiah."

"Katrina?"

Kat brought the phone back to her ear. "Yes?"

"Bart told me Agent Melbourne called him because he'd been unable to reach you. Your cousin feels you should call him right away."

"Do me a favor? Tell Bart I'll call both him and Ken as soon as I get a chance." She put the phone in her raincoat pocket.

Dayton looked at Kat over a pair of reading glasses. "Well?"

"Seems it could be a statue of a demon. At least my friend thinks it is."

"Did he know what Gorgon meant? Why would you ask him about it, anyway?"

He seems to be, for lack of a better term, our town's expert on oddities and the supernatural."

"So you think we have some kind of a cult thing going on here?"

"This statue, coupled with *The Book of Fallen Angels*, almost makes it a certainty." Kat told Dayton about the history of the book and what had befallen Ravens Cove. She explained the death of the mayor and, in what had become the accepted version of the story, she told him the new librarian in Ravens Cove had been the culprit in the deaths.

"Busy for a small town."

Kat smiled. "Never seems to be a dull moment."

Dayton yanked a piece of paper from the others on the desk. "Think I'll ask your friend if she knows any of these people." Kat caught a quick glimpse of a name roster.

Kat took her first deep breath when she and the detective were back in the study. *There was something in there. I could feel it watching us. How can I tell this guy what he's facing?*

Carson Watermill met them in the entry. "The station got a call from a pawn shop. Seems a diamond ring and a crystal obelisk made their way into that fine establishment about a half hour ago."

"Oh, my gosh! I didn't see his favorite pinky ring tonight. It had at least a one-quarter carat diamond as its main attraction." Mandy tiptoed out from behind Watermill.

"You were supposed to stay in the kitchen."

"I got nervous by myself."

"You're surrounded by law enforcement!" Watermill shook his head. "Ah, never mind. I guess it saves me a trip down the hallway to ask you about Spawldine's jewelry. Are you sure he was missing the ring?"

"No, but can't you check?"

"Hey, guys. Hold up."

The morgue attendants stopped halfway in and halfway out of the entry door.

"Which hand?" He yelled back over his shoulder.

"Right pinky."

Detective Watermill unzipped the body bag and held up the right hand. "Nothing here. I'll get some uniforms to the pawn shop. The owner said the guy's still there—holding out for more money.

"You want to go and greet this mystery fella or should I?" Dayton said.

"Up to you."

"We're done here for now. You are still my prime suspect, Ms. Thomas. Don't leave Anchorage."

"I'll keep her with me." Kat searched her pocket and pulled out an old gum wrapper and a dull pencil. She scrawled something on the wrapper and shoved it at Detective Dayton. "Here's my cell number if you can't reach her."

"Thanks—I think." He took the wrinkled rectangle, smelling of mint mixed with berries, and put it in the pocket of his baby-blue Oxford shirt.

Ken Melbourne paced his hotel room, stopped, and picked up the phone. He dialed Kat's number. It went to voicemail for the fifth time.

"Blast it!" he dialed Bart. "Where is she?"

"Calm down, Melbourne. She'll call when she gets a minute." Bart Andersen pushed the elementary school's request for new gym equipment to the side.

"She wouldn't let me know she's in trouble if I was the last person on earth. I'd have to read about her arrest in the newspaper before she'd admit a problem—and she probably wouldn't ask for help then. Can you tell me why she can't let me know when she's off to get into more trouble?"

Bart smiled. "I can see her telling you her every move just about as much as I can see you developing a little patience."

Ken dropped onto the mattress that he was sure could have doubled as a steel plank. He felt his vertebrae compress just a little and wondered if he'd lost any height. "Have you talked to her?"

"No, but Josiah did. Seems the dead guy had a secret room with a demon statue. It's like she's a magnet for this kind of stuff."

"Heck, man, it seems like your whole family attracts them!"

"See your point. Anyway, now you know as much as I do."

"Thanks." Ken hung up.

Andy Binnings picked up on the first ring. Ken explained the circumstances and asked his supervisor to find out about a suspicious death in Anchorage.

"Why's this one so important?"

"Kat's involved."

"Enough said. I'll call you back."

Binnings called him thirty minutes later. "She's knee-deep in a murder investigation alright," was how the second conversation started.

"I'm going to throttle her. Can you find out how deep is deep?"

"Already did. She's not an official suspect, but her friend is. The word from my liaison at the police department is she looks suspicious by association. Want me to make a call? I got the lead detective's number while I was on the phone."

"What do you think?"

———

"Dayton." The detective barked into the phone.

"Andy Binnings with the FBI. I hear you have a certain Katrina Tovslosky in your custody."

"Not in custody, but she is here."

"Is she under suspicion?"

"Haven't decided yet."

"Maybe I can help. It would be a grave error on your part to arrest her if you are not 100 percent sure she's involved. Such a mistake would reflect on the entire APD—and not in a good way."

"I would not railroad anyone. The fact is, she's only under suspicion because of her knowledge about some of the facts in this case."

"What does she know?"

"More than most about the occult. And this case smacks of the occult."

"Have her call me right away."

"You know where to find us." Kat whispered in Dayton's ear and headed to the door.

Detective Dayton held up his hand. "Got it. No, thank you." He punched *end* on the cell phone. "Seems a certain FBI official has called to make sure you are not in need of assistance."

Mandy looked at Kat with a new respect. "When did you make such important friends, KittyKat?"

"News to me. Who called?"

"A Chief Binnings. I assured him you were fine, but he wants you to call him anyway." Dayton retrieved the number from his recent calls. Kat punched it into her phone.

Binnings' phone beeped. Kat's number and name flashed in the Caller ID box.

"You wanted me to call?" A warm voice with a smiling lilt greeted him. *No wonder Melbourne's smitten. I could fall in love with the voice alone if I weren't already happily married.*

"Ms. Tovslosky?"

"Indeed. What did you say to Detective Dayton? He's acting a little scared of me."

"I just let him know someone is watching out for you."

"Ken called you, right? He shouldn't have! I am doing fine here."

"Glad to hear it. Just want you to know you don't have to do this alone and if you need help, I'm a phone call away. My cell phone is with me twenty-four hours a day, seven days a week."

"Thanks. I'll keep it close. Since I'm sure your next phone call will be to Ken, would you let him know I'm not happy with his involving you?"

Binnings smiled at the spunk in Kat's tone. *Her grit would have been the second trigger to fall in love with this one—the combination is rare and lethal to a bachelor.* "Sure will. Still, call if you need anything."

"How many nice-guy guardian angels does one woman need?" Kat asked Mandy.

"Somehow law enforcement and nice guy don't seem right when used together."

"You need to get a normal life. It may change your opinion of certain professions."

"If I get out of this one without going to jail for life, I will work on it." Mandy held up her right hand in a girl-scout pledge.

Dayton waited to approach Kat until she was deep in conversation with Mandy. "Everything okay at the FBI?" he asked.

"Just fine. Overprotective people are the theme of my life." Kat smiled at Dayton. She had grown to both admire and like this man in a few short hours. Anyone who could look like a present-day Co-lumbo and fool her with the act warranted respect.

Dayton smiled in relief. "Well, let's get you out of here then." He walked Kat and Mandy down the sidewalk. "Keep in touch."

"You can count on it."

Mandy slammed her car door and exhaled. "I'm in trouble on so many levels."

"You don't know trouble. If you'd stayed with Grady Spawldine, his kind of a mess would have killed you—and you would have never seen it coming—Mandy-bear." Kat used the nickname for the first time since she'd arrived.

"What do you mean? A suspect in a murder investigation trumps anything I can think of."

"Being lunch for a supernatural, invisible killer trumps anything this world can throw at you. And, my friend, if you had stayed with Spawl-dine, it looks like you might have ended up just like him—or worse."

"When did you lose your rational mind, Kat? Are you getting help?"

"Not the kind you're thinking. When we get back to the Cove, I'll introduce you to a new guy and have you sit and chat with him and Grandma over a nice lunch. Then we'll discuss the kind of help I've received."

"I can hardly wait."

"Me either, Mandy girl, me either."

Mandy jogged through the back door of the oddities shop toward the jingling telephone on the counter. She dropped the phone and whooped into the dusty silence.

"What?"

"They got the guy. He confessed to killing Spawldine—a burglary gone bad. He told Dayton that Grady came out of his study while he was looking for a TV or something he could hock. He said Grady came out of nowhere—Dayton thinks it's probably because he was in the secret room—anyway the intruder latched onto the first thing he could find and beaned him."

"Sounds a little too convenient." Kat questioned the coincidence—history told her there were none. *There you go again. Stop it! Life is not all about the supernatural.* She sighed and felt a weight lift right before a new one descended. They were returning to the Cove. Bart would be faced with Mandy and all those feelings he'd had for her. And Nyna might be in for the heartbreak of her life. Kat knew Mandy well enough to know Mandy *had* to have a man in her life, and she lived by the motto of "all's fair in love and war."

Mandy read the concern on Kat's face. "What?"

"Nothing." Kat smiled. "Let's get you ready and back to the Cove."

The entire time they were packing the car, Kat couldn't shake the feeling a storm was heading into the Cove and Mandy, somehow, was the eye of the tempest. *God help us,* she thought as she got behind the wheel of Wendy's Subaru and headed south.

Chapter 3
A Necessary Alliance

Ivy June Coistrell flopped onto the second-hand couch and tossed the gray wig and snake-adorned cane to her side. "Good riddance for now, Madame Piquant," she said. She snagged an oversized red and cream tapestry bag with her toe, dragged it close, and scooped a detailed figurine from the bag.

"You are going to make me rich, Lilith." She planted her lips on the woman's mouth.

A light *rap, rap* prompted Ivy June to stuff the small statue deep into her carpet bag.

"Ivy, open the door!" A deep voice boomed from the hallway.

Ivy swung the door open and hissed through clenched teeth, "shut up! What, are you stupid? No one here calls me by my real name!"

"Sorry, *Madame Piquant.*" Detective Carson Watermill strode into the rundown apartment and made himself at home on a worn and tattered wing chair.

Ivy June slammed the door. "Why are you here, anyway? Thought you didn't want us to be within fifty city blocks of each other."

"I don't. But this couldn't wait. Mandy Thomas has been cleared so she left Anchorage. She's a loose thread and needs to be clipped."

"If she's gone, then what's the problem?" Ivy June plopped back onto the old couch.

"You were sloppy, Ivy June. They found fingerprints at Spawldine's house."

"So? Madame Piquant was requested to hold a séance. She did."

"Those fingerprints don't belong to Madame Piquant. They belong to Ivy June Coistrell. And she's wanted for robbery and murder in Oregon."

Ivy June pulled the statue from her bag. "What should I do, Queen of the Damned?"

Watermill lunged. "How did you get that? Are you trying to get us both thrown in jail?"

Ivy June held the statue at arm's length. "This is my insurance. I don't want to end up like Mr. Spawldine." She pulled a gun from underneath the couch cushion and leveled it at Watermill's stomach. "So is this."

Watermill threw up his hands. "Okay. Keep the horrid thing! Just put the gun away."

Ivy June lowered the gun. "About the guy in Oregon, it was him or me."

"If you hadn't been robbing his house, he wouldn't have tried to take your life."

"It was still self-defense."

"Was Spawldine self-defense?"

"His demise was your idea, remember? Still, I wouldn't have agreed to arrange it if he hadn't figured out my scam—plus he had something I wanted. It sure was easy to convince that guy there was a lot in it for him. If he'd get me just one thing." Ivy June smiled at the figurine.

"You do not even know what the statue is about. I do. It's dangerous in the wrong hands."

"I know enough. You were willing to find me and use me to get to Spawldine when you knew he had it. That means it's worth a lot. And I want my cut."

"If you live to see it. There's a certain society that has kept to itself for hundreds of years. The statue is a direct link to them. Do you think they'd think twice about silencing you permanently?"

"I'm sure they'd take me out at the first chance—I would if the tables were turned. I have you, though. You know about this X-rated thing and the group who worship it."

"I do. And I know the only way to make sure I don't end up as the morgue's next client, is to keep my mouth shut." *And to find what my friends are looking for."*

"I'll take my chances. Now, about the girl. She saw me once as a decrepit old woman. Look at me. Do you see any resemblance?"

Watermill took in the dark blonde hair and wrinkle-free skin. "No."

"Then she won't either. She's not a threat."

"You forgot about the fingerprints. It won't take long to put two and two together."

"So what do you want me to do about it?"

"I want you to take care of her."

"You mean kill her?"

"What do you think?"

"Tempting. I do so enjoy that line of work, but I need to lie low after Oregon."

"Dayton's going to eventually find out about the fingerprints. I can throw him off the trail of the old lady but not Ivy June Coistrell. Getting you out of town kills two birds with one stone—you get lost, and the one person who can possibly identify you gets silenced."

"And what do I get out of it?"

"You can have the statue. I'll give you a contact for a sale."

Ivy June smiled. "When do I leave?"

"I've booked you on a tour bus tomorrow morning under the name of Etta Torrent."

"Sounds like another old lady. How boring!"

"This isn't a game! You'd stand out like a sore thumb if you go as yourself. Who'd suspect another old lady on a tour bus?"

"I guess." Ivy June looked Watermill in the eye. "After the job's done, I'll need to get out of there in a hurry."

"Already covered. I took a couple of days' leave. I'll be there twenty minutes after you call."

Ivy June jumped to her feet. "Then get out of here. I need to pack and get a good night's sleep—I like to be well-rested before I hunt."

"You're sick."

"Right now you need sick. Get out!"

Chapter 4
Lost and Found

The silver Subaru rolled to a stop in front of a mint-green fifties-style ranch.

"Exactly one week to the day," Kat said as she dropped the keys into Wendy's hand.

"Good thing. I was getting ready to report a stolen vehicle." Wendy walked around the Subaru.

"Where is your trust, Winsome? Don't you think I'd call if there was any damage to report?"

"No. But it looks as good as when you left. Except it could use a wash." She raised expectant eyes to Kat.

"It's the least I can do. I will wash it myself before winter sets in."

Mandy joined them. "Hey, Wendy."

"Hey, yourself. How long are you staying this time?"

"I told Kat three months."

"Well, we'll see. This all your earthly possessions?" Wendy pointed to the back of the tiny low-rider. Cardboard boxes lined the rear windows. An old pink and white quilt and various articles of clothing peeked out from between the stacks.

"They'll do for now."

"You got food?"

"Soup and some crackers."

"I'll drop you, Kat, and then I'll take her," Wendy pointed her chin at Mandy, "to the store in Clayton."

"I can get there myself."

"How much money have you got on you?"

Mandy's eyes fell to the ground. "Twenty bucks."

"You can get an apple and some milk if you're lucky. I'll take you."

"I'll make do."

"We're not fighting about this, Amanda Hareling-Thomas."

"You disowned me. Why do you care?"

"You disowned me first. But you are still my sister. And you're back in the Cove, which makes you my responsibility, *little* sister! You wouldn't be in this mess if you'd stayed like I told you to. So help me…"

"Can you finish this feud after I get home? If you haven't noticed, it's raining—and hard." Kat threw up the windbreaker hood and crossed her arms.

"I'm done for now." Wendy ducked into the driver's side of the Subaru, then yelled at Mandy. "Take yourself into my house and stay there. I'll be back in fifteen minutes."

The familiar sound of crunching gravel flooded Kat with the thrill of being home. She jumped out of the car and snatched her small suitcase from the back.

"Thanks, Wendy. Ouch!" Angry green eyes met her emerald ones. BC's four black feet were firmly attached to Kat's jeans. She shook her leg; the claws went deeper.

"How'd Houdini get out? I'm sure I locked his escape route." Wendy pointed to the flap-covered exit cut into the cabin's heavy wood door.

"Don' know. Right now, I need you to help me get him off."

Wendy threw open the car door and jogged toward the cabin's deck. "I got it."

Kat's head shot sideways. "Ken!" She started to run, but was stopped by the feline weight and the pain shooting up her leg.

Ken Melbourne bounded off the porch steps. He gently pushed the soft pad of BC's front and back feet until BC released his grip and dropped to the ground. His attention remained on Kat's leg.

BC launched himself at Kat's thigh. Ken caught him in midair and cradled him in the crook of his arm. "I'm sorry. I forgot to relock the cat door. He was out before I even heard the car."

Kat stood statue-still and stared at her fiancé. "You're here," she whispered.

"He's here alright. Melbourne, what in the world are you trying to do? Kill her before you can collect the life insurance?"

Ken flashed white, straight teeth at Wendy. "Not my intention." He turned to Kat. "I didn't call because I didn't even know I could come until yesterday."

"How?" Kat found a little more of her voice. In a familiar move, she held out her arm. BC walked from Ken to Kat. He kneaded her left lower arm. The gentle rhythm soothed Kat's shocked emotions.

"After what happened in Anchorage." Ken looked around. "Where is this Mandy person, anyway?"

"She's at my house. Don't change the subject, FBI," Wendy said.

"You still here?"

"Darn right. Will be until I get to hear this story. So, hurry it along, will you? Then I'll leave, and you can get to whatever you two do when you get to be alone."

"Hug."

"Right. Still don't understand your need to wait until you're married. Go on, Melbourne. The town's waiting." Wendy referred to her informal job as the procurer and announcer of any new gossip in the Cove. Since the death of the town's only reporter during the last demon siege, Wendy was the residents' only hope of getting news in a timely manner.

"You should consider taking over at the newspaper."

"You're changing the subject again."

"Right." Ken took Kat's shoulders in a gentle hold. Her fiery eyes warned him an emotional storm was on the horizon, and he was going to be the lightning rod if he didn't talk fast.

"I know you can take care of yourself. I am as surprised to be here as you are to see me. But when I found out *The Book of Fallen Angels* had been tied to the Anchorage murder, I couldn't rest. Worse, I couldn't shake the feeling something bad's heading this way."

Wendy raised her eyebrows. "You're here because of a *feeling?*"

"Call it my FBI intuition."

"You don't act on feelings, Ken." Kat's eyes had softened, but the storm still played around the edges.

"It isn't logical. Neither was the call I made to Binnings two days ago requesting a return to the Anchorage office. After a long debate of the pros and cons for my return, we reached an impasse. So I did all I knew to do."

"Which was?"

"I told him I wanted an extended leave of absence. I told him I'm considering a career in small-town law enforcement."

"Why? You always wanted to be in the Bureau. You don't want to be a small-town cop!"

"Maybe I do; maybe I don't. It gives Binnings a solution to an impossible problem—me. It's the least I can do. Any other boss would have tossed me out on my ear years ago instead of working to salvage my career." Ken remembered the first time he had tried to explain the supernatural events in Ravens Cove. The disbelief and pity in his boss's eyes were almost too much to take. "The man has given me a lot of rope, and you know it."

"It's not your fault he doesn't believe the deaths in Ravens Cove weren't by a human's hands."

"It sure would have been easier to explain if they had been. Binnings ended the phone call by giving me six months to make a decision."

Kat sighed, dropped BC to the ground, and threw herself against Ken. She took a deep breath. His smell permeated her senses. She felt safe and secure for the first time in months. Ken lifted stiff arms, pulled her head to his chest, and caressed thick auburn curls.

"Alright, I'm out of here. I can't take much more of this mushy stuff. Talk later, KittyKat. Welcome aboard, police chief." Wendy gave a quick wave as she climbed into her Subaru.

"Not police chief—consultant." Ken yelled at the back of the retreating car.

The car slid to a stop and reversed course. Wendy leaned out the window. "Think what you will, police chief!" she sped onto the road.

Kat slapped a lone tear from her cheek. "Does Bart know you're back?"

"No. Think I better let him know there's a new police chief, I mean consultant, in town? If he'll still have me."

"He'll still have you and yes, you'd better let him know—and, Josiah and Gram and—"

"I get the picture. Let's move. Wendy's got a head start."

Kat smiled at him, then dropped her eyes to where BC had been. She scanned the open field and gravel pad in front of her cabin. "Where'd he go? I'd like him in the house. Here kitty, kitty, kitty… BC, WHERE ARE YOU!" Kat's voice cracked with emotion.

The distant waves of the Cook Inlet and the cawing of a raven were the only response.

"Stupid animal." Kat stopped herself before she kicked the gravel like a two-year old.

"He's alright. Just mad you left him."

"You're probably right." Kat fought back the terror BC's absence provoked. *Please God, let him be safe.* She took a resigned breath.

"If you're so concerned, let's go looking." Ken headed to the back of the cabin.

"No, you're right. He'll come home. He always has. We'd better get to Bart." Kat headed for Ken's navy-blue SUV.

Chapter 5
Gains and Losses

Carson Watermill shoved a piece of paper into Ivy June Coistrell's hand. "When you get to Ravens Cove, head out of town and find a place to hide until dusk. Then go to this address, and get rid of Mandy Thomas."

"What about her boyfriend?" Ivy June asked.

"I have friends who will take care of Justin. He's become a liability to their, umm, corporation."

"You mean their cult, right?"

"Mind your own business, and keep those thoughts to yourself—unless you want to end up like Spawldine."

"Not me. I plan on getting out of this in one piece and a little richer."

"If you do what you are told to do, you will. Now get on the bus before it leaves without you."

Ivy June blew Watermill a kiss and hobbled up the bus steps. To an onlooker it was a sweet old mom saying goodbye to her son. Ever the actress, Ivy June immersed herself in her new character. Her bent body and well-rehearsed limp disguised her youth. She smiled and nodded at the other travelers before lowering herself into a seat next to the window.

A silver-haired man with thick glasses plopped into the chair next to hers. "First time to Alaska?" he asked.

"No, I live here. It is my first time going to Ravens Cove, though. I thought it was time to see small-town Alaska—before I can't travel anymore." Ivy June let out a shrill cackle.

The older man leaned back, nodded, and dug a book from his carry-on.

Ivy June turned toward the window and smiled. *The old crone's laugh is the best part of this character. Just enough so people think I'm a little crazy.* She closed her eyes and fell asleep. She jolted awake in response to the earsplitting volume of the intercom.

The portly driver waved to the steps. "Ladies and gentlemen welcome to Ravens Cove. You have two hours to look through the shops and have some lunch. We depart for Clayton at two o'clock. Don't be late."

"It's show time." Excitement flooded Ivy June Coistrell. She slipped out of character and jumped up with the vigor of her true age. The older man leaned back and gave her a wide-eyed stare. She feigned a loss of balance, grasped her cane, and planted it to her left. "You think I'd remember my age." She hunched over the cane and smiled at those going past her on the aisle. A young man took her arm and guided her to the steps.

Ivy June melted into the tour group until the bus and its driver were out of sight. She hobbled across Main Street and sat on a bench contemplating her next move. She paid attention to the individuals as they scattered in different directions. Some ducked into a local pottery shop and some into the hardware store. An overweight fifty-something man headed through a door. The lettering identified it as Jo's Bakery. Ivy June smiled. "Just what you don't need old guy—but it'll sure work for me. Ivy June hobbled back across Main.

"What can I get for you?" A flushed and hurried Josephina Latrell asked.

"I need a bathroom." Ivy June croaked.

Josephina took in the stooped figure and sighed. "Usually don't let anyone but patrons use it—but I'll make an exception in your case. It's all the way in the back."

"Thanks so much. You are kind."

Ivy June locked the door of the one-person restroom. She whipped the gray wig off her head, pulled the pins from her hair and shook her head. Her dark blond hair fell to her shoulders. She stripped off the brown wool sweater and broom skirt. She yanked the lid off the domed trashcan and dug a hole in the wet paper towels. She pulled a long-barreled revolver from the skirt's lining and stuffed her disguise in the receptacle. "So glad they don't check for weapons on tour busses to Ravens Cove." She patted the gun and stuffed it deep into her purse.

Ivy June ambled through the crowded bakery. She walked faster as she passed the deli counter. Once on Main, she turned left and headed toward the police station. A birch wood bowl and matching walking stick in the antique store's window caught her eye. Ruby eyes glittered from a sterling silver wolf's head atop the cane. *I want it!* She looked at her watch. *Later. I'll pick it up on my way out of town.*

She followed the well-used footpath to Ravens Ravine. The dirt trail disappeared into rust-colored moss and tan pine needles. Ivy June trudged the spongy carpet to a forest of gnarled trees and low bushes. She picked her way through the black spruce and alders.

By the time she reached the edge of the forest it was night. The full moon spotlighted a rotting wooden bridge. A wide black river coursed past the structure, making it impossible to cross.

"I was sure this was the way to Thomas's house," she said.

"Are you lost?" A disembodied voice gurgled up from the tar-colored water.

Ivy June fixed her eyes on the murky depths. "No," she answered.

"Oh but you are! You've been lost for a very long time, Ivy June Coistrell."

Ivy June yanked the handgun from her purse and pointed it toward the water. "I don't know how you know my name. You can be sure I'm gonna find out. Come out right now or I'll kill you." She shot an I-mean-business round into the river.

Malevolent laughter filled the air. Ivy June raised the firearm, spun in a circle, and emptied the bullets into the surrounding forest.

"Your puny weapon will not help you." The river churned up into a waterspout. A mummified woman with dark brown skin and shocking pink eyes surfaced. She grinned. A sticky fluid oozed from cracks in the dry lips. The liquid stretched like a rubberband, then dropped into the dark water with a heavy *plunk*. Ivy June dropped the gun and scurried backwards. Her heel caught on a tree root, and she tumbled to the ground.

"You asked who I am. I am Lilith, and I am hungry." Lilith seized hold of the younger woman's neck and yanked her forward.

Ivy June ran in place above the river. "Let me go. I'll get you anything you need," she croaked.

"Oh, how considerate. Still, I can't let you go. I want you to know how very bad I feel about you becoming my first meal in centuries."

"Not if I kill you first." Ivy June grabbed hold of the leathery arms and yanked. Rotted flesh filled her hands, then slid into the river.

"You can't kill what's already dead, foolish girl." Lilith tightened her grip. Ivy June stopped struggling and hung like a ragdoll in midair.

"I don't usually feast on women. After all, we are sisters in so many ways. So, it's unfortunate you happened upon my place of hiding before a man or tender child." Lilith turned Ivy June until they were face-to-face.

"To make it up to you, your death will be quick, and you won't die; you will have a place of honor as my servant—forever." Lilith dug her fangs into Ivy June's neck. Dark eyes turned a cloud blue. Lilith threw the corpse to the ground and sighed. "Kumrande come!"

Nihilist clip-clopped out from black woods and bowed. "As you wish, great one."

"Take this shell and destroy it. Leave it where it will be found."

Nihilist smiled. "I will enjoy it."

"Eat none of her! She gave her life so I am stronger, nothing more."

Anger filled Nihilist's eyes. "You told me I could have your leftovers!"

"Not this one! Leave her where she can be found. Make sure she brings men here so I can have my fill. Then you can have yours." Lilith flew out from under the bridge and planted herself in front of Nihilist.

Nihilist backed up and bowed again. "It is done! He dragged the corpse into the woods.

Please, God, give me strength—and a little patience if You don't mind. Bart looked at his visitor.

Annie Scofland sat ruler-straight across Bart's polished oak desk. So far, she had opined on the people of Ravens Cove, the price of antiques, and the negligent landlord who hadn't fixed the water leak plaguing her store.

The stack of memos and phone messages on Bart's desk yelled for him to get back to work. He contemplated the best way to end Annie's visit.

"Do you understand why? I sure don't."

"I'm sorry... a lot on my mind. Understand what?"

Annie Scofland's full lips straightened into a thin line. "I was saying I don't understand why someone would break in and steal a birch wood bowl and cane. There was so much of more value."

Bart leaned toward her. "You're sure the items haven't been misplaced?"

"Yes, I'm sure! I specifically put the bowl and cane behind the counter right before closing up for the night. They belonged in the window, but it had been a long day. I just wanted to get home. So, putting them away was my first order of business this morning."

"Right." Bart stood up hoping Annie would follow suit. "Well, as you probably know, I'm filling two jobs right now. I have a few calls to make before I can break away from the mayor's role. In the meantime, would you do me a favor and go through your shop again—just to make sure?

"I told you they aren't there."

Bart held up his hand. "And they probably aren't. Would you just humor me? While you're checking the shop, I'll interview your neighbors to see if they saw anyone hanging around."

Annie relaxed and extended her hand. "Thanks, mayor. I'll check the store again. I know I sound silly, but I'm a bit nervous to be there by myself after this."

"Not silly. I just wish I had someone to send over. There is only one police officer under normal circumstances."

Concern darkened Annie Scofland's bright features. "I understand."

"Jo and Horace aren't very far from your store. They'd be happy to keep an eye out. Want me to talk to them?"

Annie nodded and smiled. "Thanks so much. I sure didn't expect to have to worry about a burglary in Ravens Cove—one of the main reasons I moved here. Guess crime happens everywhere."

"Ravens Cove has its share. Sorry you had to experience this side in the short time you've called it home." Bart shook her hand. "I'll be there soon."

The demanding buzz of the intercom finished the meeting. Bart pushed the black dot of a button. "Yes?"

"Your next appointment is here, Mayor Andersen."

"*Bart,* call me *Bart,* Jenny." Silence. Bart took a resigned breath. Jenny, the all-business assistant, refused to drop the title of mayor. It had been an ongoing battle since Bart took the position. *Guess she may be gonna win this one.* Bart looked at the brown leather appointment calendar. The page was blank.

"I don't see any appointments for today."

"This one just came up."

"Be right there." Bart stared at the hill of pink messages. "Don't guess you're going anywhere in the next few minutes." He rounded the desk as Ken walked in from the reception area.

"Where'd you come from?" Bart gripped Ken Melbourne's hand and yanked him into a bear hug.

Ken pulled himself free and patted Bart on the shoulder. "Glad to see you too, Andersen."

Kat giggled. "Isn't it great?"

"I'm confused. Last we talked you were banished to LA for an indefinite length of time. What changed your chief's mind?"

"Was banished—may be again. For now, though, I am on an extended leave and have permission to offer my assistance to the town of Ravens Cove—as a consultant."

Bart and Kat reminded Ken of twins when their eyebrows shot up in response to Ken's monotone dialogue. "What'd I say?"

"Not what. How."

"Don't know what you mean."

"Never mind," Kat said.

Bart cleared his throat. "Okay, then. How would you like to join me at the new antique store for your first assignment?"

"Not another murder."

"No. Petty thievery."

Ken relaxed. "Sure thing. I'm on it. Why don't you stay here and do whatever important business you have as mayor? Think I can handle this one on my own."

"I'd say you could handle it on your own anywhere else. This is the Cove. You aren't trusted here yet. You need me, just for a while, so they'll get used to you."

"Forgot. Small town 101."

"Don't start, FBI. Bart's right. On the bright side, you already have office help." Kat grinned up at him.

"Oh, stutters. I'm gonna have to run Kat's position by the town council now. They have to be made aware of any 'relationships' working together."

"What!"

"Had to do the same thing when you came to work for me."

"They are so weird. This whole town is related somehow—almost."

"Rules are rules. Until I get an answer, steer clear of the station."

"Senseless policy, but okay. " I need to get unpacked—and find the cat.

"BC?"

"He took off."

"And you're surprised—why?"

"Nothing he does should surprise me, I guess. He's an independent little cuss and always has been."

Bart poked her in the arm. "Takes one to know one."

"Funny. Just let me know when I can come back to work." Kat looked at Ken. "And don't you even think about trying to talk Bart out of it. I won't be in danger, and neither will you." She flashed him a knowing smile.

"Wouldn't dream of it. Kind of like the thought of having you around. I can keep a close eye on you while I'm doing important police—I mean consulting— stuff for the Cove."

"Only part-time, FBI. You only have me part-time." Kat turned on her heel and almost body-slammed Wendy Hareling.

Wendy's mouth turned downward into a pout. "Oh, I guess he's already heard."

"Guess so."

Wendy brightened. "Well, then I'm off to get Mandy to Clayton, then settled at the old cabin." She waved and was gone.

"She sure can move fast when she wants."

"That was a red herring if I've ever seen one. Bet she's making a stop at Gram's beforehand. I'll give her a call." Bart headed back into his office.

"Off to home sweet home." Kat tiptoed and gave Ken a hard, fast kiss. "See you later, FBI."

Ken scanned the light oak paneling of the reception area.

"Can I help you, Agent Melbourne?"

Ken smiled at Jenny. "No."

Jenny responded with a disapproving stare, then turned back to her work. The *ticky-tap* of Jenny's computer keys filled the tomb-silence of the room.

Bart came out of his office, pulling a black, lightweight raincoat over his shirt-and-tie-clad body. "Josiah and Gram have been notified. All is right in our world." He jerked his head toward the door. "Let's go find us a thief."

Kat strolled down Main drinking in the summer light like a sun-starved rosebud. She took a deep breath of the warm salt air and grinned.

"What's so wonderful, child of my heart?" Gramma Bricken asked.

"All is right with my world today. Summer, birds, the smell of all the wildflowers…"

"And Kenneth Melbourne is in town." Josiah's sharp blue eyes twinkled with humor.

"Yes, he is."

"Where are you off to?"

"Home. I've been asked to delay going to work until Bart can clear it with the town council."

"So you find yourself with time on your hands."

"Indeed."

"Why don't you come home with us?"

"I would, Gram, but I want to get to the cabin and see if BC's come back. I'd be lost without him." Kat gave her grandmother a sheepish grin.

"Don't have to explain to me. His loyalty to you knows no bounds. Come by later—and bring Kenneth."

"If the little rascal's back at the house, I'll come right over." Kat brushed her grandmother's brown cheek with a quick kiss. She threw her arms around Josiah and held him close. "Love you, old man," she whispered.

"How can you call me old and make me feel so young at the same time?"

"Talent."

"How about we walk with you a bit."

"I'd enjoy the company." Kat stopped at the antique store. The teal-green door shouted an elegant invitation to enter. "Maybe I should check on the owner. She had a break-in last night."

"What a shame. So unusual for the Cove even with the influx of summer visitors," Alese Bricken said.

"What's more unusual is the thief took some old bowl and a cane. She has some spendy stuff in there." Kat jiggled the door handle. It held firm. She peeked through the window but didn't see movement. "Odd behavior for the middle of a workday." Kat shrugged. "Guess I've procrastinated long enough. I'd better get home. I'll be over as soon as I can, Gram."

Kat headed south at a fast clip. The sun played hide-and-seek in storm-gray clouds. Ravens soared high on the light winds, becoming almost invisible against the deep-gray background. One of the inky dots broke away. It plummeted toward Kat, then swooped up and back into the sky. *You are the joker of this world, raven.*

Kat made her way up the gentle incline leading to the top of Ravens Ravine. She threw a guarded glance to the hag tree standing watch over the alder and birch lined entrance. The very tree which came to life anytime Iconoclast and his demon army came to the Cove.

"What in the world!" Kat scrambled up the hill. The severed trunk rested in a bed of moss and wood shavings. The tree's dismembered shaft revealed an ashen interior. Kat picked a claret-red piece of wax out of the moss. Kat crouched and pressed on the rotted wood.

"Ick!" She snapped her hand backwards to avoid the tar-colored fluid gushing out of the spongy wood. The smell of rotten cabbage assaulted her senses. She threw one hand over her nose, used the other to rifle through her windbreaker pocket, and pulled out a tattered Kleenex. She swiped at the putrid-smelling substance.

Several IV bags littered the ground. Kat examined the sticky red fluid seeping from puncture marks in the bags. The smell of iron laced with a sickening sweet scent filled the air.

Kat caught a flash of white from the corner of her eye. She marched to a stand of alders and parted the gnarled branches. Red toenails gave way to a petite ankle. Kat's eyes scanned the calf and stopped at jagged red tendons shivering in a light wind. Kat threw her hand over her mouth and choked back the bile.

Bart picked up on the first ring. "Slow down."

Kat took a deep breath. "I said the hag tree has been destroyed." *Tell him the real reason you called. No!* she argued to herself. *Then the horror of what I saw will be real.*

"What do you mean *destroyed?*"

"It's in pieces. Looks like someone took an axe to it."

"Well, good riddance to bad rubbish, is what I say." Relief tinged Bart's words. "It's good to know at least one hallmark of Iconoclast and his army is gone. Now if we could just figure out what to do with Old Town." Memories of the skull-like boulder sitting in the courtyard of the ill-fated tourist attraction drifted into his mind's eye. He hadn't told anyone his sleep was filled with nightmares of demons swallowing the inhabitants of his town.

Tell him! she told herself. "Ummm, there's something else—a leg."

"Okay… what kind of leg?"

"A human one."

"Why didn't you say that in the first place! On my way." Bart hit *end* and motioned to Ken.

"Thanks." Ken said to Horace Stoddard, the proud owner of the only hardware store in town.

"Got a problem." Bart explained to Ken on the way up Main. Both were unaware of the black mist observing them from the shadows of the antique store. A look of loathing and murder contorted its features. "Soon, we will meet. This time, you die!"

⟡

Kat made a beeline down the path. "Thank goodness. I wasn't sure how much longer I could stand being here alone. Oh, I found this in the hag tree." She shoved the red wax to Bart.

Ken walked over to pull her into his arms. Kat backed away. "Not right now." She trudged up the hill.

"What'd I do?" Ken asked.

"Not a thing, friend." Bart caught Kat's arm and pulled her to a stop. "Where?"

"There."Kat pointed a shaky finger to the alders.

A stiff white calf lay on a skinny trunk, toes pointed skyward in a morbid dance step.

"Not again." Bart speed-dialed Doctor Billings, the town's physician and ME when the need arose. "Yep—at the ravine. Thanks, Doc."

"How'd he take it?" Kat asked.

"Like I'd expect. Upset and worried Iconoclast is back."

"Me, too."

"Why would he take out the tree? It's his servant. Nope, this wasn't Iconoclast," Bart said.

"Bart. Tell me what this is." Ken pointed to light depressions in the tall grass.

"They're tracks. No way to tell if the indentations are human or animal."

Ken whirled around and pointed his gun in the direction of a loud *crack*. He lowered it when he recognized Doc Billings.

Billings gave the gun a nonchalant once-over and turned his attention to the leg. He looked at Ken. "Don't take this the wrong way, Agent Melbourne, but when you come to town, death either precedes or follows you. Can you tell me why?"

"You don't seriously blame him?" Kat said.

Billings smiled. "I can, but I'm sure there must be another explanation." Billings gloved his hands and walked to the alders.

"He can be a real jerk," Kat grumbled.

Ken turned a stern face to Kat. "He has a point. It does seem I show up at the worst times."

Kat touched his arm. "You show up at the best times."

Ken patted her hand. "Thanks, KittyKat."

"Hey, come over here a minute," Billings yelled.

"Bart pointed at Kat. "Stay."

Kat stopped in her tracks. "Fine. I've seen enough gore for one day anyway."

"Was this here?" Doc Billings pointed to a fragment of beige fabric fluttering in the afternoon breeze.

"Can't say as it was. Hey, Kat can you come here for a minute?"

"Seriously?" she yelled back.

"Yes."

Kat tromped up the hill. "What?"

"Was this here before?" Bart asked.

"I don't remember seeing it. All I could think about was that," Kat nodded to the macabre limb, "so I might have missed it."

A sharp laugh escaped Billings. He grimaced. "Sorry. You guys might want to bag it. I'll be back in a jiff." Doc disappeared down the path and returned with a body bag.

"Don't see any need for the mortuary boys." Billings placed the leg in the bag and zipped it shut. "I'm counting on you two to find the rest of the body. Without it, our chances of an ID are slim to none."

"We still have quite a bit of ground to cover here. With any luck, it'll show up," Ken said.

"With any luck, the owner had a bad accident and is in the Clayton hospital."

"It'd be a miracle if someone survived losing a leg. They'd bleed out in minutes."

"One can hope," Bart replied.

"Sorry about the earlier comment, Ken. It was uncalled for," Billings said.

"Nothing to be sorry about. It is a baffling coincidence."

Billings nodded. "I'll clean the leg up and do what I can to tell you how it got separated from its owner. I'll be hard pressed to give you much more, though."

"Anything you can find will be more than we have now. Call me when you have anything, anything at all," Ken said.

"Will do." Doc Billings disappeared back down the path.

Ken gripped Kat's arm. "Let's get you home.

"I feel fine. I'd like to stay." Kat headed down the ravine pathway, wobbled, and collapsed to the ground.

"Ah, man! I didn't see that coming. Think you can get her home by yourself?" Bart looked first at his unconscious cousin and then back at Ken.

"Weight training was one of my few pastimes in LA. Besides, she isn't very big." Ken walked over and scooped Kat into his arms. A small "umph" escaped Ken. Kat's petite size belied her muscular frame.

Bart grinned. "Yep, weight training paid off for ya."

Ken steadied himself and Kat. "I'll be back in a flash." He returned twenty minutes later.

"All settled in. She came around right after I got her into the house."

"How is she?"

"Physically, good. Mentally? Think this discovery took a toll. She still had enough gumption to tell me to get out, though."

"A good sign."

"I guess."

"What'd we do before cell phones?" Bart punched in a number and waited. "Gram, Kat's had a real scare. Can you get a ride down and watch after her for a while?… I'll let her tell you. Thanks. Yes, Josiah can come too. Thanks again."

"How are she and Josiah supposed to get here?"

"Pastor Paul told her to call anytime she needed a ride. If that doesn't work—it'll work."

"Maybe I should go back to the cabin. She shouldn't be alone."

"Take it from me, brother, Kat doesn't want you there right now. If she's conscious, if she's talking, you're better off here. When she feels vulnerable, she comes out fighting."

"She did look and sound good. Just pale."

Bart smiled. "Let her lick her pride-wounds in private—and with Grandma Bricken. And let's you and me get to work." Bart scoured the bright green foliage dotted with white and purple wildflowers that lined the pathway. He stopped at the heavy boulder barricading the entrance to the high-walled gorge.

Ken joined Bart. "No sign of anything happening down here."

"Well, maybe we aren't looking for Iconoclast this time—which would be good news." The memory of the last battle with the demon and his army, and the heartbreak over the loss of good citizens and friends flooded him for a second time in a day.

"The best news I've had since we found the body," Ken said. "Onward and upward, as they say."

Ken and Bart made their way up the dark pathway and back into daylight. Amos Thralling met them, fishing pole over his left shoulder, tackle box in his right hand, otherwise nothing to show for being to the mouth of the river.

"Evenin', sheriff," he said to Bart. He nodded to Ken. "Evenin', agent."

"I'm the mayor now, Amos." He pointed a thumb at Ken. "He's the new police chief."

"Not in an official capacity. I'm just helping out." Ken sent a warning look to Bart.

"He's just being modest."

Amos raised his bushy eyebrows. "Well, ain't that somethin'? Guess we'll see if you have what it takes to take care of the Cove, now won't we?"

"Guess you will, Mr. Thralling."

"Amos, when did you go down to fish?" Bart asked.

Amos looked up at the sky. "Three or four hours ago. Why?"

"Did you come by here?"

"Always do."

"Did you see anything?"

"Like what?" Amos looked around the ravine hill. His eyes stopped on the remains of the hag tree. "The tree wasn't cut to pieces when I walked by earlier."

"You sure?"

"Don't you think I'd have noticed? The ugly thing has been here since God made the earth, I'm sure, and I've walked by the eyesore every day for nigh on fifty years. I'd have noticed."

"Got it. Did you see anyone, anyone at all?"

Amos furrowed his brow. "Well, there was a stranger on the path. Walking real slow, like he was looking for something."

"When?" Ken asked.

Amos looked through Ken, then turned to Bart. "When I was on my way to the river."

"I asked the question, Mr.—"

Bart threw up a hand. "Amos, did you get a good look at him?"

"Looked like all the other out-of-towners around here. Except—" Amos directed his comment to Ken.

Okay, this is going to be harder than I thought.

"Except what?" Bart clinched his left fist and put his right hand over his nonexistent gun belt. His hand fell to his side.

Ken smirked at the old habits of Police Chief Andersen. Bart had planted his feet slightly apart and his legs were straight as tree trunks. The only thing missing was the left hand on a flashlight.

"He was dressed in a long trenchcoat, wide-brimmed hat, and sunglasses. I remember thinking it was a bit odd, even for an out-of-towner." Amos stared into the distance. He snapped his fingers. There was an American flag on the brim of his hat."

"Anything else. Hair color? White, black, or Native?"

"He was a white guy; hair was light brown, maybe blond. He was pretty tall. I felt like one of Snow White's seven dwarfs when I walked past him."

"Did he have anything in his hands?" *Chopping concrete with a table knife would be less frustrating and definitely less painful than this interview,* Ken thought.

"No. Could have had something under the coat, I suppose."

"You're doing good, Amos. Can you remember anything else?" Bart asked.

"Nope. We done here? I want to get home and get some shuteye before the midnight run." Amos Thralling lived and breathed fishing. Nothing, not even almost being accused of murder twice in the past, stopped him.

"We're done."

Amos touched his forehead in a salute and headed toward Ravens Cove.

"Are they all going to be like Amos?"

"Oh, they'll warm up—eventually. Just got to earn their trust."

"How?"

"Don't have any idea, but it'll be fun to watch. Let's check out the other side of the ravine. Maybe we'll get lucky."

Two pairs of blood-red eyes followed Bart and Ken's trek to the eastern ridge. "They'll never know what's going to kill them or when," a misty, black figure said to its carbon copy.

"No they won't. I love the element of surprise. So much fear." They dissolved into the earth beneath them.

Chapter 6
An Unexpected Alliance

Grandma Bricken, Josiah, and Paul Lucas drove up to Kat's house just as she ducked into a distant stand of spruce trees.

"I'll go after her." Paul reached for the door handle.

"No need." Grandma pointed.

"What are you doing here?" Kat yelled from the forest's edge.

"Brought you some company."

Gram and Josiah got out of the car and waved in unison.

The terrific twosome. Kat chuckled and made her way back to the cabin.

Alese Bricken wrapped her arms around Kat. "How are you?"

"Guess blabber mouth Bart told you I had a little fainting spell."

"As well he should."

"I'd be a 100 percent if BC had come home." Kat looked at her grandmother, worry clouding the normal shine of her eyes.

Alese kissed the top of her head. The fear in Kat's eyes reminded Grandma of the first day Kat came to live with her. She had spent much of her life helping Kat heal from the abandonment she felt. Now, the same little girl stood before her. "I won't leave until we find him."

Kat wiped a small tear from her cheek and smiled. "How about you and Josiah go in and make yourselves comfortable, along with a strong pot of coffee for the caffeine monster."

"Guilty," Josiah said. "Alese is right, though. Someone should help you look for your elusive creature."

"Not necessary."

"You shouldn't be alone right now, and I want to help. I, for one, will look forward to a cup when we return," Paul said.

"Me, too. House is open."Kat trotted to the woods. Paul followed close behind.

"I do hope she finds BC—unharmed."

"I'm going to believe she will. Let's get some coffee."

"Here kitty, kitty, kitty." Paul yelled as he trudged through waist-high grass and Devil's Club.

Kat shivered. "The temperature must have dropped ten degrees in here."

"It is a bit cooler. Alaska is amazing in so many ways."

"Lord help us! We need to find BC—now." Kat's voice shook as she pointed to a rotting bridge. "Why would he have come this far in?"

"What makes you so nervous here? Is it that old bridge?" Paul looked at, then past, the wood and rope structure. Arthritic black spruce pushed against the overpass. Their trunks stood inches apart, and their twisted limbs intertwined to form a ghoulish barrier to the forest behind. "It's broad daylight. How can that part of the forest be black as night?"

"Looks dangerous, huh? My great grandmother told us any who ventured into those woods never came out." Kat laughed. "Silly. Yet a part of me doesn't want to go in and find out." Kat jumped when the bridge let out an ethereal groan. "Silly or not, something feels wrong, even dangerous here."

"Maybe it's just nerves but I feel it, too." Here kitty, kitty…"

"BC ignores being called 'kitty' when he's on a freedom run." Kat pulled a Baggie of apricot-colored chips from her pocket. "If he's here, this is the only thing to flush him out. He can smell it miles away." Kat shook the bag, opened it, and placed two salmon flakes on the ground. She walked back toward the cabin, dropping miniature wafers along the trail. Her shoulders sagged, and Kat's voice shook when she whispered, "guess he isn't here."

"I'm not giving up hope just yet. How about we say a prayer?"

"For an animal?"

"God loves them, too. He surely didn't tell us to pray about certain things. 'Come to Him with all requests' is what Saint Paul said."

"I'm game." Kat dropped her head. Tears streamed down her cheeks and ended in soft *plops* as they hit the grass and leaves below.

Paul took her hands. "Heavenly Father, this cat, Your creature, is so important to young Katrina, also Your creature and, even more, Your daughter. Please bring him home to her. In Jesus'..."

Kat's eyes flew open when she heard a familiar *meow* then felt a hard *thump* to her calf. Grass-green eyes met hers before BC trotted into a small stand of alders, sat, and looked back at her.

"Come here, you rat!" Kat ran after him.

"Thank you, Jesus. You answer our requests before our prayers are finished. You are wonderful. Amen." Paul took off after her.

BC trotted a few feet ahead and sat again.

Kat caught up to him. "You are making me so ma—." BC took off.

"Stop with the games!" Kat shouted and raced to keep up with the graceful feline. She sighted him—his tail anyway—right before he ducked under a low-lying bush.

"Come out of there, now!" Kat reached through the hole and came up with a handful of needles and dirt. She peeked into the tiny lean-to. "Now, BC!"

BC head-butted Kat. "Ouch! Stop it." She reached into the dark gap again. BC moved just out of reach.

"How about I move some of those branches aside so you can get a better look?" Paul offered.

"Good idea. I'll block this opening." She sat in front of the small opening and crossed her legs.

Paul analyzed the leafy structure, looking for a weak spot. "This looks like the best place to start." He yanked two alder branches to the side. "There's some rust-colored fur back here."

Kat rounded the natural lean-to and looked down at the copper-colored hair. An emerald BC eye appeared.

"What you got here, BC?" Kat touched the fur and jumped when she heard a yelp.

"Sounds like a dog."

"Or a fox," Kat said.

"You got a saw or something at home? It could take hours to untangle the branches by hand."

"Yes, there's an axe—a little too big for this purpose—by the front door. Beside it is a trunk. Inside is a small-toothed saw."

"Back in a jiff."

BC bumped Kat with his head and paced back and forth like a worried father-to-be.

"You heard him—right back."

BC swatted at her hand and took to pacing again.

"You're right. We can't wait, can we, Black Cat?" Kat relocated to the front of the small shelter. She pulled a penknife out of her pocket and stripped the smaller twigs from the thick branches. She sawed a cut into the stubborn wood. The limbs gave way after a few tugs.

A narrow brown face with espresso-colored eyes studied Kat. "Well, there you are." Kat cooed as she worked more branches free to widen the opening.

BC nudged her leg with his head.

"I'm going as fast as I can. Maybe you could gnaw on a few and help out." Kat worked enough branches free to get a full view of the long-coated dog's torso. Its leg was caught in a tight-knit clump of branches. A rivulet of blood stained the white of the back leg.

"Oh, you poor thing." She leaned in. The dog dug its paws into the soft earth, backed up, and shivered. "I'm not going to hurt you. Just need to take a look."

"You got quite a bit done while I was gone."

Kat threw an apologetic smile over her shoulder. "Sorry. BC wouldn't calm down until I widened the opening. Can't get this pup's leg free, though."

"Let me try." Paul pointed the saw toward the tangle of twigs and leaves. BC put himself between Paul and the gnarl of limbs.

"I'm not going to hurt him, I promise."

BC zeroed in on Paul's face. Satisfied by what he saw, he lay down, sphinx-style, in front of the dog's body.

"I think he understood me!"

"He did. What's more, he believed you. I'm impressed."

"You think he knows what I'm saying?"

'Sure. Did you know that some dogs, and in my own opinion cats, have the passive vocabulary of a five-year old child?"

"No, I didn't."

"Just ask Carl Douglas if you don't believe me." Kat referred to the one and only veterinarian for Ravens Cove.

"By the looks of the animal's leg, I'll have the opportunity as soon as we free it."

"We'd better get to work." Kat lifted the smaller branches up and away from the injured leg.

"Perfect." Paul pulled a pair of pruning shears from his pocket. "Brought these along, too. Just in case." Paul snipped each tendril, then sawed off the main branch. He reached in and pulled the small dog free. "Sure is a nasty cut."

"Definitely needs to see Carl. Come on BC—Where'd he go? BC, come *now!*" Kat yelled.

The miniature version of Lassie jumped and buried its muzzle in the crook of Paul's arm.

"Sorry." Kat scratched the soft fur and walked down the path. BC was halfway up the trail eating salmon flakes.

"Should have known." Kat scooped him up and gave him a gentle squeeze. Then she held him out so they were eye-to-eye.

"You hate dogs," she said. "What makes this one so special?" Kat kissed the top of his head. "Guess we'll find out, huh?" BC snuggled deeper into her arms and purred. She kissed his head again. *Thanks, God. I owe You.*

"I see you found the wayfarer—again."

"Indeed. Now about the injured one." Kat pointed her chin at the dog.

"Is Douglas in? It's after eight o'clock."

"That late? Took longer to get the pup free than I thought. I've got his home number—oh, man, I left Gram and Josiah all this time." Kat rushed up the trail and burst through the cabin's front door. The welcoming aroma of meat and onions filled the small house. "I'm sorry I left you so long."

"No need to apologize. I'm keeping busy, and Josiah is delightful company."

"It smells wonderful!"

"Sit. Food's ready."

"Right after I call Doc Douglas. BC disappeared because he was guarding a dog, of all things. It's got a nasty cut."

"Where is Paul?"

"Don't know." Kat stuck her head out the door.

Paul waved from his car. "Get a hold of the doc?"

"Give me a minute." Kat ducked back inside—"Carl says he'll meet you at the clinic. Sure you don't want me to come with you?"

"Not necessary. You visit with Alese and Josiah. I'll call you when I know something."

Kat smiled. "Thanks so much. Next time you need something done at church or even at home, give me a call." She joined Alese and Josiah at the claw-footed oak table.

"That was a good meal if I say so myself."

"Every meal you cook is good. Thanks for taking care of me—again."

"Always a pleasure, child of my heart." Grandma sat on Kat's overstuffed sofa looking out at the lush trees in their full summer dress.

"Never gets tiring, does it?"

"No. Of course, we don't see greened-up trees much of our year."

Kat giggled. "True—now, how am I supposed to get you guys back to town?"

"I'm not ready to go home quite yet. You need to tell me why you fainted."

"Right now?" A vision of a pasty leg, muscle and tissue floating in the wind, hit Kat in the gut. Her legs trembled, then gave way.

Josiah caught her before she collapsed, guided her to the sofa and released her. "I think you do, Katrina. Things held in secret make us weak—physically and spiritually."

Kat nodded, took a deep breath, and told Alese and Josiah what she'd seen.

Lines of worry creased Josiah's forehead, and concern whispered to his heart. "Do you think the small dog has anything to do with this?"

"I don't know how—oh, I knew I'd seen it before."

"Where?"

"At the antique store. Annie Scofland said it adopted her. She said it wouldn't leave her side." A different kind of sickness hit Kat's stomach. She reached for the phone.

Chapter 7
Déjà Vu

"This place is a dead end." Bart shook his head in frustration more than disgust." Let's make our way to the bottom of the ravine." Bart's front pocket vibrated, then beeped. "What part of *rest* don't you understand?" He growled into the phone.

"I'm a little too wound up to rest. Do you want to know why I called?"

"You're gonna tell me anyway."

"True. So here goes. When I went looking for BC today, I found him and a dog."

"Okay… so call around and see if anyone's missing a pet."

"I know the dog. Annie Scofland told me it had adopted her."

The hairs on Bart's neck came to attention. "Did Ms. Scofland happen to say where it came from?"

"No. She just said it was a stray and wouldn't leave her side—doesn't sound good, does it?" Sadness laced Kat's voice.

"Not on the surface. Where's the dog now?"

"Pastor Paul took her to Carl Douglas. She was cut pretty bad."

"Call and see if one of our summer visitors reported it missing, would you? Then REST!"

"Bart, here!"

"Gotta go. Keep me posted." Bart climbed to the top of the ravine and joined Ken.

"No way." Elf-size cloven imprints in the soft dirt screamed, *they're back*. "Kumrande." Bart spat out the name for the half goat/half man dwarfs who served the demon Iconoclast and his army.

"Could they be old?"

"I'm hoping." Bart slapped at the back of his neck. "We better keep moving or we'll be a feast for the mosquitoes."

"Okay. The prints lead there." Ken pointed to a tight-knit copse of spruce and birch. He pulled an LED flashlight from his belt. "I thought we were rid of those nasty creatures when we got rid of their master."

Bart pointed to the flashlight. "Glad to see one of us is prepared. Who'd have thought something as mundane as a utility light would end up saving our bacon more than once?"

Ken pulled his gun.

"Let me refresh your memory. Firearms don't work against those minions of the devil."

"It'll work if we come up against something natural—like a bear."

"Now, wouldn't a big grizzly bear be a nice change? I'm game if you are." Bart waved Ken to the lead.

Several feet in, a sparkle caught Ken's eye. He bagged a solitary diamond in a platinum setting. "Looks real."

"Which begs the question—where's the owner?" Bart plowed into the underbrush, parting tall grass and ferns looking for clues.

Ken spotted a pile of dried leaves and sticks. He picked up a leaf-covered branch and swept the debris off the mound. "Found her."

A pasty-white torso was in full view by the time Bart arrived. Bart frowned as he gloved his hands, stooped and brushed the leaves from the body's face. The lips and eyes were as ashen as the corpse's body. Skin fanned out away from the bones reminding Bart of grotesque wings. The lower half of the left leg was missing.

"Looks to me like the Kumrande's handiwork." Bart pointed to the deep hole in the rib cavity.

Ken shook his head. "I'm starting to think I should have stayed in LA."

"Why?"

It's safe compared to this place.

"Female." Billings stood up. "Rigor has come and gone. Looks like some evil son of a jackal actually drained her of every speck of blood. You didn't find any around here?"

"Not a drop."

Ken rubbed his hand across his face. "There's another crime scene. But where?"

Billings turned the victim's palm skyward. "These fingers look like dried apricots. I'm not sure I can get a print. The Anchorage ME's office might have a solution. I'll give them a call."

"Thanks, Doc. In the meantime, I'm hoping we'll get lucky and find an ID."

"This poor woman sure wasn't lucky." Billings shook his head and turned. "I've done all I can do until I get her back to the office. The mortuary boys will be here in short order." Billings referred to Eric and Jonas Smotherly, two brothers who worked for the Ravens Cove Mortuary and doubled as morgue attendants when the need arose.

"If the Kumrande are back, we need to get some lights." The urgency in Ken's voice accentuated Bart's growing discomfort.

Bart looked at the sky. "We have some time before it's dark."

"True, but since those," Ken pointed at the pitch-black woods ahead, "are the next logical step, I think LEDs are in order."

Bart remembered when Ken and he were ambushed by the Kumrande in the now defunct tourist attraction known as Old Town. They stood back-to-back and fired until the guns were empty. When Ken was taken down by the yellow-eyed creatures, Bart took hold of the only thing left on his belt—a flashlight. In the mayhem he accidentally pressed the *on* button. The light hit a Kumrande in the eyes. The hairy dwarf shrieked in pain and ran for the woods.

"I'll get them here. Pastor Lucas stocked up after the last run-in with those creatures."

———————◆•✦•◆———————

"On my way." Paul looked at Doc Douglas. "Will you call Kat with an update?"

"Count on it. Otherwise, she'll show up here demanding answers."

Paul laughed. "She sure can get her hackles up about animals."

"You'd think she was appointed by the good Lord as the protector of lost beasts."

"She and Saint Francis of Assisi. She could be in worse company."

"I guess. Anyway, I'll give her a call."

"Glad the pup's gonna be fine; just sorry no one has showed up for it."

Paul drove the short distance home he shared with the love of his life. On his way back out he stuck his head through the kitchen doorway. "Back later, Babe."

Tanya Lucas spied the flashlights and bible. "Be careful. Come home soon."

"I love you with all my heart."

"I love you, too—everything okay?"

"Of course. Just don't tell you enough."

Tanya Lucas grabbed his arm. "You'll be back soon. Right?"

"I promise." He blew her a kiss.

Paul parked his car in front of the police station and walked the rest of the way to Ravens Ravine.

"Have Doc Billings call me right away." Bart barked at the Smotherly brothers. "Don't come any closer, Pastor. Active crime scene."

Paul handed two flashlights to Bart. "So, where are the creatures?"

"Don't know if there are any. Saw a footprint. Need the lights just in case."

Paul tensed and studied the alders and trees lining the ravine's perimeter. He strode to the side of the pathway. "What's this?"

Bart took hold of a gold filigree triangle with a gloved hand, turned it back and forth, then shook his head. "Haven't a clue, but it looks familiar."

"Looks kind of like the corner of a folder or notebook."

Bart looked at the three-cornered object again. "I knew something was nagging me. It's the same doodad I saw on *The Book of Fallen Angels*."

"So where's the rest of the book?"

"Just another question we need to answer."

Ken joined Bart and Paul. "Didn't see anything else."

Bart shoved the small evidence bag into Ken's hand. "Look what Pastor Paul found."

"Where was it?"

Bart pointed to an alder. "Don't know how we could we have missed it."

"There are a lot of trees and brush. Seems easy enough."

"I could have sworn we checked the alders where Paul found this."

"I guess we'd better do one more sweep of the ravine path—and the floor."

"Yep." Bart looked at the darkening sky. "I think you'd better get on home Paul. Thanks for bringing the flashlights."

"Are you sure you don't need me?"

"Sure."

Paul held out the bible. "Take this. You may need it."

"It can't hurt." Bart took the bible.

Ken inspected the ravine path, brush, and earthen walls. The carbon-copies of the guardian hag tree vibrated to each footfall. "They weren't shaking before. It's like someone dug up their roots," Bart said.

"Let's move a little faster. Not a place I want to be pinned."

"Amen."

Bart forgot about the quaking hag trees when he came to a scorched spot on the path. "Seems like it was only yesterday."

Ken looked at the black earth and remembered the first Iconoclast battle in Ravens Cove and the angel who had left its holy mark on the pathway. "Why is this place such a prize for the evil foe? Not to mention God."

"If I knew the answer, brother, I'd call Oprah," Bart replied.

A twig snapped and Ken whirled toward the sound. "You've got to be kidding. Can't you ever stay put?"

"Turn that thing off!" Kat lowered her hand when she heard the click.

"You could have gotten shot!"Bart yelled.

"More like blinded," Kat mumbled.

"Why aren't you at home with your guests?"

"My guests were picked up by Paul after he left you."

"So you got bored and had to show up here?"

"No. I got a call from Gram. Tanya Lucas called her upset. I thought Paul might have come back. Tanya also mentioned something about Paul packing up flashlights and a bible—this isn't just a murder investigation, is it?"

"May not be just a murder investigation." Ken turned to Bart. "Is there no way to control a crime scene, or stop the rumors about a crime scene from flying around this town?"

"I've been trying for years, and still haven't succeeded. I'm open to suggestions."

"Are you finished lamenting your inability to subjugate this small corner of the world?"

"For now."

"Good." Kat held up Bart's jacket and tie. "I found these on the way down. Thought I'd make sure you were still wearing something."

"Well, you can see I am." Bart pointed to his shirt, then his pants. "The coat was too hot, and I can't do a good job if I'm eating a tie every time I bend over." *Why am I explaining this to her like she's my mother?*

"Well, I am relieved—hey, what's down there?" Kat nodded toward a black object a short distance from the scorched earth.

Bart switched on his flashlight. A tar-colored puddle absorbed the light, and then dissolved into the earth. "Did the black goo just vanish?"

"Looks like it." Ken stepped over the baked soil and wiped his hand across the brown earth. He held up his palm.

Bart shook his head. "Not even a trace."

Ken studied the boulder barricading the ravine entrance. "That's a new look."

"Now I *know* it wasn't this way a few hours ago." Black liquid streamed down the boulder, pooled at the rock's base, then disappeared into the earth. Small fissures formed wherever the ebony fluid touched.

"Where's it coming from?" Kat reached out to get a sample on her finger.

Bart caught hold of her hand. "What are you thinking?"

"Maybe it's water. We have a high water table in this area and it's full of iron. Makes the water almost black—look at the river."

"Except the stuff's magically disappearing into the earth. Not the other way around."

"Do you smell what I do?" Kat asked.

Bart took a deep breath. "The ole death and sulfur smell is back."

Ken pulled a packet marked 'sterile swab' from his pocket, tore it open, and caught a sample of the black liquid as it snaked down the rock. He put the swab in a clear cylinder and capped it. The black liquid dripped off the cotton and struck the bottom of the small bottle. It shimmered. The inky liquid turned a brilliant purple and then as clear as water.

Bart took the vial and witnessed the transparent liquid double in size. He crouched down and stuck the head of a cotton swab into the earth. He pulled it back out and watched the swab turn from white to purple. It swelled to twice its size. Transparent liquid dripped to the ground. "Can hardly wait to get an opinion on this stuff."

"You know there's not gonna be an opinion. Which will more than likely lead to another interview with Binnings." Ken flashed a resigned smile to Bart, then Kat.

"When I see purple and black, I can only think it's Pet." Kat shivered at the thought of the shapeshifter who had enticed so many to their deaths at the hands of Iconoclast.

"This murder doesn't resemble the ones committed by Iconoclast and Pet. Besides, Pet is Iconoclast's tempter, not the killer." Bart used the only way to diffuse Kat's fear he had found—logic.

"You're probably right. But what is it, then?"

"Don't know. We need to find out more about the victim to come to any conclusions. If the perp is another supernatural thing, this Jane Doe is the only lead we have."

"Don't you think it'd be a good idea to talk to Gram? She might know something."

"I don't want you to bring this up with Gram," Bart said.

"You don't have a choice." Grandma Bricken used her cane as support on the way down the path. Josiah followed close behind.

"How did you even hear what I said? Never mind. Why are you here?"

"Tanya Lucas called us."

"You, too?"

"Said the way Paul had left the house, she felt something was amiss and asked us to check on him. Where is he?"

"Sent him home a while ago. And I'm sending you home now." Bart waved them up the path.

"Don't take that tone with me, Bartholomew Andersen. I'll leave when I'm good and ready!" Grandma Bricken turned to Kat. "Mandy Thomas called. Told me she couldn't reach you."

"My cell's right here. It didn't ring." Kat dug in her raincoat pocket. "Shoot, must have left it at home. What'd she say?"

"A detective—I don't remember his name— called her."

"Detective Dayton?"

"Yes. Said he had questions and was trying to reach you, too."

"When I talked to Binnings he told me the case was tied up. What do you think he wants?" Ken asked.

"I don't know. I'll give him a call from the house."

"Good idea. We're all leaving now, anyway. It's getting dark and I don't want to run into any creatures of the night—if you know what I mean." Bart shooed the others up the path.

Kat turned. "There's only one reason you'd be concerned about the dark—the Kumrande! Are they here?"

Bart pushed his cell into her hand. "Why don't you call Dayton right now?"

Kat pushed the phone back to Bart. "You're changing the subject."

"I think we all should hear why Detective Dayton's calling."

"Not to state the obvious, cous, but I don't have the number."

"Oh, where is my mind today." Grandma handed Kat a piece of paper. "Here's the number."

Really? I have to call with all the overprotective witnesses present?

"Anytime now, *cous.*"

Dayton answered on the first ring. "Thanks for getting back to me so fast."

"Is Mandy in the thick of it again?"

"No. If anything, she is no longer my suspect."

"Good to hear. So, what else can I do for you?"

"Remember the statue we found in Spawldine's hideaway?"

"The one named Lilith, right?"

"Lilith?" Grandma said to Kat.

Kat nodded, then returned to what Dayton was saying.

"Yes. The next time I went to Spawldine's house, it was missing. You didn't happen to take it with you?"

"What would I want with the disgusting little half-naked thing?"

"I have to ask."

"What makes it so important anyway? The guy was hit on the head and died. Seems pretty cut and dried to me."

Ken held his hand out for the phone. Kat shook her head vehemently and mouthed, "I have this covered." She turned her back.

"It seems Spawldine not only had a knock on his head that would have killed an elephant, but he was drained of blood."

"Well, he bled pretty hard."

"Yes, he did. But not hard enough to bleed him out."

"Oh, how awful."

"What?" Bart whispered in her face. Kat held up a hand.

"So what does this have to do with the statue?"

"I don't know; just a hunch. You think your friend would have taken it for any reason?"

"I don't know how. Either you or your partner was with her at Spawldine's house or I was with her packing the shop and her apartment."

Ken yanked the phone away from Kat. "This is FBI Agent Ken Melbourne. Do you have any legal reason to be badgering this woman?"

Kat snatched the phone and glared at Ken. "As you were saying, Detective Dayton…"

"Who was that?"

"A friend."

"I've never met anyone with two friends in the FBI. Are you in witness protection or something?"

"Nothing so exciting. Just lucky—if you can call it luck."

Dayton chuckled. "Listen, her cell phone goes directly to voice-mail. If you see Ms. Thomas, tell her to call me right away."

"I will."

"Thanks. Oh, tell Agent Melbourne I'm sorry to have bothered you." Dayton's tone lacked sincerity.

"Not necessary. I'm sorry for his interference. Call anytime." Kat glared at Ken as she punched *end*.

"Seems like something's gone missing from the dead guy's house in Anchorage."

"Mandy?"

"Who else would they suspect? But I don't know how she could have done it. She wasn't alone more than a few minutes last week…" Kat's voice trailed off.

"Is there something else?"

"Dayton said the dead guy didn't have any blood in him."

"What?" Bart and Ken said in unison.

"Did I just win the prize or something? I said the dead guy—"

"Heard you." Bart looked off into the distance, lost in thought.

"Tell me this shouldn't have any effect on us here."

"We just had a body taken away. It looked to be drained of blood. And I don't believe in coincidence," Ken answered.

"It's hard to deny the connection. How many bloodless corpses has the FBI found in Alaska?"

"None," Ken said.

Josiah cleared his throat. "Gentlemen, excuse me. Lilith is a de-mon mentioned in the old texts—not the bible. She was known for drinking the blood of her victims. My only question is why would she do this to a woman? It is written she seeks to destroy children and men because she blames men for her demise and destroys chil-dren because she could never have any."

"This is getting a little too personal," Ken said.

"And the statue of Lilith is missing, too?"

"You heard right, Josiah."

"I only know of one reason to steal that statue," Josiah said.

"You telling us someone in Anchorage is worshipping this lady?" Bart asked.

"I'm thinking someone *was* worshipping this entity in Anchorage, and now they might be here." Josiah lifted his hands and dropped them back to his side. "That's what I'm thinking."

"It's tourist season so the suspects are numerous. Let's start with who we know had something to do with this." Bart looked at Kat. "Let's go see Mandy."

Large yellow eyes followed the small troop until they were out of sight. "They know too much. Where is the guardian?" Nihilist spat at his cloven-footed companion.

"Making preparations for the rise of the woman—and the spirits she will release."

"The demons still do not know of this plan?"

"No. They think we are loyal and are preparing for the return of Iconoclast," Homunculus answered.

"Good." Nihilist smiled in satisfaction. "Then the demons will help us be rid of the humans. Find the watcher; find Pernector NOW!—Wait."

Homunculus turned back to Nihilist. "You don't want me to find the watcher?"

First, find the one who can drive humans insane."

"Why not me?" Homunculus protested.

"We need the invisible one. Find Energumen."

"As you say, chosen leader of the Kumrande." Homunculus dove into the earth and disappeared.

Nihilist pulled a black and purple sphere from his robe.

"No one knows I have you. No one will know until I make my play." The thing hummed a melancholy tune. Nihilist curled his clawed fingers around the ball. "Glad we saved you from the destruction of your friends, Pet."

The small being purred as Nihilist stuck him into a sack of salt, then into the pocket of his robe. He patted it softly. "So glad."

Mandy opened the door and looked at Ken, Kat, and Bart. She took a step back and waved them in. "Excuse the mess." Mandy pointed to a mound of clothes piled in one corner of the room. A makeup case and shoes held the small hill in place. "Still haven't gotten unpacked—not to mention acquired any furniture."

Kat smiled. "Has Wendy got anything you can use to store your clothes at least?"

"Didn't ask. Hello, Bart. How are you?" Her tone was soft and inviting.

Don't you dare, Mandy. Don't you dare. Kat thought.

"Doing great. How about you?"

"Could be better." She whipped around to Kat. "To what do I owe this visit?"

"Detective Dayton called."

"Oh, for goodness sake, why won't he leave me alone?" Mandy plopped onto the only piece of furniture in the room—a folding chair.

"You are no longer a suspect in the murder of Spawldine," Ken said.

"Is that why Dayton called? And who are you? Mandy asked.

Kat's protective instincts rushed to the surface. "This is my fiancé, Ken Melbourne. Ken, meet Mandy Thomas."

Mandy winked at Ken. "If you're ever available, give me a call."

Ken gripped Kat's hand. "Not interested, Ms. Thomas. I've been looking for this woman all of my life. I'm not going to let her get away."

'Too bad." Her face lit up. "On the other hand, glad I'm no longer a suspect."

"Not in the murder but something of Spawldine's is missing."

"Missing? You were with me the whole time, Kat. Why would he suspect me?"

"It's logical. He asked me about it, too. I don't know how you'd have gotten it, but I think you should call the guy. Otherwise, he could show up and drag you back to Anchorage for more questioning."

"What's missing?"

"A statue from Spawldine's house."

"Was it a woman with a snake?"

"How do you know what it looks like?"

"You *do* think I stole it! For your information, I saw the ugly thing the day it came in the mail." Mandy shivered. "It is the scariest 'work of art' I've ever seen. Do you know I was sure I saw the snake move one time? Anyway, he told me it was part of a rare collection."

"You only saw the statue once?" Ken asked.

"Yes. When I asked where it had gone, he said it was in a safe place. I never asked again."

"If it was rare, maybe there was someone else who wanted it. Anyone come to mind?"

"Look, I didn't know much about Grady's personal life—other than the part I played in it." Mandy dropped her head to her hands. "And I am trying to forget our, umm, association."

And looking for another one as fast as you can, Kat thought.

"Did you ever meet any of his friends?" Bart asked.

"He didn't exactly show me off to anyone. But one time I showed up early. Five or six people were just leaving. He rushed me into the kitchen and shut the door."

"Did you get a good look at any of them?"

"No." Mandy twisted the hem of her jacket. She raised her eyes. "I do remember this one lady. She was old. Her back was hunched and she used a cane. I'll never forget the stick she had."

"Why?"

"A silver snake wound around the full length of the cane. It reminded me of the one on that horrible statue."

Kat sighed in frustration. "Mandy, can you just offer some of this information without the twenty questions?"

"Sorry. Still feel like I'm a bad guy." She lifted pleading eyes to Bart.

Bart ignored the appeal. "Do you have any information to help Detective Dayton find the thief?"

"I remember Grady calling the old lady Madame something... like a title. Let me think." Mandy pursed her lips then snapped her fingers. "Piquant. Her name was Madame Piquant—I think."

"Okay. Now we have something to work with."

"Here's Dayton's number. He said to call him as soon as we reached you."

"Fine. I'll do it in a minute."

Kat took Mandy's cell from the small counter dividing the living room from the kitchenette. She plopped it into Mandy's hand.

Mandy looked at the phone. "Guess I'll do it now."

Dayton answered on the first ring. Mandy explained what she had told Kat and the group, then handed the phone to Ken. "He wants to talk to you."

"Melbourne, is it?"

"Yes."

"Madame Piquant has a reputation with the police here. I'm going to try and find her. I don't expect her to head in your direction, but I'll send you her photo just in case. Got a fax?"

"Uhhh..." Ken remembered the copier at the station. It had fax capability. He just prayed it was functioning. "Yes."

"I don't know why she'd show up in Ravens Cove but if she does, trouble's sure to follow. Keep an eye out."

"Will do."

"Oh, and if she does surface there, I'd appreciate a call."

"Will do." Ken just didn't say when.

"Seems the old lady has made quite a name for herself with the APD. Think we'd better do some checking on our own."

Bart nodded. "Good thing you still have connections in high places."

"Gonna find out if I do first thing in the morning. Right now, I think we'd better call it a night. I'll drive this one"—he pointed to Kat—"home and meet you later, Bart."

Kat climbed into the SUV. "Where are you staying, fiancé of mine?"

"Bart offered me a place to stay. I was pretty sure you weren't going to."

"You were right."

"One can only hope." Ken smiled at Kat.

"Keep hoping, my man, keep hoping."

Mandy watched the trio leave. "It could have been different, Bart. It could have been so different," she said under her breath. She picked up the cell phone and dialed. "They know."

"They don't know enough. Keep your mouth shut." The line went dead.

Chapter 8
Divide and Conquer

Kat waved to Ken and watched the SUV's headlights fade as he backed down the driveway. She took a close look at the flowerpots lining her small deck. The orange and yellow marigolds had become black silhouettes in the deep-blue dusk.

The dark outline of something or someone tall rocketed past the corner of Kat's eye. She whirled to her right and scanned the logs for the source of movement. "Hello?" She crept over to the rough-hewn beams. She touched the timbers. They were still warm from the sun. Kat shook herself. *I need sleep.*

She crossed the threshold and tensed for the usual hide-and-attack by her feline friend. It didn't come. *Darn cat. Probably still out looking for fresh game.*

"No presents tonight, BC. I couldn't take it. The last time almost killed me." She remembered the mutilated gift from BC—a dead shrew. Black Cat had placed it squarely in front of the threshold. She saw the bloody corpse, jumped backwards and managed to regain her balance right before she tumbled down the deck steps. "I still don't know how I stayed upright."

Kat made her way to the bedroom. "I was sure I had put those on the bed before I left." She snatched up two sage and burgundy bed pillows, tossed them onto the closet floor, and made her way to the bathroom.

A rustling sound brought her back out. She shrieked. The pillows were on her floor again, in a neat line against the bed frame, and facing the bathroom. She heard a loud *thwack* and stared in disbelief when a photo of Mount Denali took on a life of its own. It jumped off the picture hanger, slid down the wall, and came to a stop with a light thud. Memories of the first Iconoclast siege sent chills up her spine. She saw the dead—purple and yellow oozing from their eye-sockets—and the purple and black shapeshifter called Pet who had almost lured her into eternal slavery.

A vision of the second time Iconoclast came to Ravens Cove slammed her brain. A Kumrande had found its way into her bedroom, intent on taking her to Iconoclast and his nasty man-eating boulder named Dacoit. She remembered watching Wendy entranced by Pet and waiting to be the horrible demon's next meal. Fear turned to fury.

"You're kidding, right?" she yelled into the empty room. "What is it about this one little town? Why can't you leave us alone? And another thing, is my bedroom just the hotbed of activity for the demon army? If so, then bring it on you nasty thing, bring it on. I'm too tired to be fighting something I can't see! In the name of Jesus, show yourself!"

Nothing happened. Anger turned to humiliation. *I am so glad no one was here to see me make a fool of myself. I definitely need sleep.*

Kat snatched up the pillows and stopped. A normal-looking shadow on the wall fluttered in a nonexistent wind. Kat's eyes widened when a torso, then arms and legs formed out of the dense silhouette. Malevolent red eyes burned through the inky mass, followed by two pinpricks for a nose, and a blood-red hole of a mouth. It grinned, revealing its barbed teeth. "As you command," Energumen stepped into the light.

Kat scrambled backwards to the closet wall. She reached behind, took hold of a hanger and lunged.

Energumen blasted to the ceiling. He waved a gnarled hand. The coat-hanger vibrated, then jerked itself from Kat's hand. Energumen dove and hovered a few feet above her.

"If this is my end, so be it!" Kat stood straight-backed and glared at the demon.

"So be it!" Energumen flew at Kat.

Kat squeezed her eyes shut. "I won't hide from this!" Her eyes popped open. She focused on the blade-like claw barreling inches from her nose. Kat threw her arms over her face. Searing pain traveled to her shoulder. Blood gushed from the wound, making a sickening *plop-plop* sound as it struck the floor.

Energumen hovered a foot above her head. "I'll take my time—the other arm, then your legs. Don't worry, though. It won't take you too much time to bleed to death—just long enough for you to regret calling me out." He sniggered and raised a gnarled, long-fingered hand.

"Ahhhh! Release me!"

Kat saw a semitransparent rope wind through Energumen's arms. The mist yanked Energumen down and through the floor. She stood paralyzed—unable to move while her brain digested the incomprehensible event she had been through.

Pain shocked Kat into movement. She jogged into the bathroom, snagged a towel, and covered the oozing arm in a makeshift bandage. Waves of nausea slammed her stomach and drove her into the bathroom for a second time.

———◆—◆◄►◆—◆———

"You showed yourself to a human! Tell me why I shouldn't send you plummeting into the abyss!" Pernector hissed.

"Oh, Watcher, she commanded me in *the Name!* I had no choice," Energumen whined.

"Not good enough!" Pernector raised his arm and pointed to the ground. It began to vibrate. "This place is too important to our master! Now, the Gorgon has been released *and* the humans will know we are here."

"Maybe. I left a package in the vile woman's home which will make her question her sanity—better yet, others will question her honesty."

Pernector lowered his arm and the earth quieted. "I am listening."

"I was told to discredit one of God's faithful ones. I have."

"You were told to drive one of them insane."

"Is this not better? The others will think one of their own is untruthful or crazy. Divide and conquer."

A smile played at the corners of Pernector's mouth. "Will it be found?"

"Oh, yes."

"I have always counted on you to make a bad situation worse. Get away from me before I change my mind."

Energumen bowed and shot into the night sky.

"That hurts!" Kat leaned back against her bed pillows and glared at Doc Billings.

"If you'll hold still it won't hurt as much." Doc tied off the knot.

"She's always been a baby when it comes to needles and things." Wendy let go of Kat's hand and wiggled her fingers. "For someone almost in a puddle on the floor when I walked in, you sure got your strength back in a hurry."

Doc Billings taped large gauze pads over the wound and wrapped it in an Ace bandage. He pulled a syringe out of the old-fashioned doctor's bag. "Roll over."

"You're kidding right? Can't I just get some pills?"

"Roll over!"

"Told you—needles and doctors," Wendy said.

"Fine." Kat rolled onto her stomach. She grimaced at the sharp prick of the hypodermic.

"All done. And, yes, you need an oral antibiotic, too. I'll give you a prescription for penicillin. Get it filled at the pharmacy tomorrow. The wound is already inflamed."

"Will do." Kat gripped her left jean pocket and yanked the pants over her hip.

Kat heard a loud bang on the entry door.

"Who could that be?"

"KAT," Bart shouted.

"How did you manage to call Bart without me knowing?"

"It's what I do." Wendy turned and yelled. "Back here, Bart."

"I'm not happy with you, Wendy. Now my lug of a cousin is gonna go into protection overdrive. Just what I need." Kat flopped back against the bed pillows.

Bart stomped through the front door. His foot came down on something with the consistency of a drenched washrag. He released the flashlight from his belt and pointed the beam at a bloody lump of gray fur. "What in the name of..."

A black streak seized hold of the gory mass and dashed toward the bedroom. "No, BC!" Kat yelled as he trotted toward the bed, a mutilated shrew dangling from his mouth. He dropped it.

"Oh, yuck." Wendy took the last clean towel from the bathroom and picked up the small corpse. "Be right back. Looks like the ravens will be having a complimentary breakfast."

"Yes, let's look at the bright side." Kat grimaced and considered another run for the bathroom.

Doc Billings took in Kat's pallid complexion and sunken eyes. "Not to be obvious, but you need to rest. You were in a mild state of shock when I arrived, and you've lost quite a bit of blood."

"You tell her, Doc. Back in a flash." Wendy headed to the front door and came back holding Bart's forearm.

"Look who I found standing in the living room when I was taking out the, umm, collateral damage."

"Good morning." Doc nodded to Bart, and turned back to Kat. "Want you in my office first thing tomorrow."

"Again I ask you, Wendy. Why did you think it was a great idea to call Bart? I just want to go to sleep!" Kat rolled onto her side.

Wendy marched to the side of the bed wagging her finger at Kat's back. "There's some crazy on the loose and you're gonna sleep? Since when?"

"Where is everyone?" Ken called from the front.

Kat sat up and turned to Wendy. "Him, too?"

Ken looked from the bandage on Kat's arm to the blood on the floor. "What happened?"

"Someone attacked her."

"More like *something,*" Kat whispered.

Wendy rolled her eyes. "She insists it wasn't human."

Bart walked over to the bed. "What makes you say *something*?"

"Humans don't usually materialize out of thin air or fly!"

Bart turned to Ken. "Maybe a little too much for her today," he mouthed.

BC wound himself around Ken's feet then walked to the closet and sat down. Ken followed.

"Whatcha you doing, little big guy?" Ken pushed the clothes aside. He brought out a small statuette. A semi-naked woman gleamed in the sunlight. A dark, green snake encircled the figure from its neck to its feet.

"How'd that get here?" Kat's voice rose to a shriek. "HOW THE HELL DID THAT GET HERE?"

"You didn't take it from Anchorage?" Bart asked.

"No!"

"Maybe you thought it would help Mandy," Ken said.

"I didn't take the statue!"

"What's going on here?" Grandma Bricken walked into the already crowded room. She made her way to the bed. Kat fell into her arms and murmured. "They think I'm losing it—they may be right!"

Grandma Bricken held Kat at arm's length. "Why would you say such a thing, child?" Grandma Bricken turned to Bart. "Bart?"

"She's talking some odd stuff, Gram. And we found this." Bart held up the statue.

Grandma Bricken looked long and hard at her granddaughter. "Pshaw, this girl is sane as any of us in the room. Now tell me what happened and you police types"—she nodded at Bart and Ken—"get back to doing whatever you do to find out who did this to her."

"Well, it started with the pillows." Kat leaned toward Alese Bricken. "They were moving on their own."

"See what I mean, Gram?"

"Hush, Bartholomew! Go on."

"I saw a shadow, but not a shadow, in the corner. It started weaving. I told it to show itself in the name of Jesus."

"Oh, my. What did it look like?"

"It had red eyes…"

"Red eyes, you say?" Josiah joined Grandma Bricken.

"Should I expect anyone else, Wendy?"

"I think this is everyone I called."

"I know those eyes, Katrina," Josiah said.

Kat narrowed her eyes. "How —you're not just trying to humor me, are you?"

"No. I saw them in the ravine. I saw hundreds, maybe thousands of them when Iconoclast met me for battle. They materialized, too."

"This is the first you talked about this part of your confrontation with Iconoclast," Ken said.

"It is a detail I didn't remember until now. Funny, I forgot something so terrifying."

"I want to hear this one." Wendy joined the small group at the foot of Kat's bed.

"When the mountainous rock rose from the earth and closed the ravine to the world, I saw them. First, only the eyes—glinting like ruby stars in the tar-black ravine. Then, Iconoclast materialized and so did they. All different shapes and sizes; yet the eyes were the same, glittering red. So mesmerizing in their color and so cold with hatred." Josiah shivered like a frigid wind blasted into his very soul. "They lined the ravine walls, hovering on invisible bleachers. They shouted, 'more, more,' at the first wound I took. Just like those who enjoy watching a wild animal tear apart its prey. I fought until I had no more strength."

"So, why didn't you die?"

"I don't know why, but God sent one of His angels to save me. So, yes, Katrina, I believe you."

"Ah, which reminds me of Psalm 91. One of my personal favorites. 'If you make the Most High your dwelling—even the Lord, who is my refuge—then no harm will befall you, no disaster will come near your tent. For He will command His angels concerning you to guard you in all of your ways.' My friend, you saw what we only hope to see when we leave this earth. You are blessed." Paul smiled at Josiah.

"And you a blessing," Josiah quipped.

"Do you have God radar or something?" Wendy looked at Paul Lucas.

Paul chuckled. "Nothing so exciting. How do you think Alese and Josiah got here today?"

"In all the hubbub, it just seemed natural."

"Excuse me," Bart said. "Does anyone know what succubus means?"

"It's a mythical creature, a woman who sucks the life force or blood out of its victims."

"Seriously, Kat? You know about those things? You've got to get a life."

"I read a lot, Winsome. You should try it. Why are you asking?"

Bart held the figurine base toward Kat. "It's scratched into the bottom of the statue."

Wendy read aloud, *"Lilith plus Succubus.* What does it mean?"

"Well, since this Lilith liked to suck the breath out of children and drain the men she killed of their blood, seems they could be one and the same." Josiah turned to Ken. "Do you know Lilith was supposedly the first wife of Adam?"

"Interesting. I just don't see how this thing," Ken pointed to the statue, "has any relevance to the dismembered body we found yesterday. Unless you're telling me this Lilith is alive and well in the Cove and has changed her tastes to include women."

"Anything's possible," Josiah remarked.

"It seems too coincidental for another supernatural being to have taken up residence here. Iconoclast went to the depths where he belongs after his last effort to take the Cove. As far as I'm concerned, case closed."

"I would agree except for this attack on Katrina," Josiah said.

"Let's not forget about the hag tree," Kat piped in.

Ken threw his hands in the air. "Am I the only voice of reason here? Maybe the person who destroyed the tree didn't stop there. Maybe the victim saw the perp and he panicked. Maybe, just maybe, we aren't dealing with ghosts this time."

"Demons, Kenneth."

"Or those either! I am going to investigate this like the murder it is until I'm proved wrong."

Bart put a hand on Ken's shoulder. "Okay. Where do you want to start?"

"The statue is the only common denominator we have right now." Ken turned to Kat. "So, the first thing is to find out how it ended up in your closet. Is there something you want to tell us?"

Kat bolted upright. "Are you accusing me of lying, FBI?"

"The thing was in your closet."

Kat threw back the covers and stood up. "You doubt me after all we've been through? Have I ever lied to you? Have I ever given you reason to think I'd steal?"

Ken answered her tirade with a silent stare.

"I'll answer for you—NO!" Kat held the injured arm close and tugged her windbreaker on with the good hand.

"What are you doing? You heard Doc Billings' tell you to rest." Gram walked after Kat who was already on the cabin's deck.

"I'm going to find out who set me up. While I'm gone you can ask Mr. Logic if he thinks I ripped my arm to the bone just to have an alibi," she yelled as she walked to the road.

"I don't think it's a self-inflicted wound," Ken whispered.

"You are still a major piece of work, Fibber. You do not deserve her." Wendy shook her head in disgust and headed for the door. "Wait up, Kat, I'll drive you."

"You could have handled that one better," Josiah said.

"The facts lead here—and to Kat."

"How do you know that the statue wasn't put here by someone else?"

"My job is to find the truth. I can't overlook the facts just because I'm in love with her."

"She isn't going to forgive you easily, Kenneth. Her integrity is her shield. More, it is what she lives by." Grandma Bricken leaned on her cane and stared into Ken's eyes.

"I was being honest. How else did it get here?"

"You'd better try and find out."

"Why do you think I'm still here?"

"I'm sorry to interrupt but I told Tanya I'd be home by now. Let me get you two back to Gram's." Paul interjected.

"We're done here—for now." Gram shook her head at Ken. "This is a very sad day."

The whispered scolding knifed Ken in the stomach. *I'm doing my job!* He thought.

"Sometimes the job comes second." Grandma answered.

"I'm going back to work." Ken stepped into the bedroom.

"I've checked all the windows, and there is no evidence of forced entry," Bart said.

"There would be no forced entry if it was a demon," Josiah remarked from the doorway.

"I've told you my feelings about demons returning to the Cove. Why are you still here, anyway?"

"I felt it important to say you had better tell that beautiful young woman you believe her before you lose her—again—Agent Melbourne."

Ken bristled. "I'll take it under advisement. And would you stop calling me agent? I'm not here on FBI business."

Josiah gave him a quizzical look. "As you'd like, Mr. Melbourne."

"Enough," Bart said. "Don't take him too seriously, Josiah. You are looking at the walking definition of stress in Melbourne. By the way, he is now the acting police chief of our fair town."

"Oh, I see. Well then, chief, welcome to your new position."

"I am only a consultant."

"Temporarily on assignment as our new police chief." Bart's phone chimed. He glanced at his watch. "Already? I'll be right there. Hold them off, Jenny." He snapped the phone shut. "I've got a council meeting and completely forgot. You got this, Melbourne?"

"Sure."

"I'll catch up with you as soon as I can." Bart threw himself against the doorjamb right before Kat's good elbow hit him in the stomach.

"You still here?"she said as she passed by.

"Why are you back?"

"BC. Maybe a wild animal tore up the woman at the ravine. I don't want to be worrying about him while I'm trying to prove my innocence. Did one of you let him out?"

Ken leaned on the bedroom doorframe. "Not on purpose."

"So you say. How do I know I can *believe* you?"

"I've always told you the truth."

Kat raised her eyebrows. "Have you?"

"Okay, I should believe you for the same reason. I get it."

"Do you?"

Ken sighed. "I care about the black terror. I wouldn't do anything to hurt him."

"Keep digging yourself that big hole. Jump in when it feels comfortable. He'll come back, he always has—I'll just have to TRUST him." Kat glared at Ken.

"I let my investigator take over. I should have let my love for you do the talking."

"You bet you should have. I accept your apology. I don't know if I can… "

"I will help you find out why the statue ended up here. Then maybe we can put this behind us and get on with our future."

"Don't know, FBI. I was scared before. Now I'm terrified of a long-term commitment to you."

"Because I was doing my job? It's who I am."

"Because you doubted my integrity. It's who *I* am!"

"What can I do? I want us to have a future."

"I'll let you know when I figure it out."

The sadness in Ken's eyes tugged at Kat. *I love you so much, and you cut me so deep.* "Right now, let's just drop it. There are more important things to do."

Ken sighed. "Okay—for now."

"Later." Kat headed out the front door.

"Don't suppose I can talk you into coming to the office and typing up a report?"

Kat strolled back inside. "I'd be going against town policy."

"You'd be doing me a big favor—besides maybe Bart'll have it through the council before they find out."

"I suppose I might see something in your notes to help me find the creep who set me up."

"It's possible."

A mischievous grin lit Kat's face. "I'll take my chances with the council. See you at the station, FBI."

Chapter 9
Where's the Connection?

Kat flipped the power switch. The fluorescent lights of the station hummed to life. Kat welcomed the usually annoying buzz. It quieted her jangled nerves. The off-key duet of the jangling phone and tinkling door chime shattered the calm. Kat jogged to the phone. "Ravens Cove Police."

"Mornin' again, KittyKat," Wendy's cheerful tone greeted her.

Kat waved to Ken and lowered herself into the desk chair. "How did you even know I was here?"

"Where else would you be with a dead body showing up in the Cove? You, my friend, are a creature of habit."

"Thank you for the compliment—Ms. Free Spirit. Let me just head this conversation off by saying I have no information for you."

"I'm not calling *for* information. I'm calling *with* information."

"Which is?" Kat held the phone between her shoulder and chin, leaned down, and pushed the computer's *on* button.

"BC's at the vet."

Kat gripped the receiver and leaned forward. "Is he okay?"

"He's just fine. Carl, I mean Doctor Douglas, says he yowled and scratched on the front door of the clinic until he was let in. Once inside, he ran for the kennels in back. He won't budge."

"Wendy, when did you become the vet's assistant? Where's Nyna?"

"I'm just helping out. He and Nyna are in emergency surgery."

"I'll be right there."

"Not necessary. BC is happy as a clam lying in front of the stray's cage. And Carl thinks he's good for the dog. Seems your wildcat has a calming effect on it. Go figure."

"Well, I guess there's no harm in him staying. I'll come by and check on him after I'm done here."

"That works. Talk later." The phone went dead.

The door's bell chimed again, breaking Kat's concentration. She looked up at Bart. "What are you doing here?"

"The question is why you are here. I don't remember telling you the council okayed your return." Bart crossed his arms and scowled.

"Work calms my nerves. I couldn't see any harm in helping out and…"

Bart's face broke into a wide grin. "They approved it. Go to work at full speed, O great police chief's assistant."

"Oh, thank goodness. I didn't want to train someone else—the only one I could think of being Wendy, and you know where that'd go."

"We all know where it would go," Ken said from the doorway of the police chief's office.

"Thought you'd still be at the cabin."

"Just finished up," Ken answered.

"How's the office feel? Like home?"

"It feels like an office."

"Give it some time. It'll grow on you."

"We'll see. You here for a reason? You could have called with the okay for Kat to go back to work."

"I was thinking. The best place to find someone who doesn't want to be found—if they are here—is someplace no one wants to go."

"Tell me you aren't talking about Old Town."

"What better place to hide? It's spooked everyone in town." Bart referred to the happenings in Old Town where Iconoclast had taken a last stand to capture and murder as many as he could in Ravens Cove.

"It *is* completely abandoned. The council even coughed up the money for a chain-link fence to keep out the curiosity seekers," Kat added.

Ken sighed. "I suppose it should be the next stop."

"Seems logical." Bart smiled. "But it's your decision."

Ken hefted himself off the door jam. "You coming or am I doing this one on my own?"

"My calendar is clear. Jenny can handle the mayor's office with her hands tied behind her back. She'll call if anyone needs a face-to-face with me."

"And you're going in those clothes?" Ken looked at the well-used houndstooth sports coat and charcoal gray dress pants.

"I threw a change of clothes in the truck after our excursion into the woods yesterday." Bart held out a black sports bag. He ducked into the back. He returned clad in jeans, a black T-shirt and his signature utility belt. The .357 Magnum sat on his right hip and an LED flashlight on the left.

"All you're missing is a hat."

Bart plopped a black baseball cap onto his head. A silver-threaded mountain range sat below the words *Ravens Cove.*

"Sums it up nicely." Kat swung around and started typing.

"What? You're not gonna beg to come along?"

Kat whirled back around. "I've had enough of the heeby geebies for a while. I'll finish this and get to Doctor Douglas's office to retrieve BC."

"BC's *at the vet?*"

"He's okay. He isn't letting the stray out of his sight. Strangest behavior on Black Cat's part I've ever seen."

"Has nothing on his owner," Bart said.

Kat stuck her tongue out.

"How grown-up." Bart and Ken got through the door before the box of tissues hit it.

Bart stuck his head back in the door. "Missed." He slammed the door shut and heard a loud thud at his back.

"You do live dangerously, my friend."

Bart grinned. "She needed to get her spunk back, and I'm always happy to oblige."

The buildings of Old Town sagged as if invisible weights had been tied to their roofs. The windows swallowed the daylight into unfathomable darkness.

"This place looks worse than after the siege."

"It sure does." Bart singled out a small black-topped key and handed it to Ken. "You want to do the honors?"

"Don't think I'll need it." Ken gave the gate a gentle push. It glided open.

Bart gloved a hand, picked up a heavy chain, and examined the rings. "Cut clean through."

"So, we can safely assume someone wanted into Old Town. If you were going to make this home, where would you take up residence?"

Bart pointed at the five-spired house on the right end. "The mansion."

"My thoughts exactly."

They walked over quartz and brick stones, giving the boulder in the center of the courtyard a wide berth.

"It's still here?"

"You want to move it? I say let sleeping dogs lie." Bart looked at the rock and shivered in spite of himself.

Ken followed Bart's line of sight. He took in the skull-like features. He remembered the glowing eyes and the menacing beak of a mouth devouring is victims like candy. "It can stay right there."

Bart tried the mansion door. "Locked up tight. Give me the key ring."

He flipped through several keys, found the one he was looking for, and aimed it at the lock. The door popped open.

"What was that?"

"Hoping it was the wind." Dark wood floors glistened through a dull layer of dust. A trail of ghostly footprints led to the ornately carved mahogany staircase.

Ken pulled his gun.

Bart pushed the barrel of Ken's gun to the floor. "Maybe it's kids looking for a place to have a good time." Bart's words echoed in the tomb-like silence.

Ken lifted a finger to his lips and tiptoed to the staircase. He heard a click. Blue light flooded the stairs. Bart directed the light to a barely perceptible splatter of rust-red liquid. Another drop lay on the cream-colored stair runner.

"*That* doesn't bode well." Ken threw out Bart's well-used phrase.

"Couldn't have said it better myself."

Ken rooted through his windbreaker pocket and pulled out a bag with a cotton swab and a jar.

"Still the Eagle Scout, I see."

"Always be prepared—FBI training drove it home for me." Ken swabbed and contained the evidence before they continued to the second floor. A balcony overlooking the entry served to connect the right and left wings of the house. A larger pool of chocolate-red greeted them. The trail of red led to the right wing.

"Couldn't it have gone the other way? I hate attics—especially this attic."

"Let's get this over with." Ken raised his gun and headed up the short flight of steps.

Bart released the .357 from his belt. "I've got your back."

Ken poked his head into a small room with a dormered ceiling. "It's clean."

"I don't think we can say the same about the attic." Bart pointed to the doorway. A small pool of blood lay in front of it like a gruesome welcome mat.

In contrast with the bright sunlight outside, the attic was steeped in deep darkness. The smell of iron, mixed with a sickening sweet scent filled the air. Bart flicked on the flashlight. The walls were splattered with red droplets. "Guess we found where the victim met her end."

Ken reached into his other pocket and pulled out four plastic booties. "Thought we might need these."

"Man, I forgot all about those. Shoddy police work to say the least." Bart slipped the blue plastic bonnets over his tennis shoes.

"Someone could have come in there." Ken pointed to a broken window.

"It never got fixed. This town was shut down and boarded up right after Iconoclast was sent to hell where he belongs. There was a board over it." Bart walked over to the small opening, and took a breath of the fresh air coming through the window. The clean scent was a welcome contrast to the death scent surrounding them.

"Okay, so who needs a window unboarded?"

"Someone who wants a quick escape?"

"Not unless they can fly." Ken looked out the small window at the one-foot roof edge. "The drop's at least twenty feet."

Bart ran his eyes over a honey-colored oak table filled with antique snowshoes and ivory carvings. "Doesn't look like someone broke in here for quick cash. This stuff would bring a pretty penny in any pawn shop."

"Something's missing." Ken pointed to a circle of clean wood on the otherwise dusty table.

"The miniature of the rock," Bart said.

"You know, this is feeling way too familiar." Ken picked up a book with his gloved hand. "*The Book of Fallen Angels*," he read aloud.

"No way! It disappeared a month after the battle with Iconoclast." Bart tucked it under his arm. "Won't be disappearing again."

"Seems less and less likely this is where our victim died." Ken pointed to mounds of shrew carcasses scattered about the pinewood floor.

"Who would have taken the time to do this?"

"I'm going with the crazy person who killed our Jane Doe. Looks like practice."

Bart snapped pictures of the tiny corpses. He turned angry eyes to Ken. "Let's go find this sick son of a gun."

———————————

Kat hurried through the incident report and shut down her computer. She pulled her windbreaker off the back of her chair and strode to the breakroom to check the coffeepot. The brass bell announced a visitor. "For the love of all mothers." Kat clip-clopped to the reception area.

Mandy Thomas stood at the door. "I think I had a break-in."

"Something stolen?"

"No."

"Well then why do you think someone broke into your house?"

"It's more like something was put there."

"I don't have time for this." Kat headed for the door.

"I know, I know. It sounds crazy." Mandy held up a bejeweled white stone jar.

Kat walked around the railing separating the waiting area from the work area and took a closer look. She raised her eyes to Mandy. "Seems you'd remember something like this."

"I sure would."

"Do you have any idea what it is?"

"Never seen it before." Mandy stuck the object back in an oversized carry bag.

The door chimed again. "Detective Dayton?"

"Just the girls I came to see."

"I'm not sure I can say the same to you. What's so important you needed to show up in person?"

"I got a call from Chief Melbourne. He said the statue showed up here."

"A statue showed up here," Kat said through clenched teeth. "We could have shipped you the statue so I still don't understand why you're here."

"We've had another homicide connected to you, Ms. Thomas." Dayton fixed his eyes on Mandy. "I don't believe in happenstance. And I just can't shake the belief that your town is connected to what's happening in Anchorage."

"What do you mean by 'what's happening'?"

"The recent death in Ravens Cove is too similar to the Spawldine case to dismiss."

"Anything else?"

"As a matter of fact. It seems, Ms. Thomas, you knew this last victim, too."

"Who?"

"A man named Justin Roverson."

Mandy paled and lowered herself into a waiting room chair. Tears sprang to her eyes and streamed down her cheeks. She buried her head in her hands. "It can't be."

Detective Dayton produced a crime scene photo and shoved it in Mandy's direction. "Does this man look familiar?"

Kat caught Dayton's hand and lowered the photo. "Let's do this in the back."

He slapped the snapshot to his side. "Lead the way."

Kat guided Mandy through the swinging gate. "Show him to the breakroom, will you, Mandy? I'll be right there."

Mandy and Detective Dayton disappeared inside the small space that doubled as the interrogation room. She punched numbers into the desk phone and whispered. "Get here and quick. Detective Dayton is in the office and has Mandy under interrogation."

"Two minutes away." Ken gripped the SUV's steering wheel. "Call Wendy. Then, get in there so she has a witness," he told Kat.

"What's up?" Bart read the cloud of anger on Ken's features.

"The detective from Anchorage has shown up and has Mandy in our office."

"What are you waiting for? Let's go."

"Don't you have a mayor's job to do?"

Bart's shoulders sagged. "Probably. I'll walk from the station. Just get there."

"I know Anchorage is connected. But how?"

"You just asked the question of the year." Bart turned and faced Ken. "This is going to sound bad, but I'm glad it's not just Ravens Cove this time. I was beginning to think we are all under a mass hallucination or we were in some kind of alternate reality."

"I've felt that way more than once about this town."

Ken wheeled the SUV up to the curb in front of the police station. He turned off the ignition and kept his hands on the steering wheel. He contemplated three ravens coming in low, one tipped a wing at his vehicle, then all three flew upward toward the blue sky. *What's it like to be carefree? Maybe someday I'll know. Until then, I'll fight this battle and any other that comes my way!*

———◆·✦·◆———

"Our people are on the way." Kat's sweet smile contradicted the challenge in her eyes.

A tight grin crossed Dayton's face. "Glad you thought to call. Don't think it was necessary, though."

"I think it was *very* necessary." Ken leaned against the doorway and crossed his arms.

"And you are?" Dayton asked.

"Kenneth Melbourne."

"Why does is the FBI need to be here for me to talk to Ms. Thomas?"

"I am a consultant to Ravens Cove in the absence of a full-time police chief."

"I see."

"So what brings you to our fair town, Detective Dayton?"

"Seems another of Ms. Thomas's acquaintances has met a tragic end."

Ken leveled his gaze on Mandy. "Is this true?"

Mandy raised red-rimmed eyes to Ken's piercing blue ones. "If it is who he says, yes."

"I was trying to show her the photo so she could ID the victim before I ask any more questions."

"Mind if I take a look?"

"Be my guest." Dayton held out the print.

Ken pushed the photo back into Dayton's hand. "You have nothing a little less graphic?"

"Not with me."

"Of course not." Ken gave Dayton a knowing look. "Mandy, this photo is, for lack of a better term, gruesome. You need to be strong."

"NO. Why do I have to identify him? His family can confirm who he is!"

"His family did. I need to know this is the same Justin Roverson Ms. Thomas knows."

"And if she doesn't give you what you want?" Kat whispered.

"I'll take her back to Anchorage until I'm sure she's not involved."

"Can he?" Kat asked Ken.

Ken nodded.

Kat took Mandy's hand and squeezed. "I'm right here."

Mandy gave a slight nod. Dayton put the photo on the laminate table top.

The lifeless eyes of a young man stared skyward. A deep cut started at one ear, traveled across his throat, and ended at the opposite ear. The pale flesh revealed tissue the color of bone. Mandy threw her hand over her mouth. "That's him." She burst into fresh tears.

"How did you know him?" Kat asked.

"He was another one of the many men you had your claws into. Wasn't he, Ms. Thomas?"

Ken tilted his head. "Another one?"

"I see you don't know this lady's arrangements with men. Let's just say she had a few gentlemen who saw fit to be generous enough to provide her with a very comfortable lifestyle." Dayton spat in disgust.

"Mandy? Tell him it's not true." Kat searched Mandy's eyes.

"You make it sound much worse than it was." Mandy glared at Detective Dayton. "I cared about Justin. We were going to get married."

"Convenient—since your supposed fiancé is no longer able to speak for himself."

"Back off a little, detective. When did you find this man?"

"Yesterday. And you know who had to find him like this?" Dayton pounded the eight-by-ten photo with his index finger. "His mother!"

"Poor woman." Kat's voice cracked with emotion.

"Why do you think Mandy's involved?" Ken asked. "She was in Ravens Cove."

"I don't know how. I just know she is."

"I'm not involved! I *loved* Justin. I wouldn't hurt him!"

"So you keep saying. If I had any hard evidence, I'd whisk you off to Anchorage, throw you in jail, and lose the key. Believe me when I say, if you're involved I'll make sure you don't see the light of day for years—maybe a lifetime."

"This is the real reason you made the trip?"

Dayton turned to Kat. "Yes—and to take a look at the figurine you have in your possession."

Kat jumped up and marched over to Ken. "You called him and didn't think it was important to let me know?"

Ken cringed."It slipped my mind. I'm sorry."

"Slipped your mind?"

"Yes." Ken turned to Dayton. "It's not in her possession. I have it in my office." Ken ducked out and returned with the snake-adorned statue.

Dayton donned a pair of reading glasses. He scratched on the surface of the cream-colored stone, then looked at his nail. Nothing came off. "Looks real."

"What a relief," Kat said. Sarcasm dripped from every word.

"What does this mean?" Dayton pointed to the name under the statue.

"Some kind of vampire-like woman, from what I'm hearing." Ken sighed. *Here we go again—X Files eat your hearts out.*

"Okay, then. So, someone wants us to think there's a beautiful vampire murdering men in Anchorage?"

"Maybe."

Dayton scratched his right cheek. "Well, they're doing a pretty good job. The Anchorage ME found no other reason for the complete loss of blood from Justin except for a bite mark—with human characteristics. His throat was cut as an afterthought."

Ken shook his head. "I'm beginning to understand why you think Ravens Cove is connected to your murders. Come with me. There're some photos I think you should see."

Kat spun on Mandy. "What have you gotten yourself—and me—into? What are you doing, Mandy, and who are you doing it for?"

"I don't know how the statue ended up here. I don't know anything except the men in my life are dying."

"Why don't I believe you? I'll tell you why! Because every time I do, I find out you've been keeping something else a secret."

"Sorry, Kat."

"Let me tell you something, Amanda Hareling-Thomas. If I find out you're involved in these atrocities, you'll wish you'd never set foot into my life again. I'll personally drag your skinny body to this jail and call Dayton to come and get you!" Kat crossed her arms glowered at Mandy.

"Understood."

"Time will tell. Right now, you need to tell Ken about the break-in."

Mandy dug the jar back out of her bag and shoved it into Kat's hand. "Give it to him. I don't care if I ever see it again."

"Can Mandy leave?" Kat yelled out.

"Yes. Just not the town."

"I know the routine. I'm not going anywhere," Mandy said.

The slamming of the station's door almost succeeded in drowning out the annoying chime of the brass bell. "WHERE'S MANDY?" Wendy shoved the gate and walked through.

"Calm down. I'm right here."

"What have you gotten yourself into this time?"

"Nothing I can't handle."

"Seriously?" Kat looked at Mandy then to Wendy.

Wendy dug her fingers into Mandy's arm and shook it. "Up until now I've shut my mouth about your stupid choices. I thought you'd outgrow this wild side. I guess I'm the stupid one. You are in trouble, Mandy. Do you understand? You could go to jail. Are you hearing me?"

Kat gave Wendy's hand a gentle shove. "Stop, please. She's had a bad shock. Take her home." Kat held up her hand. "Let me finish."

"Fine. Finish what you need to say."

"Mandy, you tell your big sister *every*thing—and I mean everything. You need family now."

Mandy's lips narrowed into a hard line. "I don't."

"If you don't tell her, I will. You won't like my take on what's going on here."

Mandy crossed her arms and glared at Kat. "I'll do it."

"When?"

"How about right now?" Wendy said.

"How about right after you tell Ken about the break-in?"

"You had a break-in and you didn't call me?" Wendy screamed.

Ken appeared at his office door. "What break-in?"

Kat sighed and held up a large evidence bag. "Mandy says someone left this at her house."

"So, nothing was taken and something was left?" Ken cocked his head to the left and raised an eyebrow.

"It happened to me; why not her?" Kat asked.

"We'll talk about your break-in later." He turned to Mandy. "Did you handle the jar without gloves?"

"Yes."

"Of course you did. Hopefully we can still find a fingerprint that doesn't belong to you. How'd you get it here?"

"In this." Mandy held up her oversized tote bag.

"Dandy." Ken took the evidence bag from Kat and looked it over. "Where's the missing piece?"

"What missing piece?"

Ken pointed to jagged edges of red wax on the jar's lid.

"I didn't open it!"

"Don't lie to me."

"Okay. I opened it and there was nothing inside. It was missing a piece when I found it."

"I'm going to need to see your house. You gonna make time?"

"You bet she is," Wendy said.

"Mandy?"

"I don't see why not."

"Good. While I'm there, take her somewhere, Wendy. Jo's, your house—I don't care, just keep her out of trouble before she's thrown in jail for a long, long time. I'll get in touch with you when I'm done."

"Can I get a copy of this?" Dayton shook the police report.

"I think we can manage." Ken looked at Kat.

"I'm sure you can manage, police chief. I'm off the clock." She smiled sweetly at him.

Ken took the report from Dayton's outstretched hand. "I'll be right back."

Dayton turned to Mandy. "Stay in touch, Ms. Thomas."

"Sure thing." Mandy pushed through the gate.

"See you later, KittyKat," Wendy said as she and Mandy disappeared out the door and into the late-afternoon sun.

"Here you go." Ken handed the copy to Dayton.

"Thanks. I'll be going too." Dayton stopped. "No matter what you think, Ms. Tovslosky, I would like Mandy Thomas to be innocent. Your friend just happens to be in the middle of a brutal cyclone and keeps surfacing as the eye of the storm."

"I know you have a job to do. Doesn't mean I have to like it."

Dayton nodded to Ken. "I'm going to be around—at least until tomorrow. Is there a way I can talk to the doc who autopsied your victim?"

"His name is Doctor Billings. Shouldn't be a problem unless the body's already on its way to Anchorage."

"Here's my number." Dayton handed Ken a business card. "Call me when you know?"

"Wait a minute!" Ken ducked into his office and returned with a small evidence bag.

"What you got?"

"Think it's the jar's missing piece."

Ken removed the red wax and placed it against the hole. "Perfect fit."

"Is that the piece you found at the ravine?"

"The same."

"You telling me Mandy was there?"

"I don't know. I do know this jar was. But why?" Ken was speaking more to himself than Kat.

"It sure looks old."

"Was it something the antique dealer had in her shop?"

"I didn't see it when I was in there."

"Can you ask Annie if she'd stop by and take a look at it? Just in case it's related to this case, I'd like to keep it out of the public eye."

"Can do." Kat looked at the wall clock. "Oh shoot, I'll stop by her shop, then I've got to get to Doc Douglas' office."

"BC sick?"

"No. BC won't leave the stray's side. He's been there long enough, though."

"Shouldn't take me too long at Mandy's house. Meet me at your grandmother's as soon as you can? I'm feeling the need to talk to her and Josiah about the goings-on here."

"You thinking this more than a natural event?"

"I just can't shake the feeling. If it is, I want to get a jump on it. Meet me soon?"

Will do."

———————

Nihilist clip-clopped into the shadowy attic of Old Town's mansion. He centered a burlap bag inside a pentagram etched into a rough-hewn rectangular table. He hastily circled the five-pointed star with salt.

Nihilist hopped backwards when the burlap sack vibrated to life and crumpled into a heap. A purple and black witch ball twitched, then hummed and uncoiled. Rings of amethyst and onyx stretched to the ceiling and snapped back toward the table. "Why do you contain me?"

The gurgling voice sent a chill through Nihilist. "You may fool others, small demon—not me! I will keep my life." Yellow eyes glinted off neon-red ones.

"You are afraid of *me.*" The imp stretched upward. "How delightful."

"Where is the skull?"

"Look out the window." Pet mocked.

"The miniature."

"Well, if you could see fit to let me out of this prison, I might be able to help you."

"I'm not a fool!"

"Oh, but you are."

Nihilist clip-clopped forward and stood just out of Pet's reach. "I'm not imprisoned by the Kumrande."

"This?" Pet glanced around at the salt. "You think it will contain me forever?"

"Yes."

"Just know when I am free, your punishment will be eternal." Pet shivered with delight.

"You won't get out of there."

"We shall see. Onto more pressing matters. Where is the she-thing?"

"What do you speak of?"

"Do you think I'm deaf? I heard you talking among your comrades. Now, where is the tree-dweller? She is no longer in her prison."

Nihilist put weight on one hoof then the other, like a small child caught in the act of stealing a cookie before dinner.

"WHERE IS SHE?" Pet roared.

"I don't know," Nihilist's jaw tightened.

"You *are a fool!* She is not of the demons; she is not of the humans. She has no allegiance and seeks to destroy us. Why do you think we left her in the tree for these centuries?"

Nihilist stared into the hate-filled red eyes. "We will find her."

"You have an original thought? Since what time?"

"I can think for myself! The Gorgon's imprisonment left her starved for human food. She will reveal herself. Then we will find her."

Pet pulsed through his yellow and purple colors as he thought. "Bring me the she-thing."

"Why would I?"

"Because if you don't, I will destroy this trinket." Pet turned his clawed hand toward the floor. A miniature skull dropped to his feet. The demon morphed into a purple and black hammer and hovered over the sculpture.

"You would not destroy that. You need it as much as we do."

Pet became a lavender vapor and streaked to the ceiling. "True."

Nihilist backed up several feet, the clippity-clop echoed through the oppressive silence.

The mist rocketed toward the table, then disappeared. A small arrowhead lay in the center of the pentagram. "I can find a stupid human to release me."

"Not as long as you are alone."

"Do not underestimate me, *slave.* I was made to destroy those filthy and arrogant humans. Mark my words, I will have one—soon."

"How is it you escape the abyss when the others in Iconoclast's dark army do not?"

"It is none of your concern. This skull is."

"What do you want me to do? The woman demands it. Or she demands my death. I must have it."

"I would like to see Lilith take you." A vision of blood and shredded flesh glazed Pet's red eyes. "Very much."

"Don't say her name. She'll come here!"

"Which won't work to my good until I am free of this prison." Pet tossed the dark brown skull to Nihilist. "The book is gone—again. Find it."

Nihilist caught the ivory orb. He never saw the claw until it cut halfway through his hand.

"You horrid creature. I will send you to the abyss myself!" He threw his arm up, blood splattering the walls in a wide arc.

"If you could send me there, you already would have. Bring me the book. And show me respect! I AM your master." The snarl and bared teeth revealed Pet's lethal nature.

"As you wish." Nihilist bent forward in a shallow bow and walked backwards.

"I want the book AND the spirit here no later than tomorrow this time." Pet screamed.

Nihilist scampered into the courtyard and up to Homunculus. "I will be rid of him, I swear by the gods of darkness!" Nihilist said to Homunculus.

"So be it!" Homunculus replied. The two Kumrande dove beneath the boulder and disappeared.

Chapter 10
Two for the Price of One

"Off, Benny, off now!" Kat pushed against the barrel chest of the white wolf. He didn't budge. She sighed and stared at the ceiling. She grimaced when a wet tongue ran up her left cheek.

"Benny, for heaven's sake, get off of her." Bernice Tellamoot yanked the canine's leash. Clear amber eyes met chocolate brown ones. He stepped rearward and sat down.

Kat pushed herself off the floor. "Guess I should come out and visit more often," she said as she dusted the back of her pants.

Doctor Douglas's waiting room went tomb-silent when Benny put both paws on Kat's shoulders with such force he almost dropped her to the floor a second time.

A Yorkshire terrier barked as if to applaud Benny's actions. Kat gave the terrier a stern look, then perused the waiting room. Every chair was occupied.

"Who are all these people?" Kat asked Bernice.

"Haven't a clue. It was like this when I got here. I think you and Alese need to come for a visit. I've heard about the"—Bernice's voice dropped to a whisper—"deaths."

"You know something, Mrs. Tellamoot?"

"Not saying I do. Just saying it's not natural. Just like the ones in Old Town weren't natural."

"You have an idea, don't you?"

"More, Katrina, you have an idea. We need to help you remember."

"Remember what?"

"Just bring your grandma. We'll talk." Mrs. Tellamoot waved, and with Benny in the lead, headed out the door.

"Hey, happen to come for a small panther disguised as a cat?" Nyna managed a tight smile before the threatening growl of a black lab stole her attention. The black canine had the Yorkie in his sites like an owl with a mouse.

"Just a second, Kat." Nyna walked out from behind the reception desk. "Sir, please get control of your animal."

The owner, a man in a wide-brimmed cowboy hat and boots to match planted his feet. He and the dog looked like twins.

"If you don't, I guarantee you won't be seeing this vet—today or ever."

Cowboy hat relaxed and heeled the lab. It sat at his feet, and cast threatening looks at the terrier.

Kat leaned into Nyna and whispered, "You tell 'em."

"People like him get under my skin." Nyna walked back behind the desk.

"Mine too." Kat pushed back off the desk. "So, what's going on?"

"Seems there's an outbreak of kennel cough. Worried tourists heard the rumor and almost ran each other down to get here."

As if to emphasize Nyna's point, a long-haired blonde in dark sunglasses raced through the door and to the counter. The black eyes of a teacup poodle stared at Kat from the rim of a leopard-print hobo bag. "My baby needs a shot. Now!"

Nyna ran a hand through her hair. "I understand. Please have a seat. We'll be with you shortly."

"I'll just let myself in the back," Kat said.

"Good idea. Carl will join you as soon as he can."

The smell of antiseptic hung in the air. Kat scanned the stainless-steel kennels lining the room. Her eyes came to rest on a furry black ball on a pink fuzzy rug.

"BC."

One lime-green eye opened. BC stretched like a Halloween cat, trotted to his owner, and bumped her leg with his head. He jogged back to the kennel.

Kat followed BC and crouched down. She came eye to eye with what she swore—again—was Lassie in miniature. The sincere, gentle eyes never left hers.

BC stuck a paw through the kennel bars. "No." Kat gripped his forefoot.

The dog gave the paw a small lick. BC rubbed the kennel bars with his head and looked up at Kat.

"So what do you want me to do?"

"I think he wants you to take her home." Carl Douglas strode toward Kat, removing purple examining gloves and tossing them into a waste can. "BC only lets me examine her and give her food and water. Otherwise, he growls and blocks my way. You're the closest anyone's gotten to her."

"Oh, I don't know, BC." Kat looked at her long-time feline companion. "I can hardly keep you in food and other things. How am I supposed to take care of two of you?"

"BC seems to think it's not a problem." Douglas smiled at the cat's half-closed eyes.

"He doesn't have to pay the food bill." Kat sat on the floor and crossed her legs. The pup sprang to its feet and wagged its beautiful full tail, tipped in black.

"Not fair." Kat reached through the bars and gave the dog a scratch on its head. "Not fair at all."

BC walked into her lap and purred.

"Look, I wouldn't push anything so serious. But there is an outbreak of kennel cough, and I don't want to see a healthy dog in harm's way."

"Life is a bit crazy right now."

"I can't fix everything, but I can help with the food bill."

"The food bill is not my only concern."

"The owner may show up yet. I've already given her the shot to protect her from kennel cough, but I still don't want her exposed before it takes full effect. Think of it as a foster service."

Kat took a deep breath. "What about the leg?"

"It's fine. Didn't even need stitches. The bandage can come off in a couple of days."

Kat felt like all eyes were on her. Doc Douglas, BC, even the small dog in the kennel seemed to be waiting for her decision. "If it doesn't work you'll take her back, right?"

"Right. And I'm looking for the owner."

"You got a lead?"

"Not yet. But I'm sure someone is missing her. She looks to be a purebred Shetland Sheepdog, and she's been well-cared for." Carl smiled and disappeared into an exam room. He reappeared with a royal blue leash attached to a black leather collar.

"Are you giving away expensive collars now, too?"

"This one was on her. Just couldn't see it under all the fur."

Kat inspected a miniature bronze key hanging from the leather band. "What's this?"

"Don't know. If anyone calls to claim her, though, it's a great way to identify her."

"Good idea."

Doctor Douglas opened the kennel door, snapped the collar in place, and handed the lead to Kat.

"All yours. Oh, wait."

He disappeared into the supply room. When he came back, he held out a bag of dry dog food. "As promised."

"I think I'm gonna need some help. Can you take her a minute?" Kat handed the leash to the doctor and pulled her cell from her coat pocket.

Bart came in a few minutes later. "Thank goodness you needed me. Jenny had me in a budget planning meeting. She wasn't gonna let me out of there before sunset—which is around, what, nine these days?"

"We still on for dinner tonight?"

Bart smiled at Nyna. "Planning on it. What time?"

"I'll be off at six-thirty. Pick me up?"

"You bet." Bart picked up BC, who in an out-of-character moment, settled into his arms as content as if he were in Kat's. Bart shook his head. "Wonders never cease."

Bart opened the passenger door. "This animal better not have an accident in my ride."

"It's rare an animal does, Bart. And who'd notice? It's not like your truck hasn't seen better days. There's always a weird smell."

"It's a manly smell."

"Sure it is. I'd call it O de Stink." Kat picked up the sheltie. "You're a hefty one for your size." She put her in the back well of the truck and followed her in.

"You aren't going to sit in the front?"

"She could get scared."

"You are such a lunatic—about animals. You need help. Want me to call someone?"

"You could use a little sweetness yourself. Of course, Nyna seems to be helping in that department."

"I'm the same as always!"

"You just keep telling yourself that. Can I ask a favor?"

"You can."

"I just remembered I told Ken I'd meet him at Gram's. I can walk from here. Would you drop BC at the house?"

"Sure. How do you think your soon-to-be-mate is going to take a new addition to the family?"

"The key phrase is soon-to-be. I'm not sure how long we'll have this addition anyway. She probably has a family waiting in the wings. I'm just the sitter."

"You keep telling yourself that."

Chapter 11
The Key

"Come on, little dog, finish your business. We need to get to Gram's before Christmas." Kat pulled on the leash. The canine kept its nose glued to a grassy mound.

"Yeah, gossip is a real business in a small town." Mandy's familiar voice was followed by a slamming door.

"Oh, man. Come on dog." Kat yanked harder, and her companion followed.

"Always good to see you, *little sister.*" Wendy wiped her right eye and hurried down the steps.

Kat jumped backwards right before Wendy body-slammed her. "Whoa, friend. I was hoping I'd find you here."

"Not if you'd waited any longer." Wendy turned misty eyes to Kat.

"She did it again, didn't she?" Kat threw her free arm around Wendy. "What happened?"

"She's acting weird, Kat."

"She's always acted—"

"No, she's different. You didn't see the hate in her eyes. For a minute, I thought it wasn't Mandy. Stupid, huh?"

"Not stupid. You know her better than anyone. What do you want to do?"

Wendy shrugged. "What can I do? She doesn't want my help."

"Makes me wonder why she came back," Kat whispered.

Wendy shrugged again and pointed toward the ground. "Have you taken up pet sitting for some extra cash?"

Kat smiled. "It's my foster child. Your boyfriend asked me to take care of her for a bit."

"He's not my boyfriend—although I might consider it." Wendy winked.

"I bet. Anyway, I've acquired a new pet—for a time. Since she's so new, thought I'd better keep her close. I'm on my way to Gram's. Want to come along?"

"What's up?"

"Not sure. Think it's important, though."

"I'm always game for breaking news," Wendy said. "I suppose you want me to let the little beast in my car."

"Well, I sure don't want her running alongside it. I'll even use my windbreaker as a seat protector."

"You think of everything. Get in."

<hr />

"That may be the noisiest animal I've ever met. My ears are still ringing," Wendy said in disgust as they started up the steps.

"She does have a shrill bark."

"Shrill? She could be heard in Clayton without a megaphone. Really, every tourist we passed was a threat, really?" Wendy directed her question to the dog at Kat's feet.

Kat giggled. "I don't know much about the sheltie breed, but I'm beginning to think they're barkers."

"Ah, Ms. Sherlock, what was your first clue?" Wendy popped her ears and opened the storm door.

Kat heard Ken's warm baritone. Sadness flooded her heart. *You don't believe me. How can I stay with you forever?* Anger inched out the sadness. She threw her shoulders back and started toward the kitchen.

"I was wondering when you grew claws." Grandma Bricken scanned the petite dog hiding behind Kat.

"Long story, Gram."

Alese Bricken sighed. "Bring it along. I'll find a bowl for some water."

"Sounds like we're late for the party," Wendy whispered.

Kat sniggered. "I like to think of it as right on time."

"Where did you get *that?*" Ken looked from the small canine to Kat.

"Don't like dogs?"

"Not much."

"You have fought a demon-army—twice I might add—and you're uncomfortable with a dog? Just another tidbit to add to the 'what I don't know about Ken' list."

"Meaning?"

"You're the detective. Figure it out."

"So, why the problem with dogs?" Wendy asked.

A slim smile crossed Ken's lips. "Long story."

Wendy plopped into the chair beside Josiah and cupped her chin in her hands. "I'm all ears."

"Suffice it to say, I'm bad luck for dogs. They know it, and they bite me."

The small canine stepped toward Ken. "Might you get control of the beast?"

"It's a dog for heaven's sake. Say hello."

"Hello. Now get a hold on it."

The dog yanked the leash from Kat's hand and bounded over to Ken. "What part of control don't you understand?"

"Oh, get over it." Kat took the leash and gave it a gentle yank. "Come on, dog. You're not welcome."

The dog braced itself against Ken's leg and pulled backwards.

Kat dropped the leash. "Deal with it, FBI."

"If I might continue?" Josiah winked at Ken.

"Please do continue this history lesson on the name Lilith." Ken caught Kat's eye and mouthed, "we need to talk."

Kat shook her head side-to-side and mouthed back, "nothing to talk about."

"As I was saying, if these murders in Anchorage and Ravens Cove are connected, Lilith becomes important."

"For the sake of argument, let's assume these events are, umm, supernatural. Just hypothetically, I mean," Wendy chimed in.

"After what I've seen, you can take it to the bank. There's more than a human involved here." Ken considered the discovery of the *Book of Fallen Angels* and the chameleon-like liquid in the ravine.

Josiah cleared his throat. "As I was saying…"

"Let the man talk. I want to catch up," Kat said.

"The story of Lilith is older than the narration of Adam and Eve. You won't find a mention of her in the bible, but she is alluded to in other ancient texts. In those documents, she was Adam's first wife."

"You've got to be kidding? Adam got divorced?"

"This is no time for a joke." Grandma Bricken peered at Wendy over her glasses.

"Thought it was," Wendy whispered to Kat.

An impatient sigh escaped Josiah. "Lilith was rebellious. She did not like being controlled by Adam, and she ran away. Adam loved Lilith and appealed to God. God sent three holy angels who ordered her to return in the name of the Almighty God. She refused. As you can imagine, her rebellion increased. She changed from a beautiful woman to an ugly and demonic figure."

"All because she didn't want to do what she was told?"

"Yes. And because she was arrogant and self-centered."

"She got turned into a demon because she left Adam?" Kat thought about her impending marriage and what she'd do if faced with a no-win battle with Ken.

"No, Katrina. God looked into her heart and saw only evil. He spoke to Lilith about what He saw. He told her she was to become what she desired—pure evil. Then, He told her she would be cursed throughout eternity because of her wickedness."

"Seems harsh. She just didn't like the situation."

"She chose darkness. Rebellion seems so innocuous. It lies to us. It tells us we have a right to do what we want, and we can still live in peace with our God. Yet, it is the root of all murder, greed, and hatred. When we choose rebellion, we tell God we know better than He does." Josiah's eyes sparked with an inner fire.

"Still seems harsh."

"Consequences of our choices can be harsh. Lilith proclaimed she had been created to cause illness, to kill children because she'd never have them, and to murder men because they were the cause of her condemnation—not herself. She completed her transformation to a demon and became a succubus."

"I'd heard of a succubus but never Lilith." Kat pondered this. *Funny where myths and legends come from.*

"I have no doubt there are people today, and surely in the past, who worship such a being. And I do not question that such an evil spirit could exist." Josiah stopped talking.

"I'm living the *X Files.*" Ken dropped his head into his hands and shook it from side to side. "Just call me Fox."

Kat patted his hand in feigned sympathy. "I've still got your back, big guy."

"Thanks for the support."

"You've got mine, too." Wendy smiled at him.

"I am feeling more and more uncomfortable."

The small dog leapt to its feet and growled at the far corner of the kitchen. Ken pushed away from the table. The chair teetered on its back legs. Just before he fell backward, Ken threw himself forward and caught the table. "See why I don't like dogs?"

"No," Kat said without taking her eyes off of the yellow and white buffet in the corner. The fur on the back of the sheltie's neck rose to attention. She lowered her head and jumped forward. The dog bounced in a semicircle around an invisible threat. All eyes turned to Kat.

"Okay, so maybe it has a crazy gene." She pushed back from the table and headed toward the cabinet.

The dog yelped. Kat's eyes widened when the dog moved forward while its small legs pushed backwards. "Something has hold of this dog!" she yelled.

"What?"

"I don't know. Look!" Kat pointed to the collar. The front of it formed a V. It looked like an invisible finger was crooked through the band. Kat willed herself to move and could not. Instead, she stood helpless and watched the collar twist until it had a chokehold on the dog. The small animal levitated and flailed in midair.

Ken's eyes bounced from Kat to the canine. He snatched a paring knife from the kitchen counter. "Hold still," he commanded. The dog went limp.

Kat broke free from her paralysis, wrapped one arm around the dog and worked her finger under the collar. Ken wedged the dull edge of the blade against the dog's fur, and jerked the knife forward. The leather split and the dog fell into Kat's arms.

The band hung in the air and swayed in a nonexistent wind. The hushed room amplified the eerie tinkling of the brass key striking the collar's D ring.

Josiah's voice thundered into the deathlike quiet. "In the name of Jesus, be gone from this place." He stood, picked up his bible and opened it. The neckband twisted into a figure-eight and stilled.

"I said be gone!" Josiah let go of the bible. It fell to the table. The pages rustled. Josiah dropped his eyes to the book and read, "*After Jesus had gone indoors, his disciples asked him privately, 'Why couldn't we drive it out?' He replied, 'This kind can only come out by prayer.'*"

The collar glided toward the small animal. It snarled and lunged.

"Jesus, help us." Josiah cried out. "You are sovereign over all the earth, seen and unseen, the master of creation, the beginning and the end of all things. Stop this evil from occurring, and take this thing's power away. I ask this in Your mighty name."

The collar trembled and dropped to the floor. An inky silhouette materialized against the bright white wall, then dissolved.

The dog bolted to Ken and plastered itself against his leg. "What?" he asked.

"Pick her up."

"No way."

"You saved her, and she knows it. Let her know it's okay." Kat picked up the small sheltie and held it out to Ken.

"Fine." He hoisted the animal into his arms. "Only for a minute." The dog nuzzled into the space between his neck and cheek.

"Any lingering doubts about what we are up against here?" Grandma Bricken asked.

Wendy, Ken, Josiah, and Kat shook their heads at the same time.

"Well, then, Kenneth, you need to do your police work, and find out what the connection is between Anchorage and the Cove. If you do, we will find the person or persons responsible. Then, we will know how to stop this evil before it gets any uglier—and we all know it will."

"Where's Bart?" Ken asked.

"I think he's out with Nyna," Kat answered.

"He needs to know what we're up against. Otherwise, he could walk headlong into the arms of death." Grandma Bricken stood up and headed for this hallway.

"Already on it."

Grandma walked back into the kitchen. "Oh, please pick up, Bartholomew," she prayed.

"Bart? Listen…" Ken walked into the hallway.

"Mandy was acting more secretive than usual today," Wendy whispered, almost to herself.

"How?" Kat asked.

"I'm sure she was making a phone call and didn't want me to know."

"Why do you think that?"

"She went to the bathroom and stayed in there a long time. I thought she might be sick so I put my ear to the door. I'm sure I heard her talking. I checked around for her cell phone and couldn't find it." A sharp laugh escaped Wendy. "Little sisters never learn big sisters know everything."

"Do you know who she was calling?"

"No. Why would she hide a phone call from me?—unless, she's in bad trouble." Wendy searched Kat's face. "She is, isn't she? This is my fault."

"It is not, Winsome. Mandy's a big girl. If she's in trouble, it's her fault."

"I was supposed to take care of her. I blew it."

"You were only a child yourself when you lost your parents. You did the best you could." Grandma Bricken set the coffeepot in the middle of the table and put her hand on Wendy's shoulder.

"Then why do I feel like I'm such a failure? Look at her life—the men, the alcohol and drugs, the running away—and look at the trouble she may be in now—involved in murder and maybe with demons?" Tears spilled down Wendy's cheeks.

"You don't have to do this alone anymore." Josiah patted Wendy's hand. "And we'll do everything we can to help her."

"What'd I miss?" Paul stood in the kitchen entry.

"Oh, the usual—death, demon attacks, Ravens Cove under another siege, you know." Wendy wiped her eye with a finger and smiled up at him.

Paul examined Wendy. "What did I really miss?"

"The trials of sibling rivalry."

"I don't think that's all, but I'll let it go for now."

"Thanks. Besides, we have bigger fish to fry, "Wendy said.

"We do?"

"Yes. People are dying, demons are appearing—we just had one try to kill this dog." Ken raised his arms, the bundle of fur heavy and asleep.

Paul picked up the severed collar. "This key looks familiar. I'm sure I saw it attached to a small box at the antique store."

"How'd it get here?" Fear hit Kat's stomach like a fist. "I think I better get in touch with the owner." She walked to the hallway, then stuck her head back in the door with the phone to her ear.

"Please tell me Annie Scofland isn't a succubus."

"Unlikely. I forgot to mention this creature only roams in darkness," Josiah said.

Ken looked at Josiah. "Kind of important. Thanks for sharing."

"We did get interrupted."

Paul took the chair Kat had vacated. "A succubus? You mean like Dracula? What makes anyone think they are real?"

"They, as most or all human myths, are based in some kind of fact," Grandma said.

"Have you ever heard of Lilith?" Josiah ventured.

"Adam's supposed first wife?"

"One and the same."

"The name only."

"Well there is a longer and more interesting story. Let me tell you." Josiah leaned close to Paul.

"I got a machine. I left my cell number and asked Annie to call as soon as she got the message."

"Well, I'm not waiting. It's going to be dark in a couple of hours, and I'd like to talk to Annie before something starts roaming the streets."

"What's your plan?"

"To get Bart and head to the antique store. I'm hoping Ms. Scofland can fill us in on this box."

"Won't be easy. Bart's having dinner with Nyna."

"Now I understand why he was so abrupt. He'll have to break free or they may not get to have another dinner together—the way things are shaping up, I mean."

"I need to feed BC before he goes and finds his own dinner, then I'll be ready to go."

"How about you stay home and feed yourself, too?"

"How about in your dreams, *Fox?*" Kat replied.

"On second thought, I'll be happy to wait for you."

Kat's eyes narrowed. "Why the change of heart?"

"Perfect time to clear the air."

"For heaven's sake, would you two just get hitched? Then, you can fight anytime you'd like." Wendy shook her head. "This is not, as they say, rocket science."

"Right, Winsome. In a perfect world that would solve everything." Kat turned to Ken. "Nothing to talk about. I'll try Bart again. Don't want to disturb sleeping beauty." Kat raised her chin at the dog who had just begun to open its eyes. It let out a quiet squeak as it yawned and snuggled closer to Ken's chest.

Kat snickered and then dialed.

"I beg to differ, we have a several things to discuss."

Kat help up a hand. "Nice of you to answer."

"Can't a guy get a few moments of free time?" Bart barked into the phone.

"No—guess what's been happening while you are having a nice dinner out?"

"Do I want to know?" Bart sighed and threw an apologetic look to Nyna. The red glow of the sun laced Nyna's blonde hair in crimson. He ached to reach out and touch it. *Not now. Maybe not ever—at least until I know where I want this to end.* "So, tell me."

Kat launched into the story from Josiah and the attack on the dog. "I'll be at the station in an hour."

Chapter 12
Rebirth

Purple and yellow throbbed against the pewter-gray attic walls. With each pulse, a new cluster of lava-red droplets burst through the decaying wood and fell to the floor. The fluorescent violet, amber, and red fused to cast a ghoulish spotlight on a one-footed creature hovering within the confines of a five-pointed star.

"I'm tired of this game now," Pet said. He searched the room. His eyes stopped on a whiskbroom lying in blackness. "Perfect." The swirling colors gave way to crusty brown skin. A second leg popped from the dark torso. Pet stretched his neck until his head touched the ceiling. He unfurled a gnarled claw and crooked it toward the broom.

The sweeper shivered to life and danced to the table. Pet brushed his hand from side to side. The bristles mimicked the movement and swept the salt to the floor.

"Not bad. Not bad at all." A shadow drifted in the window, clapping ethereal hands.

Pet bowed. "You could have helped, you know."

"And miss seeing you in true form and power? Never. Besides, I was busy, remember?"

"You got it?" Excitement laced the gurgling voice.

"No." The shadow bent its head. "The man of God had help. The book told him what to do."

"Unfortunate for you. You must go back."

"No! I'll have another chance. The collar is free of the mongrel. I can get it without being seen."

"I suggest you prove your words, Adumbration. Otherwise, you go into the abyss."

"Do not say my name. It is forbidden."

"Not by other demons, you fool. Only by those who serve us."

Adumbration's shadow arm reached behind its back. "I have something for you."

"What could you possibly have that I would want?"

A small, beige object appeared and hovered in midair. "Where did you find it?" He snatched at the miniature skull.

The shadow hand drew it back. "I am a shadow. I can take what I want. The Kumrande are arrogant. Easy targets." Adumbration dropped the skull into Pet's hand.

Pet purred a melancholy and unholy tune. "Maybe you are worth keeping around—at least for now." A ghostly mist snaked through the floor. "I bring tidings from the great one and your master Icono-clast who is awaiting release." The being threw down a heart, still beating, in front of Pet.

"What good is this to me?"

"It is from a worshipper of the abomination Lilith. The power is invincible."

Light dawned in Pet's eye. "Do the others come, too?"

"They come. They seek their goddess. They will meet an end like this one." Estafette grinned. Rusty foam dripped off his dagger-sharp teeth and sizzled as it hit the floor.

"This is good. They play into our hands. We will feast again."

"When will you have the key?"

Pet gave Adumbration a scornful look. "Yes, when will we?"

Estafette turned his attention on the shadow-demon. "You had it?"

"No—I almost did. A man of God threw me from the place before I could complete my task."

"You spawn of a worm. You let the man of God know you were there!"

"The mongrel attacked me! I can defend myself!" Adumbration protested.

"You were not in danger. Your vain attempt to terrorize has put us all at risk. I will return with the masters' decision regarding your punishment. Do not leave this place until I return." Estafette dissolved through the floor.

"I would leave this place," Pet remarked. "I would find the key and be here when Estafette returns. It is the only way to save yourself."

Adumbration considered Pet's advice. "What's in it for you?"

"Just some free counsel. Take it or leave it."

"I cannot find fault in your words. "It shall be done." He melted into the wall.

"You'd better hope so," Pet sneered. "In the meantime, I have a date with a Kumrande—it's time they know who owns them."

"Enough of the silent treatment. We need to talk."

"I already told you there is nothing to talk about." Kat yanked the door handle.

Ken hit the lock button. "I disagree."

Kat wheeled on Ken. "How are you going to change what you have already done? How? You believed, and probably still believe, I stole something in a police investigation. You don't know me at all, Kenneth Melbourne. I don't want to marry someone who thinks I'm capable of thievery or any dishonesty, for that matter." Kat crossed her arms and threw herself against the seat.

"I think this is about more than my questions to you."

"Then, pray tell, what would it be about?"

"You think I'm going to leave you—just like your mom and dad."

"How dare you mention them!"

"I am not trying to make you angrier. I want you to look at it, though. You've been running from me since we fell in love."

Kat turned her attention to the fiery red sunset illuminating the black, jagged outline of Mount Redoubt. "I'm not the one who keeps leaving."

"No, but you won't go with me."

"This is my home."

"I know it is." Ken caught hold of Kat's hand. "If my moving to Ravens Cove is all it takes for us to close this chasm between us, consider it done."

"No. You need bigger things."

"I need you."

"Not good enough. Your need to be with me won't always be this strong, and I won't be the one responsible for making you unhappy."

"To be honest, Kat, this town is my home now, too. I have tried to deny it. I can't. Your family is the closest thing I've ever known to having one of my own," Ken whispered.

Kat searched Ken's face. "You aren't kidding."

"Not in the least. You aren't the only one who has trouble with commitment."

"We are quite a pair."

"Yes, we are."

"I love you so much, Ken. You broke my heart when you questioned my motives."

"And I'm sure I'll hurt you again—not because I want to but because I'm just a man. I'm sure we'll fight and even question our decision to get married."

"Then why would you want to get married at all?"

"Because I'm *more sure* that we can make it through anything—together." He squeezed her hand.

Kat wiped a tear away with her free hand. "What if you die?"

"I haven't yet. And it sure isn't for the lack of trying on the demons' part."

"True. Maybe you are tough enough for me to take a risk on." Kat threw herself against Ken and kissed him hard.

Ken held her tight. "Just know I'm with you for the duration."

Kat buried her head into his chest and nodded. "Okay, then. Let's fight the bad guys. Then we get married."

Kat squinted at the closed miniblinds in the large window of the police station. A shadow drifted by once, then glided past again. She crept up to the glass door and peeked inside.

Bart Andersen came into view, hands clenched behind his back as he twirled on his heel and started in the opposite direction.

Kat smiled and yanked the door open. "Been here long?"

"As a matter of fact, yes. I cut my date short, and she is mad."

"A bit smitten, are you?"

"I enjoy her company."

"This inability to express one's true feelings is at epidemic proportions today—first Wendy, now you." *Not to mention myself.* Kat looked up into her cousin's chocolate-brown eyes. "Not having any twinges about Mandy?"

Red crept from the bottom of Bart's neck to his jaw. "Not in the least."

"Why don't I believe you?" The telltale red and the faraway look in Bart's eyes told her a different story. *Memories of times gone by and dashed hopes of what could have been, cousin?*

"Not in the least," Bart growled.

The chime of the door stopped the conversation. "Strangest thing," Ken said.

"Stranger than demons and Kumrandes?"

"No. But guess who's running the antique shop?"

"I give."

"Mandy."

"Mandy Thomas? Where's Annie?" Discomfort slammed Kat's stomach.

"Mandy says she had to leave town for a bit. Says Annie hired her before she left."

"I did tell her to get a job. Maybe she took my advice for once."

"Maybe."

"So, why is she in the shop now? It's the middle of the night."

"Says she was nervous about running the shop. She wanted to check it one more time."

"That is out of character."

"That's what I thought. She reported another theft."

"Of course she did. Did you check her person?"

Ken opened his mouth. Kat held up her hand. "Wait, don't answer."

A rare laugh escaped Ken. "I won't."

"So what's missing now?"

"A small box. You know the one Paul said had the brass key in it? Mandy said she couldn't find a receipt for it."

"Did she happen to say if she called Annie to see if she sold it and forgot to leave the receipt where Mandy could find it?" Bart asked.

"She said she couldn't reach Annie."

Kat cocked her head toward Bart. "I think the lady wants attention. Probably hoped Bart would show up."

"There's a history I need to know about?"

"A very old history—done and done again. So why am I here and not on a date with my current girl?"

"Seems we have an answer to the bloodless corpse."

Bart's eyes lit up. "Great. Does it happen to be related to one human murdering another?"

"Not in this town's lifetime. Seems the statue and everything else going on are adding up to a succubus."

"We don't do vampires. Not even in this town. Not even at Halloween," Bart said as he, Ken and Kat walked to the back office.

Ken dropped into the chair behind the desk. It protested with a loud squeak as he turned it to the front. "I'd agree but Josiah related the name on the statue to the queen of the blood-suckers."

Bart's shoulders sagged. He sighed. "So where do we start? I haven't seen any fresh dirt or new graves hereabout."

The familiar tinkle of the front door interrupted the conversation. "Does it ever end?" Kat headed for the front office.

A breathless Arnie Thralling met her. "There's some old witch hiding in the bushes outside my shop."

Kat narrowed her eyes. "That's a terrible thing to say! No matter how mad a woman made you."

"No, Kat, I mean an old witch—bent over, gray hair, hook nose— the whole thing!" Arnie's words ended in a shout.

Bart reached the reception area in two steps. He took in Arnie Thralling's red face and wild eyes. "Someone dying, Arnie?"

"I almost did, and Kat's not listening to me!"

Kat looked at Arnie for the first time. She took in the wild-haired, crazy-eyed man. She looked at Bart and Ken, then burst into laughter. "Why not? Weren't we just discussing something even more unbelievable?" She leaned on the banister and wiped her eyes.

"This is not the time, Kat." Ken's scornful look did nothing to stifle Kat's laughter.

"See what happens when you ask for an answer? We get a witch." Kat giggled and cleared her throat in an attempt to gain control.

"Man, this isn't funny. She was scary and I thought she was going to attack me!"

"Sorry, Arnie." Bart quashed the smirk playing around the corners of his mouth. "At your shop you say?"

"I was putting out some garbage and she barreled down on me like a bat out of—well, you know. As far as I know she's still there. I didn't hang around to find out."

Ken opened the door. The street was empty, dark threatening to cover the whole town in minutes. "No one out there, Arnie. How about you sit down, and I'll get you a glass of water?"

Arnie plopped into a waiting-area chair. "I'm not hallucinating!"

Ken handed Arnie the water. Arnie gulped it down and set it on a small end table.

"Want another?"

Arnie shook his head. "I'm good for now."

"How about you stay here with Kat, and we'll go take a look around your shop?" Bart smiled at Kat.

"Stay here?" Kat asked.

"I like the idea," Arnie said.

Kat sighed, clenched her jaw, and sent a sweet smile Arnie's way. "Not a problem. I have a good book to read in instances just like this." Kat walked around her desk, yanked the bottom drawer open, and took a dog-eared novel from a file folder. She plopped into her chair.

"I'll call when we know anything," Ken headed out the door.

"You know where I'll be."

"Thanks for doing this, Ms. Tovslosky. I'm not usually a coward but the old lady—or whatever she was—would have scared the holy angels."

Guilt nibbled at Kat's conscience. She put her book to the side. "You're welcome, Arnie. There's some old copies of *Time* and *National Geographic* sitting there. Help yourself." The phone on Kat's desk warbled.

"Hey, KittyKat, I can't find Mandy. You guys have any luck?" Wendy asked.

"She's not at the antique shop?"

"No. The place is locked up tight."

"Maybe she went to get something to eat. Did you talk to Jo at the bakery?"

"I didn't think of it. Mandy has me so upset."

"Can I help?"

"You already have." Wendy hesitated. "Kat?"

"I'm here."

"It's a good thing Mandy has a job, right? Maybe she's starting to turn around?"

"It's a wonderful thing. Where are you, Winsome?" Kat heard the distinct sound of Bart's truck through the phone.

"Just leaving the antique shop. Why did I just see your cousin and fiancé speed by?"

"Long story."

"I'll bring you mocha and you can tell me all about it."

"Not necessary."

"I need to see if Mandy's at Jo's so it's no trouble."

Kat smiled. "I'd love it. Would you bring a coffee for Arnie Thralling, too?"

"Arnie's there? This *must* be good. Coffee and mocha it is."

Kat looked at Arnie. "I can hardly wait to hear the gossip on the streets of Ravens Cove tomorrow."

The oversized shop door gaped open and spilled fluorescent light into the deepening twilight.

"Something spooked Arnie. He's too money-conscious to leave every light on. The original Scrooge," Bart said.

Ken ducked into the Quonset hut Arnie used as a workshop. A quiet whistle escaped Ken's lips as he took in the stacks of wood planks and boards. "He likes his wood."

"He's obsessed with it." Bart pointed to an unfinished boat sitting on a makeshift scaffold.

"An old one, isn't it?" Ken looked at the teak railings topping the sides of the sailboat.

"Refinishing aged watercraft is his specialty." Bart ambled over to the pile of rough lumber and unclipped his cell from the belt.

"Need my help?" Kat asked.

"As a matter of fact."

"I'll be right there." Kat stood up and released her windbreaker from the back of her chair.

"Not here."

"Oh." Kat dropped back into her seat.

"Ask Arnie if he picked up the hag tree at the ravine."

"Just a second."

"Well, I'll be. It sure as heck looks to be the same." Ken touched the wood. "Right down to the weird hollow."

"The man won't pass up a free anything—just look around." Bart pointed his chin at the sacks of sand and various tools lining the walls. Fishing nets were stuffed in between a stack of wood and steel.

"Bart, you there?"

"Right here."

"Arnie says he did. Didn't think it'd do any harm, and he always needs scrap wood."

"Thanks." Bart put the phone back into his pocket. "It's the hag tree." Bart touched the pale-gray bark. "Is it me or is this thing seeping?"

Ken followed Bart's finger. A black and red liquid oozed from the trunk. Ken pushed an index finger into the soggy wood. Yellow light sparked in response.

"That does not bode well." Bart shook his head. "Not well at all."

The tree shivered, then quaked. Ken jumped back when a gnarled root burst out of the trunk's base and snaked toward the corrugated metal of the workshop's ceiling.

"It's regenerating itself!" Bart hit speed dial on his phone.

"Who are you calling—a tree service? The thing's lying on its side."

Bart punched *end* and pointed again. "Not anymore." The root dropped to the floor. It burrowed through the sawdust covered wood planks. Half of the tree pulled itself upright.

A deafening *crack* filled the air. "You've got to be kidding." Ken's face paled when the twin half of the trunk sprouted a large tuber and tunneled into the floorboards. Ken and Bart shuffled backward in an unprepared dance step when the trunk sprouted tendrils and knitted itself back together.

"How can this be happening?"

"What do I look like? A dictionary for the strange and awful?"

"You are cursed!"

Ken whirled toward the shrill scream. An old woman shook a chopped-down cane and birch wood bowl at Ken and Bart, then vanished.

Bart turned to Ken. "Well, I've seen stranger things."

"Maybe she's the hag from the tree? It would explain why she was after Arnie."

"I don't think so —she reminds me more of a messenger."

"From who?"

"Well, I'd say Iconoclast, but that's a no for obvious reasons. From Lilith?"

Ken sighed. "Why not?" He turned back to the tree. "Damnation, did Arnie have to bring the whole thing here?" The top of the tree hung in midair. Four ashen cords erupted from the base, reminding Ken of jagged tendons on a severed neck. The tree's headpiece floated toward its base and slid onto the trunk. The gray sinews wove in and out of the trunk, filling gashes left by Arnie's saw. Dead leaves snapped open.

Bart shook himself. "Wrong on so many levels."

The ground quaked, then heaved. The roots yanked up and out, and the tree lurched forward.

Ken jogged over to Bart."Got the tree service number?"

"Don't have one here, brother, and don't have a saw, either. I think we'd better make a run for it."

"Agreed." Ken bolted toward the door.

"Don't stop!"

"No choice." Ken pointed at three silver-furred, yellow-eyed creatures blocking the exit.

Bart slapped his hip where a flashlight should be. The loop was empty. He whirled around and heard the distinct groan of bending metal. The tree jerked forward. Pieces of steel and plastic lay in its wake. Bart turned back to the door.

The Kumrande stepped forward, whirled around, and scattered.

"What made them run?"

"Don't know. Just grateful."

Ken and Bart took off into the night toward the police station.

"Mortals are so gullible." Pet came out of the trunk.

A black shadow unwrapped itself from the tree and stretched skyward.

"Get this tree back to its home and find the spirit who inhabits it!"

"As you wish." Adumbration bowed.

Pet lifted his hands and Adumbration twisted like a sooty cord around the trunk. The tree rose from the ground and floated forward. It bent to clear the Quonset's doorway then streaked into the air, plummeted to the ravine, and stopped a few feet above ground. The roots burrowed down into the hard dirt at the head of the pathway.

A creaking wind announced Pet's arrival. He jetted around the tree and hovered at the gaping hole in the trunk. "Find the one who murdered the tree and released the spirit. Bring him to me." Adumbration nodded and flew into the night.

Chapter 13
An Unlikely Victim

The violent bang of the glass door brought Kat to her feet. Ken rushed into the waiting area, doubled over, and took deep breaths. Bart plopped into a chair next to Arnie.

Kat's eyes went from Ken to Bart. "What happened?"

"Hag tree—moved." Bart blurted out between fast breaths.

"The sucker's in pieces—ain't no tree anymore," Arnie spat.

"It's whole now." Ken's dilated eyes sent an electric shock up Kat's spine.

She gripped Ken's arms. "What happened?"

"The tree put itself back together—and then it walked! If we hadn't gotten out of there, we'd be roadkill right now."

Kat crossed her arms. "Okay, this has crazy or stupid practical joke written all over it. Which one is it?"

"Neither," Bart and Ken said in unison.

Bart turned. "Arnie, you were right. Some old witch-like broad came out of nowhere, shook a cane and bowl at us, threw a curse our way, and disappeared into thin air."

"Told you I ain't a coward."

"The sight of a walking tree could have made me screech like a little girl, I'll tell you," Bart said.

"I'm sure I heard a high-pitched shriek—and it wasn't from me."

"Wasn't me, either," Bart blasted back.

"Glad you've recovered your sense of humor so quickly but enough, you two." Kat shoved a glass of water into Ken's hand, then Bart's.

"Did you say a bowl and cane?" Kat asked.

"I did."

"Like a birch wood bowl and cane?"

Ken raised thoughtful eyes to the ceiling. "As a matter of fact, yes."

Bart's eyes lit up. "You think they're the ones reported missing by Annie?"

"Could be."

"Well, one mystery solved."

"Only to have it replaced by a more terrifying one."

Bart shrugged and gulped the water before handing the glass back to Kat. "Thanks. I didn't realize the run from Arnie's shop had made me so thirsty."

"Anything happen while we were on this latest excursion into the macabre?" Ken asked.

"A few things, actually."

Ken massaged his right temple. "Okay. What have we got?"

"Doc Billings called about the one-legged corpse. Seems it's gone missing."

"The leg?"

"No. The whole body."

Ken brought his other hand up and began to massage both temples. "I suppose he's sure it didn't get picked up by the Anchorage ME's office while he was out?"

"I asked. He called them. It was on their schedule for tomorrow."

"I'll add finding a missing body to the to-do list. What else?"

"Doc Billings said he got the results back on the IV bags at the hag tree—they were filled with Grady Spawldine's blood."

"I'll check that part of our mystery off the list. Next."

"Josiah called. Said Paul remembered something about the box's key."

"Guess Pastor Lucas's house is our next stop." Bart turned to Arnie. "How about I drop you off at Amos's?"

"That'd be good. I should tell him what's happenin'."

"Think we'd better stop at Gram's first. She called. Says we never eat right, and she's holding a late dinner for us."

Bart sighed. "We need to find Paul."

"Well, I'm not incurring her wrath. Drop me first."

Bart's stomach rumbled. "I can call him. Let's go."

Kat grabbed the mocha off her desk. "Wendy brought us some refreshments while we were waiting." She lifted her cup to Ken and smiled.

The heavy aroma of chocolate and coffee drifted through the air. He took the cup and a big sip, then handed it back to Kat. "Get in the truck."

Kat shook the empty cup in Ken's face. "You could have left me some," she said and headed out the door.

Kat tossed her windbreaker onto a coat hook. "Hey, Gram, we had another weird thing happen tonight."

Alese Bricken wiped her hands down her apron before pulling her granddaughter close. "You can tell me all about it at dinner."

Kat rushed to the table. "I'm famished."

Alese squeezed Ken's arm. "When you're married, you better make sure she eats."

"I'll do my best."

Grandma cupped Bart's head in her hands. "Glad to see you, sweet man."

"Hope you guys aren't hungry. I think there's just enough for me." Kat stabbed a large chunk of moose roast and deposited it on bright yellow plate.

"I'd better get to the table before there's none left." Bart sat down across from Kat.

"Katrina, wait for the others."

"Sorry," Kat said through a full mouth.

"While one of us is quiet for a moment, let me tell you what Paul said."

A muffled, "Funny," escaped Kat's full mouth.

"Even food doesn't stop your tongue," Grandma laughed and shook her head.

"Paul said he remembered something about the box at the antique store. When he commented on the color of the stones, Annie told him it was new to her collection—she told Paul Russian antiques are her passion."

Kat set her fork on the table and looked at Josiah. "Did Wendy ever get back with you on what might have happened to it?"

"Yes. Mandy told Wendy she knew where it was. It was her mistake, and she found it."

"She actually called Wendy?"

"No, Katrina. Wendy called her."

"She's hiding something."

"You are being cynical again, child. She may just be confused. Mandy's had several shocks lately."

"Maybe—but she's been…" Kat's voice trailed off.

A loud quack, quack burst into the room. Alese Bricken's eyes centered on Ken's pocket.

Ken responded with a sheepish grin. "Guess my new ring isn't working." He yanked the cell phone from his pocket.

"Guess not," Kat replied.

"Be right there."

"Now what?" Kat asked.

"Detective Dayton's been attacked at the Ravens Cove Inn."

Kat yanked her windbreaker off the hook. "I'm coming."

"You," Ken pointed his finger at Kat, "stay here."

"Why?"

Ken took hold of Kat's shoulders. "Because I don't know what we're walking into. Because it's a crime scene. Because I need to know you are out of harm's way so I can concentrate on my job." He dropped his hands to his side.

Kat chewed her bottom lip. "If you put it like that…call me?"

"Bet on it."

Bart pulled in close to the curb behind a smoke-black Audi. "Doc made good time, I see."

The inn's owner burst through the mahogany-red doors and pointed a shaky finger toward the second floor. "Room 210."

Ken took the stairs two at a time. Room 210's door stood ajar. "Doc?"

"In here," Doctor Billings answered.

"Looks like a war zone," Bart said. The desk chair and the hotel-issue lamp were on their sides. A painting in hues of oranges and yellows hung sideways above the bed.

Billings looked over his shoulder at Ken and Bart. "He has a nasty wound on his neck and arm. Whoever did this was intent on doing major damage."

"Is he conscious?"

"Yes, I'm conscious. Searing pain tends to keep me awake."

"You still have some fight in you, I see. You'll be okay."

"I'll be better when you find the creep whose sole aim was to make this my last day on earth."

"How'd the attacker get in?"

"I went down the hall for ice and left the door open. My mistake. Thought this was a safe town," Dayton said.

"Looks can be deceiving."

"Tell me something I don't know! I came back and shut the door. Someone snags me from behind, and pain shoots up my arm. I reached over my shoulder, got hold of a handful of hair, and snatched out a bunch. Didn't even phase the son-of-a-jackal! Instead, the freak latched on like some overgrown leech."

"Get a look at him?"

"Who said it was a man?"

"At whomever it was?"

"I never got to turn around. Lucky for me the innkeeper heard the noise and banged on the door. The creep spun me around, shoved me at the door and took a nosedive out the window."

Ken leaned over the sill. "Long drop. The bushes don't even look disturbed."

"I saw what I saw."

Ken whispered to Bart, "if I hadn't seen a tree mend itself and walk earlier, I'd say this guy had gone over the edge."

Bart nodded. He shined his flashlight onto the bushes below. "Could have broken the fall, I guess."

"Could have—or, the lowlife's not human," Ken's said loud enough for Dayton hear.

Dayton shouted, "Is this whole town crazy? First, Kat Tovslosky and later Mandy Thomas report someone's broken into their houses and left presents. Now, the one person I thought was rational thinks some other-dimensional leech attacked me?" Dayton caught hold of the headboard and pulled himself to a sitting position.

"Lie down, detective. You're not strong enough to move yet."

"I'll get strong! I've got to get away from this town before I'm sucked into this mass hallucination." Dayton stood and smiled when his legs held. He took a step forward and crumpled to the floor.

"Dayton, you haven't seen half of what I have. If you had been here—"

Bart rammed Ken in the side and hissed, "shut up, Melbourne, before we both land in the psych ward of Clayton's tiny hospital."

Ken doubled his fist, then relaxed it. "Let's talk about you, Dayton. How bad is he, Doc?"

"Suffice it to say, if the owner hadn't shown up, I'd be autopsying another corpse. So all in all, he's doing great."

"Hear that, Dayton. Today is your lucky day."

"If you want to get well, Detective Dayton, heed what I'm about to say. You are going to have to recuperate in Ravens Cove—"

"Not on your life!" Dayton tried to stand up and crumpled back to the floor.

"As I was saying, you're going to have to stay here for a while. You've lost too much blood. You're obviously too weak to drive, or even fly, to Anchorage. You need rest and a possible blood transfusion—at the hospital."

"No one's putting me a hospital! I'll never get home."

"You need a hospital."

"I'm not going to any hospital and that's final."

"There may be another solution," Bart said.

"Which is?" Doc Billings asked.

"Grandma Bricken's."

Doc Billings looked at Dayton, then back to Bart. "That's a viable option."

Bart turned to the Detective. "Don't worry, Dayton. We have ways to heal people here. You'll be back on your feet in no time."

"Just what I want—to be a sitting duck in Podunk, Alaska."

"Hey, watch what you say about this town! We're proud of the Cove."

"Well, you're just as nuts as the rest of them. Thought you had a little more sense to you."

"As I said, looks can be deceiving." Ken jerked a notepad from his pocket. "It's time for me to interview the owner."

"Good plan. I'll stay with our friend here."

Ken jogged down the stairs. *Why am I so mad at him? I've said the same thing since I came to the Cove.* A small voice whispered, *But this is my town now.*

The owner rounded the reservation desk. "I don't know how the attacker got in here. I was only in the back for a couple of minutes. I always hear the door."

"This isn't your fault, Mister…?

"Timmons. Ed Timmons." He held out his hand.

Ken shook it. "I never got your name when I stayed here before. Sorry."

"Nothing to be sorry about. Innkeepers are invisible by nature. At least the good ones." Mr. Timmons smiled with pride.

"Good to know," Ken replied. "So, did you see anything at all?"

"Well, when I came out from the back," the owner pointed behind him at a curtained doorway, "I saw the hem of a tan-colored pair of slacks at the top of the stairs. I thought it was one of the guests."

"Nothing else?"

"Like what?"

"Was it was a man or woman? Did you see a hat? The color of the skin? Hair color maybe?"

"Nope. Only the pants."

Of course it can't be easy. Ken put a card in the innkeeper's hand. "Call me if you remember anything—day or night.

Ed Timmons looked at the card. "FBI, huh? The guy in 210 must be important."

"I'm not here on FBI business. The cell phone on the card is my number."

"I see." Ed Timmons stuffed the card in his pocket. "I'll call if I remember anything."

Ken started toward the staircase. He turned back to the innkeeper. "Mr. Timmons?"

"Yes."

"Until we find this guy, stay vigilant."

The owner flashed a .38 revolver at Ken. "Always am."

Ken shook his head and jogged back up the steps. "Does everyone in this town own a gun?"

"Most everybody. Small town. Big animals."

"Well, maybe we should rethink that." Ken felt sure, if given a chance, the owner of the Ravens Cove Inn would take a potshot at anyone in tan-colored slacks.

"Not in this town's lifetime. Besides, with this kind of stuff happening, the hardware store's going to see an increase of gun sales, not a decrease."

"Great." Ken looked at Dayton. "What are we going to do about him? He can't stay here. Don't want a sitting duck now, do we?"

"I'm just fine right here."

"You're in my town, and I won't be responsible for another attack." Ken turned back to Bart. "So what do we do with him?"

"I called Gram. She offered to keep him, of course. Second to the Inn she's housed more strangers than anyone else in this town."

"You're really taking me to some old lady's house? How's some senior citizen supposed to prevent another attack?"

"You'd be surprised. By the way, don't you ever call her an old lady again. You will show her the utmost respect. Or you'll deal with me, and it won't be pleasant," Bart growled.

Dayton raised his eyebrows. "Won't happen again."

"Get him settled in the truck. Then come back and talk to me," Doc Billings said.

Ken and Bart met Billings in the inn's lobby. "I didn't want to say this in front of Dayton. These puncture wounds are clean and deep. Not jagged edges like I'd expect when a human tries to tear out someone's jugular. And there's something else."

"Good news, maybe?"

"Unfortunately, no. Those wounds atrophied before I arrived. I had to cut away the rotted skin before I sewed him up. Last, he didn't even need a local anesthetic—the area around the wound was numb."

"Nice. A thoughtful vampire."

"I don't know what we've got here. But this is nothing I've ever seen before. And it was strong. Dayton weighs at least 230 pounds. Not to mention he's a trained police officer. It would have been hard to hold onto him."

A shiver marched up Ken's spine. "Do me a favor, Doc. Call me when you get to your place. Don't need to lose one of the Cove's finest."

"Fine. Talk later." Doc Billings climbed into his black Audi and pulled off into the night.

Chapter 14
Bloodsuckers and Boxes

"Which of you horrid abominations let my servant attack before she was ordered to?" Lilith growled at Nihilist.

"I swear, my queen, we kept her in the caves. We stood guard at the doors." Nihilist clip-clopped away from the swirling apparition of wrinkled flesh.

"Fools! I made her like me! She can change form; she can walk through a wall."Nihilist bowed his head and murmured, "you didn't tell us."

Lilith flew off the bridge, latched onto Nihilist's sinewy neck and dragged him to eye level. "Tell me why I should not eat my fill of your lifeblood right now?" She leaned toward the throbbing vein in Nihilist's neck.

Cloven hooves ran in midair. "Because I am the only one who can give you the information you need to defeat Pet and the demons."

Lilith calmed. "What you say is unfortunate but true. Do you have the box to contain my servant?"

"Yes."

"Do you have the key?"

"No."

Lilith dropped the Kumrande and returned to the darkness under the bridge. "Get it or you die."

"What makes this box and its key so important? Both you and the demons wish possession."

"It is the twin of my prison. They were made by the evil ones to contain me forever." Lilith smiled. "I guess they wanted a backup in case the first was somehow destroyed. They so fear me. Anyway, the box is the only thing strong enough to contain my servant. I suggest you find it. If the demons get it first, I will have no choice but to tell them of our alliance."

Nihilist's yellow eyes widened with fear. "It is done." He bowed and ran into the forest.

———•◦)•(◦•———

"This must be Detective Dayton." Josiah held the door open for Bart and Ken. They guided their charge into the entry hall.

"My, oh, my! You do look a little green around the gills," Grandma commented on her way down the stairs. She motioned to Bart and Ken. "Bring him to the living room."

The hall ended where a large room began. A small oak desk greeted them. Tidy stacks of correspondence lined its backboard; a pen and paper sat in the middle of the gleaming wood. Black and white photos adorned the top shelf of the writing table.

"You had to leave this one out, Gram!" Kat pointed at the picture of a petite child with dark ringlets and bright eyes.

"Kat! How'd you get in without me hearing you?" Gram smiled.

"You know I'm sneaky when I want to be—wow, you don't look so good, Detective Dayton. Let's get you in bed." Kat pushed Bart, then Ken to the side and guided Dayton to the sofa. She let go of his arm long enough to fold back the dark-blue quilt and light blue sheet covering the overstuffed couch.

"He's been through quite a battle." Bart shot a knowing look to Josiah.

"Oh, I see." Josiah came over to the detective. "You're fortunate."

Dayton pointed at his bandaged neck.

"Do I look like I've fallen into some great luck here?"

"You are breathing and can speak—you're not only fortunate, you're blessed."

"If you say so. And you are?"

"Josiah Williams, at your service."

"I'll keep it in mind." Dayton turned his attention to the woman Kat called Gram. Her brown skin was weathered but her eyes sparkled with youth. *This is no old woman—no matter what her age.* He looked at Kat. Her eyes mirrored those of the older woman.

"This must be your mother." Dayton fumbled his words.

Alese chuckled. "I am her grandmother, but I thank you for the compliment."

A red flush crept up Dayton's neck to his cheeks. He hung his head. "Welcome," he mumbled. The words slurred to make it hard to understand.

Alese crossed her arms. "Has this man been drinking?"

"No, Gram. Doc Billings gave him a mild sedative," Bart said.

"Oh, I see. Well, you just rest here. When you wake I'll fix you a big plate of moose liver and onions. Best thing to start rebuilding your blood." Alese left the room.

"I'll help you, Gram." Kat looked at Dayton. "Make yourself comfortable, and see if you can get some sleep."

Dayton settled onto the couch, his head on the softest pillow he ever remembered. "Doubt I'll be sleeping," he mumbled as he drifted off.

"Welcome to Grandma's nest," Bart said.

———◆◆◆———

Familiar footsteps caught Kat's attention right before Ken gripped her arm. "I'd like to know why you are here."

Kat steadied the teacup in her right hand. "Careful. You almost scalded us both!"

"Don't change the subject. Why are you here?" Ken's voice shook with anger.

"Why am I at my grandmother's house?"

"No. Why are you walking the streets of the Cove in full dark when there are creatures just waiting for the cover of night so they can kill?"

"What wants to kill me? This thing likes men—Arnie, Dayton—men."

"The Kumrande don't care about gender."

Kat set the teacup on the counter. "I forgot about them."

"What if you'd been critically injured? Worse, what if you'd been killed? I need you to…" An ear-splitting bark drowned out Ken's last word.

"If you ever had any doubt, be assured you are my best friend in the world," Wendy yelled from the hall. "I would not tolerate this creature for anyone else." Wendy dropped the leash and glared at Kat. "This animal doesn't *ever* shut up! Jo isn't speaking to me because it ran off a couple of her late night customers before they got in the bakery, and I'm not sure Horace from the hardware store is talking to me either!"

"Carnelian!" The dog ran to Kat, sat, and looked her in the eye. Kat cradled the dog's head in her hands and kissed its forehead. "She's a wonderful dog, Winsome. Look how gentle."

"Sure, now she is." Wendy whirled and stalked out the door.

"Since when did you name the beast?" Ken asked.

"Just now."

Grandma shook her head. "Oh, dear. You've let yourself become attached to this noisy angel."

"Here's the other beast." BC leapt to the ground, trotted to Kat, and sat down beside Carnelian.

"I'm confused, Winsome. You were supposed to check on them."

"Oh, I did. Your house is a mess, KittyKat."

"What happened?"

"Looks like a cat and dog left alone to me."

"I never thought they'd get unruly in just a few hours."

"On the bright side, looks like BC taught the beasty there how to use the cat door. Good thing she's small enough to make it through."

Kat scooped up BC and looked him in the eye. "Aren't you an excellent papa? Teaching this little girl such good manners."

"You are hopeless, worse than hopeless," Wendy spat.

"Anyone home?" Tanya Lucas called from the entry.

"In the kitchen." Grandma Bricken answered.

"Is this a town of insomniacs?" Ken asked.

"Where's the party?" Tanya didn't wait for an answer. She pulled a piece of paper out of her wallet. "Paul says this has something to do with the box and key. He was so obsessed by it he went on the Internet at the library and found the information." She handed the paper to Kat.

"Says here the key fits a box said to have been the mate to a certain jar from Russia." Kat looked at Ken.

"Go on."

"Well, seems the missing box and the key are actually part of a set. Oh, not good."

"What's not good?" Wendy asked.

"The box and jar are purported to have been created by a stonemason who dabbled in the normal bad stuff—spells, alchemy, animal sacrifices. So, he gets the idea to create this box to represent the Ark of the Covenant and the jar to symbolize the Tower of Babel in hopes he can call down the spirit of God. Seems he wanted to have a face-to-face with the Almighty."

"That's a bit farfetched—even for the Cove," Bart said.

"Anyway, these two implements are rumored to have been created at the direction of the evil foe. The stonemason thought it was his own idea. The evil one didn't tell him different. What was happening, though, was the guy was creating a prison for the spirit Lilith. Seems Lilith is an enemy of Satan and his army.

"So what happened to the stonemason?"

Kat scanned the document. "Witnesses said he headed into the deep woods one day. When he didn't come back, some of the villagers went looking for him. And guess what?" Kat looked up from the story.

"What?"

"When they found him, he was drained of blood!"

"Sounds too familiar," Bart said.

"Something doesn't make sense here. I thought God turned her into a devil. Why would the demons consider her an enemy?" Ken asked.

"In this same legend, it says the evil ones see her as an abomination and less than they are because she began as a human. To make matters worse, they can't control her, which makes her a threat."

"So how'd they get her in jar?"

"The article doesn't say. It just says she was."

"Darn. Thought we'd be able to do the same thing—if Lilith is who we're dealing with."

"Here's an interesting tidbit."

"More interesting than the rest?"

"I'd say. After the stonemason's death, the box disappeared. The legends says it was been stolen by the devil himself, and buried it in a secret place to keep as a backup prison for Lilith. Then, his underlings took the jar and threw it into an uninhabited land. Seems the two together make for some bad, ummm, juju as they say."

Ken looked at Bart. "So, what if the jar Mandy brought in is Lilith's prison?"

"And the box is sitting in the antique store," Josiah said.

"Thinking back I *know* the chest is at Annie's store. Cranberry-colored jewels were melted right into the stone—just like the jar Mandy brought to the station. I saw those gems turn to a deep blue right before my eyes."

Ken stood up. "We'd better get those two things under lock and key." He turned to Bart. "Coming?"

"You bet."

Ken brushed Kat's forehead with a kiss and disappeared into the night.

Chapter 15
Kumrandes and Corpses

"Pick up the blasted phone!" Carson Watermill yelled into his mobile. Ivy June Coistrell's recorded voice told him to leave a message. Watermill hit *end*, threw the cell phone on the bed, and strode to the hotel room's window. He tapped his forehead with an index finger. "Think, Watermill. Think!"

The detective stared blankly at the Cook Inlet glittering in the bright sun, snapped his fingers, and tromped back to the bed.

Mandy picked up on the first ring. "Where have you been?" She asked. "I thought you were going to call yesterday."

"Unexpected business." *Like your murder—why are you still alive?*

"Well, things are heating up here. Seems they found a body."

"Who is it?" Watermill clinched his teeth to disguise the concern he felt.

"How do I know? And I had the little chest you wanted, but it disappeared."

"How did that happen! You can't do anything right!"

"It's not my fault it's gone! And I don't appreciate your nasty comment, either. I kept my part of the bargain; go find that box yourself!"

"I'm not finished with you yet. You'll do what I say, or I'll make you go to jail for a long, long time."

"I'm cleared, remember? You can't do anything to me."

"Oh, but I can. How hard would it be to pin this latest tragedy on you? A few clues in the right place and presto! You're the main suspect."

Mandy lowered herself into the folding chair in her living room. "What do you want me to do?" she whispered

"I want you to stay put."

"Only stay put?"

"No. Get me the name of the victim. If you do, I'll consider letting you stay free."

Kat ducked when a mud swallow swooped over her head in hot pursuit of its breakfast. "Well, one less mosquito we'll need to worry about," she said.

Wendy smiled. "Every little bit helps."

They stopped in front of Jo's Bakery. "Would you look at this crowd?" Kat glanced at her watch. "Hope we don't have to wait forever. I'm supposed to be at the station."

Josephina Lattrell set two large white cups on the glass counter. "You're late, Kat."

"How'd you know?"

Jo lifted her chin toward Wendy. "Someone called ahead."

Kat smiled and raised her cup. "I owe you one."

"Yep, you do. Let's go."

Wendy peeked into the window of the antique store. "Mandy? She never gets moving before noon." She walked inside.

"Hey, big sister." Mandy flashed a sweet smile at Wendy.

"What brings you in so early?"

"Have a bunch of inventory to do—per the boss lady. Oh, that reminds me. She sent a fax this morning. It's for the police chief."

"I'll take it."

Mandy's fine-china features contorted in thought. She shook her head. "No, better not. It's addressed to him, and I don't want to get in any trouble."

Kat punched some numbers into her phone. "Ken? Mandy needs your permission to let me bring you a fax. Hold on." She handed the cell to Mandy.

"Hello?" Mandy said. "Oh, hi, Police Chief Melbourne."

The words grated Ken's nerves like fingernails down the proverbial blackboard. "Give the note to Kat, would you? I am up to my eyeballs and waiting for a phone call."

"I don't know —"

"The note's for me, right? Give it to Kat! And when you see the shop owner, have her call me."

"Okay." Mandy frowned and put a beige envelope in Kat's outstretched hand.

"Thanks. I'll get this to the station. Coming?" she said to Wendy.

"Give me a second. I want to talk to Mandy."

Mandy's eyes narrowed. "Why do you need to talk to me?"

"I want to know how you managed to get this job when none of us have seen Annie Scofland for a while."

"I told you she's out of town and asked me to cover for her."

"And I want to make sure she really is just out of town."

"Are you accusing me of making her disappear?"

"Did you?"

"No!"

Kat pulled Wendy close and whispered, "let Ken take care of this."

Wendy looked at her best friend. "Fine." She turned on her heel and marched out the door.

Kat caught up with her, ran in front and jogged backwards. "Wendy, don't do something you'll regret. Ken will take care of it if he finds out she's had any part in the murders and thefts."

Wendy stopped. Tears coursed down her cheeks. "She's involved, alright. I can see it in her eyes. How can my own blood be such a liar and cheat—not to mention giving her own body away for money?"

Kat threw her arms around Wendy. "I don't know. I promise you we'll find out what Mandy has to do with all this. I promise.

———◆———

The door to the police station stood wide open. A fan sat two feet in, blowing warm air toward the back office.

"It must be ninety degrees in here," Kat said.

"Maybe hotter." Wendy fanned her face with one hand. "Good thing you have at least one short-sleeved shirt."

"And I wore it today."

"I'll be back in a jiff with another drink—iced this time."

"Sounds heavenly. Get one for Ken, too?"

Kat made her way to the back office. Ken took in the khaki-colored capris and a cap-sleeved T-shirt the same color as Kat's eyes.

Kat looked down at herself then back at Ken. "What?"

"You look amazing." Ken opened the envelope and read aloud:

> *Dear Police Chief,*
>
> *I wanted to set a couple of things straight. I was called out of town by a family emergency. I did hire Mandy to watch the store. She had been in a day before and left me a note with her number because she was looking for work. The family emergency wasn't such an emergency after all. Since I am already in Idaho, I'm extending my leave for a short buying trip. By the way, not only are the bowl and cane missing, so is a valuable casket. I had put the key to it around the stray dog's neck. Seemed the safest place for it. What good is a box if you can't open it, right? Can you see what you can do to find it? Thank you so much. Warmly, Annie Scofland.*

"So, do you believe this is her handwriting?" Kat asked.

"Don't have any reason to believe it's not, and I don't have anything to compare it to."

Kat walked out to her desk and came back with a small piece of note paper. "Will this do?"

Ken looked at the paper. "How fortunate."

"She liked my engagement ring so much, she wrote out the description and the price she'd pay for it. She even signed it."

Ken examined the note, then the facsimile. "Well, I'm no handwriting expert, but these signatures look identical to me."

"Glad something's resolved."

"I didn't say this is settled. Since I have no facts to the contrary, I have to believe this is from her."

"Somebody save me from the enemy and its name is bureaucracy." Bart's voice drowned out the loud hum of the fan.

"Can't help you there, buddy. It's an octopus and you are smack-dab in the middle of its tentacles," Ken yelled back.

Bart appeared at the door. His dress shirt was soaked, and his face was flushed from the heat. "This one's gonna break a record."

"Maybe you could requisition an air conditioner. The town council would feel terrible if its mayor died from heat exhaustion."

"Love you, too, first cousin of mine." Bart yanked on his shirt collar. "Got anything we can do so I have an excuse to get out of these clothes? I feel like I'm living in a sauna."

"As a matter of fact. I thought I'd be heading back over to Old Town."

Kat slammed her hands on the honey-oak desk. "No you're not!"

Ken held Kat's eyes, then turned to Bart. "As I was saying, I want to head back to Old Town—and I probably shouldn't do it alone."

Kat plopped into the guest chair and crossed her arms. "Why do you need to go there? The place is nothing but trouble."

"Because Old Town is the best lead we have right now. Maybe we missed a crucial piece of evidence. If we find some, it could lead us to the killer—or Lilith. How about you go check on Dayton?" Ken asked.

"Why me?"

"He likes you."

"You're trying to keep me out of your hair."

"Do you blame me?"

Kat sighed. "I guess not. But I want you to call me in thirty minutes. And every half-hour until you're out of that place."

"Not necessary."

"It is. If I don't hear from you, I'll be there, and you don't want that."

"And you know she will," Bart said.

I'll call in thirty minutes. Happy?"

"Not yet. One more thing…"

"Hello? Anyone here?"

"Back here," Ken shouted.

Wendy handed a frosty cup to Kat, then Ken. "Well, guess I'm going back to Jo's." She handed the last one to Bart. "What'd I miss?"

"Nothing. Just these knuckleheads are taking risks I don't like—again." Wendy pointed to the drink in Kat's hand. "Take a sip and cool down. It's their job, whether you like it or not."

"Whatcha got?" Kat nodded to a brown grocery sack in Wendy's hand.

"Almost forgot." Wendy shoved the bag at Ken. "Jo told me she found this in the bathroom trash. Thought you should see it."

"What is it?"

"I'm not opening it! Could be a head or something worse."

"Doubtful." Ken opened the bag, reached in, and yanked out a gray wig and a broom skirt. He held them up to Bart. "Either we have a naked tourist running around town or someone made sure they couldn't be identified once they got here."

"Where is my head today?" Wendy said. "Jo said an old lady from the tour bus came in yesterday and asked to use the restroom."

"And this is relevant how?"

"Jo's sure she was wearing this skirt."

"I'll make some calls before I head to Gram's. See if we can find a tour driver who remembers her."

"Thanks, Kat."

"As I said, there's one more thing. Take Carnelian with you."

"I don't need an animal along."

"I think you do. She knew that nasty spirit was in Gram's kitchen before we did. Besides, she'll let you know if there's something there you bullheaded guys are too stupid to notice."

"Bullheaded? Stupid?" Bart clenched his jaw. "Take a look in mirror."

"I'm not the one risking my life at Old Town."

"It has to be done. End of conversation."

"Then you're taking Carnelian with you. I'm sure it sounds irrational, but I can't shake the feeling you need her there. So, if you don't, I'm coming instead."

"I still think it's a bad idea, but if it will keep you out of Old Town, I'll go get her."

Kat stuck her hands in her pockets. "Okay, then."

"Now please go check on Dayton."

"On my way."

Pet glided through the underground tunnel toward the Kumrande's lair. A glint of fiery red brought him to a stop. He dipped low and took hold of a cream-colored box sitting at the rough-cut archway. "Well, well. Who do we have here?" Pet turned the box over several times. "You are not the one I seek. Still, I have a plan for you!"

Voices echoed off the deep cavern walls. Pet moved to the side of the doorway, just out of sight.

"We will take the town ourselves," Nihilist said. "We do not need to share our treasures with anyone—the demons called us to life as slaves, but we can make sure they do not keep us as such!"

A cheer rose from the small crowd. "Long live Nihilist," a lone voice yelled out.

"What about the she-devil?" another screamed.

"We imprison her just as we did her servant. Then, we truly will be free!" Nihilist answered.

"Long live Nihilist, long live Nihilist," the crowd chanted.

"You are mistaken. Nihilist dies now." Pet dropped the small box to the ground. He transformed into a purple and black saw. The demon blade shrieked and raced forward. The purple and black cutter slowed when it hit Nihilist's neck and passed through muscle and bone.

Nihilist's head teetered from side to side, then tumbled to the ground. His eyes blinked twice, and the wide mouth froze in a ghoulish O.

"Run to the caves," Homunculus screeched. The band of dwarfs split into small groups and fled through a trio of archways to dark-walled tunnels.

"Come out, you cowards. Come out now unless you all want to end up like your leader."

Homunculus stepped in the room and fell prostrate before Pet. "We are at your command."

A satisfied smile lit Pet's gargoyle-like face. "Who commands you was never a question. If you'd like to keep your head, tell me who found the box?"

"He did." Homunculus pointed at Nihilist.

"Where is the key?"

"Nihilist hid it in his cave."

"If you are telling the truth, you will live—for now. If not, you'll join him in the void of nonexistence. Adumbration! Estafette! Come."

A shadow appeared on the wall, and a mist rose from the dirt floor of the cavern.

"This Kumrande says their former leader," Pet pointed to Nihilist's head, "stole this box. Is it true?"

"It is. The spirit who has been spying on them confirms it."

"Where is the key?"

Adumbration held up a bronze object. "It was where this slave said it would be."

"Lucky for you, stupid, soulless being. You can live—for now. Know I will send you and all of your kind back into nothingness if you betray me again."

"I told Nihilist it was a mistake," the small being whined.

"Did you? He should have taken your advice. Get out of my sight!"

The Kumrande bowed and galloped into the depths of the cave.

"Take the box to the mansion."

"Done." Adumbration disappeared into the wall. He rematerialized moments later. "There are intruders at the house in Old Town!"

"Take the box to the old fish building. I will deal with the intruders. "Kumrande, come!"

"We are here." Homunculus stepped out of the dark tunnel. Hundreds of silver-haired, yellow-eyed creatures followed.

"Surround Old Town from deep within the woods. Attack when I call. Do not fail!" Pet levitated, dissolved into a mist, and shot up through the courtyard in Old Town.

———————◆◆◆◆———————

"Where do you think you're going?" Kat shoved Detective Dayton back into Grandma Bricken's hallway.

"I'm getting out of here. My partner's missing, and I need to get back to Anchorage."

"You've got 'gonna pass out' written all over you. Get back inside." Kat pushed harder this time.

Dayton caught hold of the doorframe. "Touch me again, I'll arrest you!"

Wendy grabbed Kat's arm in midair. "She's quite harmless."

"And stubborn," Grandma said. "Still, she's right detective. You do need to come back inside." Alese Bricken took Dayton's arm in a gentle but firm grip and led him to the kitchen.

Wendy let go of Kat. "You have got to quit taking those kinds of dares, KittyKat."

"He makes me so mad I see red. He is so arrogant."

"What lawman isn't?"

"Well, Bart, Ken—" Kat thought about the times they had both treated her like a five-year old. She looked at Wendy. "Come to think of it, I don't know any without an 'I know better than you do' attitude."

Wendy giggled. "Let's see how this one stands up to Grandma."

"My bet's on her."

"Not taking that bet. You'll win for sure."

Kat stood in the hallway and watched Detective Dayton's introduction to breakfast at Grandma's house. Kat's nose wrinkled when she caught a whiff of liver and onions. The more appealing smells of eggs, sausage, and sourdough toast brought her to the table.

Grandma set the plate of liver and onions in front of Dayton. "This will help you heal."

Dayton pushed the plate away. "I don't think I need this."

"I don't care what you think. Your blood needs feeding. Now eat!"

Josiah lifted a cup of fresh-brewed coffee to Dayton in a mock toast. "I'd do what she says, if I were you."

Alese Bricken touched the plate with a spatula. "Eat!"

"She made me eat it yesterday." Kat lifted her bandaged arm.

Humor them so you can get out of here, Dayton thought. He took a tentative bite. His eyebrows shot up. "This is good." He dove in.

"Where's my patient?" Doc Billings called out from the front of the house.

"Come on in, Doc. Breakfast is ready."

Billings nodded approval at Dayton's plate. "You have an appetite, I see."

"Contrary to what these people think, I'm feeling good. When can I get out of here?"

"I need to take a look at the wounds. How about we go into the other room for some privacy?" Billings pointed to Kat's arm. "Then, it's your turn."

Paul Lucas stepped into the kitchen. "I was walking by and saw this package by the door. It's for Josiah." Paul extended his hand. "I'm Paul Lucas."

"Where are my manners?" Kat said. "This is Detective Dayton from Anchorage."

Paul looked at the bandaged neck and arm. "What happened to you?"

"He had a run-in with a vampire last night," Wendy said.

Kat backhanded Wendy on the leg.

"Ouch. What else could it have been?"

"A vampire." Paul sat down. "Tell me about it."

Grandma Bricken handed Paul a bright orange stoneware plate and silverware with matching handles.

"I really shouldn't. Tanya did feed me a wonderful breakfast this morning—maybe just a little." Pastor Lucas dished his plate full of scrambled eggs, reindeer sausage, and sourdough toast.

Kat leaned over to Wendy and whispered, "it's like the whole town knows when breakfast is ready at Grandma's."

"Most of them do," Grandma answered.

"This is exactly what I've been waiting for." Josiah held a small book in the air.

"What do you have?"

"An answer from an old friend who happens to be an expert in situations like ours."

"What situation?" Dayton asked.

"The statue, the mysterious containers, deaths…"

"You mean the murders—there's a real crazy on the loose. So, what could your friend tell you unless he or she is involved?"

"This is a man of the cloth. He has great knowledge in demonology. He has made it his life's work to study legends—specifically Russian legends pertaining to demons."

"You mean like with tails and horns?"

Josiah looked up from the book."Sorry, I was distracted. What did you ask?"

"Nothing. Have you found out anything?"

"My friend's note says there is a legend in Siberia about a succubus who was trapped by a Russian nobleman. Someone, possibly a servant, smuggled it out of the country."

"Why?" Alese asked.

"I would think to take it somewhere it couldn't hurt anyone else. He talks about a lot of death in the nobleman's village. Oh, dear."

Kat leaned forward. "What?"

"He also says there is a secret society which has been searching for this entity for hundreds of years because they seek its favor—and power."

Dayton leveled his gaze on Josiah. "And you think this spirit is here?"

"I'm thinking so."

"You want to give me a logical reason?"

"We have a bloodless body. A jar like the one mentioned here. Then, of course, I believe God is leading us to the answer, and this may be it."

"That really isn't a logical explanation, Mr. Williams."

"Do you have an explanation for what happened to you last night?"

"Some hyped-up junkie with the munchies mistook me for a T-bone steak."

Doc Billings stuffed his cell phone into his front pocket. "Where's Melbourne?"

"He and Bart are at Old Town. Why?"

"Got an ID on the ravine victim."

"Who is it?"

"You know I can't tell you." Doc saw the concern in Kat's eyes. "But it's no one you know."

Kat smiled. "Thanks, Doc."

"Let's get you to the back and check your wound," Doc said to Dayton.

The front door slammed. "My, we are busy today."

Amos Thralling ran through the kitchen door, almost body slamming Doc Billings and Detective Dayton. "The blasted tree is back! It's back at the ravine."

"I never knew it was gone." Wendy looked at Kat.

Amos turned wild eyes on Wendy. "Well, Missy, it was in pieces in Arnie's shop last night; today it is back in its spot pretty as you please—like nothin' ever happened!"

"Okay, deep breath, Amos," Kat said.

"You take a deep breath! Trees don't resurrect themselves overnight—and they sure don't replant themselves!"

"I know, Amos. Is Arnie playing some kind of practical joke on you?"

"Not this time. The dang thing has new leaves! Like its spring or somethin'."

"Well, this is an amazing turn of events. I need to get to town," Wendy jingled her keys and headed for the door.

"Now?"

"Got to let some people know—maybe I can help solve this mystery."

"You want to put the whole Cove into an uproar and run off the tourists?"

"I know how to be discreet!"

"You do?"

"Yes. I'll start at the vet's office to see if they've heard anything about a practical joker. It's the quietest place in town—now the kennel cough scare is over."

"The vet's office?"

"Nyna hears a lot."

"I can't believe you need to go and flirt with Douglas at a time like this."

"I can multitask."

"Since you have your mind made up, do something productive while you are there—tell Carl Carnelian is doing great and she and BC are like lifelong buds."

"Will do. Catch you later."

Kat turned to Amos. "How about we go up to the ravine and have a look at the hag tree?"

"I'm coming, too." Grandma Bricken took her cane from a hook by the doorway.

"What about the detective?"

"He'll just have to come with us. We'll leave as soon as Doc has finished with him."

"Doc says I'm healing fast. So, don't worry about me. I don't need to be part of this mass hysteria. I'll be fine right here."

"Can't leave you alone."

"She's right. Whatever came after you may want to finish what it started. Good thing my car seats six," Paul said.

"You're coming, too?"

"Wouldn't miss it."

"Word sure got around fast." Kat pushed her way through the gawking crowd and toward the ear-piercing and now familiar bark of Carnelian.

"Not you, too?" Bart said.

"Thought you were at Old Town."

"Almost inside. Then Horace"—Bart pointed to the owner of the hardware store—"met us at the gate waving and pointing toward the ravine. He couldn't put two words together, so here we are."

"Would you look at it! Amos wasn't kidding." Kat crept up to the hag tree. It stood straight and tall. The only hint of its destruction was the black and decaying hole in its trunk.

"If the rot is any indication, this tree is way past dead. How can it be growing leaves?"

"One of many questions we need to answer."

"Can you people move back, please?" Ken's pleading tone carried above the buzz of conversation.

Kat smiled. "He's having a little trouble controlling the Cove, isn't he?"

"He's way too polite." Bart faced the crowd and yelled, "Do what the man says, now!"

The noise dropped, and the sea of people stepped back just enough to make a small path to the tree.

"Thanks." A begrudging tone laced Ken's words.

Kat crouched down and scratched Carnelian behind the ear. "You're such a good girl. Helping the big, bad policeman control the crowd."

Carnelian jumped onto Kat's knees and licked her nose.

"Don't encourage her," Ken snapped. "I've got a headache—not sure if it is the crowd or the pitch of her bark."

Bart rubbed his chin. "It *looks* like the tree we saw at Arnie's shop."

"It was acting strangely," Ken replied.

"Any tree that levitates and walks on its own is strange."

Ken pointed to a thick stream of liquid flowing down the trunk. "What's running down the side?"

"Hoping it's sap."

"Since when is sap purple?"

"Since Ravens Cove became the paranormal hotspot of Alaska?"

The crowd pushed closer. Ken whirled. "Give us some breathing room—and I mean now!"

The throng inched backward.

Arnie jogged forward and pointed. "My tree!" The onlookers inched forward again.

Ken pointed at the crowd and then Arnie. "Not another step!"

"Hey, Arnie, seems the tree doesn't think you own it," Horace yelled. Nervous laughter rippled through the gathering.

Bart stepped between the tree and the crowd. "Alright, folks, go back to town—now! You're interfering with a police investigation."

"What, you gonna arrest someone for replanting a tree?" Kat whispered.

"Not helping," Bart hissed from the side of his mouth. He raised his voice. "Go on back to town. There's nothing more to see."

"I'm losing money standing here anyway." Horace made his way down the hill. As the self-proclaimed leader left the hill, the crowd lost interest and went separate ways.

"What's going on here?" Detective Dayton asked.

"Well, while you were fighting battles of your own, we were witness to an odd phenomenon. We saw this ugly old tree become whole and walk. Any theories?"

"My guess is someone's playing a joke on gullible people." Dayton walked over and gave the tree a push, expecting it to fall over. It shivered and shot sickly-yellow sparks toward his hand. Dayton jumped rearward.

"It's back," Bart said to Ken.

"What's back?" Dayton asked.

"The tree—it kind of has a mind of its own."

"It's the guardian of this ravine."

"Some kind of Native lore, right?"

"More like a curse," Ken answered.

"Man, didn't the FBI teach you how to deduce and reason?"

Ken glared at Dayton. "They did. I have."

"I'll say it again. You people are crazy."

The leaves of the hag tree moved in a nonexistent breeze, and more sickly-yellow sparks fell to the ground. Purple sap, mixed with black fluid, coursed down the tree's trunk.

"Okay, that's just not right!" Dayton said.

"You haven't seen the half of it." Bart shook his head, remembering the two Iconoclast attacks.

"You look kinda pale." Kat offered Dayton an arm. "How about I help you to the car?"

"How about you get me to Anchorage? I'm done with this place." Dayton took two steps forward, weaved, and lurched forward.

Bart caught him by the shirt. "Not until someone shows up for you."

"Let's get you to the car." Paul led Dayton away.

Bart turned to Kat and Ken. "So we have Iconoclast again?"

"I saw him go into the depths of the earth with my own eyes." Ken thought back to the battle at Old Town. He visualized the blue energy jettisoning from angelic swords and the hair-raising screeches as the evil ones fell through the earth.

"Then who?"

"The only demon I don't remember in the battle or seeing plummet into the ground was Pet," Kat said.

"Come to think of it, I remember watching that purple and black ball fall from Iconoclast's hand but don't remember seeing it hit the ground."

"This liquid contains his hallmark colors. Do you think he's still here?"

"Thought he was just a pet—for lack of a better term. He never seemed dangerous."

"All evil is dangerous, Mr. Melbourne." Josiah said in a hushed tone. "The deception of this one is to be harmless. I think we have underestimated him."

"Where did you come from?" Ken asked.

"I came with Paul, too. I waited until the crowd left. Seemed more discreet."

"How did he avoid the abyss?" Kat asked.

"By doing what he does best. He avoided the battle. He changed shape and waited for a time he could move undetected," Josiah answered.

"God help us."

"Yes. As always, He is our only hope."

The annoying ring of a cell phone got Ken's attention. "Melbourne."

"Glad to finally get you. The ravine victim has been identified."

"You're breaking up, Doc." Ken walked out onto the path away from the hag tree.

"I said the victim in the ravine is a certain Ivy June Coistrell. Funny thing is her name's connected to a murder in Oregon."

"Okay. She found her way to Ravens Cove. Is that all?"

"Not quite. The detective I spoke with asked me about a Madame Piquant. Seems those same fingerprints were found at Grady Spawldine's home in Anchorage. The APD ran them through the database and the fingerprints for Piquant and Coistrell were identical. He faxed the wanted poster of Coistrell. It's a match to the corpse."

"Hmmm. Can you get her picture to me? I'd like to show it to Dayton."

"I'll have someone run it up to you."

"So Coistrell and Piquant are one and the same," Ken said.

Kat grasped Ken's arm and whispered. "Madame Piquant is the one who held a séance at Spawldine's a bit before he died."

Ken shoved a finger in his right ear and walked up the ravine pathway. "So, Madame Piquant is an alias?"

"Seems like it."

"I know that name! I need to get back up there." Dayton pulled free of Paul. Paul caught his arm before he fell to the ground.

"Not a good idea, my friend."

"I'll crawl up if I have to."

Paul shook his head and guided Dayton to Ken. "He insisted."

"Stubborn son of a gun, aren't you?" A half smile lifted Bart's mouth.

"When I need to be. I told you about Piquant. There's trouble wherever she goes. Now she's here and connected to this corpse?"

"Seems she is the corpse."

"Are you sure?"

"The fingerprints are a match."

"I want to see the body."

"I'd be happy to show it to you, except it went missing late yesterday—not very long before you were attacked."

"Your ME lost a body? Why wasn't there an attendant on duty? Is this whole town not only crazy but incompetent as well?"

"Doc Billings saved your miserable life. I would suggest you re-think your opinion of him."

"What's Billings got to do with anything?"

"This is a small town, Dayton. He is both the doctor and the ME. Being a small town, there certainly isn't a budget for an attendant which makes Doc a one-trick pony. He has to sleep sometime."

"Okay. So what made this body so important someone had to steal it?" Dayton mumbled to himself.

"You just asked the million-dollar question," Ken answered. "It was drained of blood, it was mutilated and the heart is missing. What else would someone want to do to the poor creature?"

A breathless Eric Smotherly ran up the hill. The twenty-something mortuary attendant shoved an envelope into Ken's hand.

"Thanks."

The kid saluted and jogged back toward town.

Ken opened the envelope and studied an 8½-by-11 sheet of paper. "She was so young." He handed the photo to Dayton. "Ever seen this girl?"

"Once. I ran into her with my partner on my day off. She's his cousin. Think her name is Vera or Myrna… "

"Her name's Ivy June Coistrell."

"Impossible! She's Watermill's cousin."

Ken raised his eyebrows. "Facts don't lie."

"Maybe Watermill's cousin has a look alike. Maybe…all I know is when I can get in touch with him, he'll straighten this out."

"Maybe he will," Bart said.

Dayton turned troubled eyes to Bart. "With the extensive mutilation of the corpse, I'm thinking the killer is someone in the medical field who has gone over the edge."

"I'd agree with you, if there weren't additional facts that make that unlikely."

"Like what?"

"Let's take this tree for an example. How many trees have you seen that resurrect themselves. Or, spark and ooze violet sap? Kat asked.

"Still think that's a practical joke."

Kat's apple-green eyes flashed. "I wish detective. Open your ears and your eyes. This is not human!"

"The Kumrande maybe?" Bart asked Ken.

200

"Doc said the arteries were cauterized—the heart wasn't just ripped free from the chest like the Kumrande's handiwork."

"I know I'll regret this question but what is a Kumrande?" Dayton asked.

Bart looked at the hag tree. "Let's just call them another piece of local lore."

"So, my dead suspect was killed by folklore?"

"Nope. Our lore would have left her arteries wide open. It's something else."

"Reminds me of those quacks who supposedly remove disease by putting their hands right through the skin. Those guys use chicken parts and such, though."

"Well, since we are missing a heart, and it doesn't look like anyone was trying to heal that poor creature, I'd say we're talking about two different animals. Wouldn't you?"

"You have a point."

Ken turned to Josiah. "So, if Pet is here and if he's planning an assault, why take a heart? Why take the body? The Iconoclast clan likes to leave evidence and terrify everyone."

"You've forgotten about Lilith," Josiah said.

Ken ran a hand through his hair. "She does add a new suspect to the mix."

"You have more than one fictitious bad guy?" Dayton shook his head in disgust. "I don't know why I'm even standing here."

"Think what you will, Dayton. I believed the same thing not so long ago."

"I see why you aren't with the FBI any longer."

"Didn't say I wasn't."

"Word gets around."

The sting of humiliation hit Ken in the gut. "Thought gossip was only believed in a small town."

"Guess not."

"Until you've seen the horrors we have, Dayton, keep your character assassinations to yourself." Bart nodded to Ken. "Stick around long enough, and you may find out what we're talking about. Now why don't you go rest? You don't look so good."

"I need to get hold of my partner and clear up this mess about his cousin. Then I need to talk to your ME."

"You can make calls from Paul's car. Right, Pastor?"

"Sure can. You ready, detective?"

"I expect to be notified as soon as you find something tangible." Dayton took a step toward the pathway. He caught hold of Paul's forearm when his knees buckled.

"If I do, you'll be the first to know. Now, I'm going back to *my* town's problem."

Bart patted Ken on the shoulder. "Well said, brother. Well said. Now, back to business."

"Remember the wig Wendy brought into the station?" Ken asked. "It was the same color as the hair on the old woman. You know the one at Arnie's workshop last night."

"I was thinking the same thing. But what's the wig got to do with Ivy June Coistrell?

"What if the old crone was Ivy June?"

"I've never heard of a ghost wearing a disguise. Seems pointless."

Ken tipped his head to the side and looked at Bart. "Since when is a ghost solid as a human?"

"This Lilith is a new addition to my knowledge of evil," Josiah said. "In the legend from Siberia, she took the form of a beautiful woman to tempt men. She also must take on her physical form to feed."

"We're talking about a recently deceased human—not a few-thousand-year-old demon."

"Yes, but Lilith usually kills men—and children. Luckily, she hasn't taken any children here. Still, if she was imprisoned in the tree and someone set her free, it follows she would have been starving for human blood—any blood. From what you've said, this Coistrell was a young woman and almost qualified as a child. Maybe this girl did not die—maybe Lilith can revive a corpse."

Bart looked from Josiah to Ken. "Well, as farfetched as it sounds, it answers some of the questions."

"I still think Old Town is somehow connected to all this. The malevolent boulder, too. We never found its ivory likeness, did we?"

"Nope. Just another reason we need to go back there."

Kat shoved Carnelian's leash into Ken's hand. "Call me."

Ken held the leash out to Kat. "Please take her home with you. I don't think taking this dog in there is such a good idea."

Kat snatched the strap and gave it a gentle tug. "Come on, girl, the big bad guys want to be alone." Carnelian sat down and looked in the direction of Old Town. Kat pulled again. Carnelian backed up, arched her neck and trotted over to Ken. Kat stared at the empty collar then to the dog at Ken's feet.

"Is there no way to control this animal?"

"I need a harness, and she thinks you need a bodyguard." Kat snapped the collar back around Carnelian's neck and handed the leash to Ken. "Whether you like it or not."

"Didn't you put the key on the new collar?"

"Couldn't find it. I thought you'd put it somewhere."

"Nope."

"Maybe it's still at Gram's. I'll check when I get a chance." Kat took a step onto the path leading to her cabin.

"We need to talk about strays as soon as we get a chance, Kat." Ken yelled. He looked down at the nutmeg face and black eyes. "Come on, dog." Carnelian heeled at his left leg and trotted in time with Ken's footsteps.

Kat turned around and smiled. "You are a perfect couple." She called after them, then made her way down the hill with Gram and Josiah.

Chapter 16
Old Town

Steel-gray clouds hung low over Old Town and drank the afternoon warmth from the air. An uncontrollable shiver snaked up Bart's spine. "Okay, then. Let's say this drop in temperature is coincidence and move on—fast."

The porch step groaned under Ken's shoe. "Ouch!" Ken pulled his foot back and bent down. "Looks like we found the missing ivory." A miniature of the boulder in Old Town's courtyard lay face up. Its empty sockets stared into Ken's eyes.

"One mystery solved." Ken dropped the ivory piece into a small Baggie and walked into the house.

Carnelian growled and lunged at the staircase. "Easy, dog." Ken pulled on the leash.

"Ouch!" Bart slapped at the back of his neck. "Something stung me!" He looked around for a bee. A shadow caught his eye before it faded into the wall.

"Man, you have a bear of a welt."

"Did you see a shadow?"

"I didn't. But it seems like Carnelian did." Ken pointed at the floor. Carnelian's legs were rod-straight, and the hair on her neck stood up. She growled at the wall.

Bart took the stairs two at a time. He leapt over the rust-colored stain in front of the attic door. "This is a different look," he shouted back to Ken.

"It didn't look too good the last time. What are you talking—oh, I see." Ken surveyed the room. A dark red fluid materialized on the attic ceiling. It plummeted at missile-speed to the pine floorboards, shimmied, then melted into the wood.

Bart sniffed and doubled over in a coughing fit. "What's that smell?"

"I think it's coming from there." Ken pointed to a rectangular table covered in a tar-like substance. A cherry-red pentagram floated in the sea of black. Two laser-red dots bounced up and down in the five-pointed star.

"How did that get there?" Ken pointed to a miniature skull hovering in the star, then shoved his hand in his pocket and yanked out an empty Baggie.

"Welcome." A voice echoed around them.

A shrill *bark* reverberated off the walls and ceiling in the noiseless room. Ken resisted the urge cover his ears.

"We are in a world of trouble," Bart said.

A one-legged creature materialized then vanished. "You are expected," a disembodied voice said.

A sharp pain ran up Ken's back. He looked over his shoulder and was met with a razor-sharp claw.

"We are definitely in a world of trouble." Ken grasped the base of his flashlight. It ripped itself out of his hand and bounced off the far wall before it skidded to a stop. Bart's light rose from his belt and did the same.

"You won't need those." The small creature reappeared. "You are here to witness my supremacy—then to die." Pet waved a gnarled finger in a circle. Yellow light appeared out of thin air and bounced up and down in front of the pentagram.

"What is it with all this need to show off? We get it. You have powers we don't."

A bolt of electricity flew at Bart. He bent toward the floor. Pain shot through his torso when a Kumrande's claw dug deep into his skin.

"Shut up and watch." Pet pulled his hands apart. The yellow light grew until it touched the attic walls. A woman materialized. She was bound hand and foot to a wooden, spindle-backed chair. A serrated dagger was taped between her hands and pointed toward her chest. The knife shivered and forced itself downward. She wrestled the knife, throwing it to the left, then the right, and up toward the ceiling. Her upper torso heaved from the effort it took to keep the dagger at bay. When the blade halted in midair, she relaxed her grip. The weapon buried itself in her chest.

The air sizzled and snapped. The sallow light faded. "You have been a witness to my true power. Now, the Kumrande will feast."

Homunculus spun Ken to face him. He pressed a stiletto shaped claw into his chest. "You will scream for death before I'm finished with you."

Ken grabbed a hairy wrist and yanked it back toward the Kumrande's body until it snapped. He dove toward the flashlights. Two Kumrande gripped his lower legs, flipped him on his back. One took hold of his right knee and upper calf and bent it toward his head.

Carnelian broke free and latched onto a Kumrande's leg. The Kumrande screamed, snatched hold of the small canine and lifted her over his head.

Piercing blue light flooded the attic. The Kumrande dropped the dog. Carnelian skittered to Ken's side.

The group of dwarfs fell to their knees and covered their yellow eyes.

"Take that, you under grown goats!" Two LED flashlights rested on Kat's hips.

"In the name of Jesus, you are bound." Paul thundered into the darkness.

Ken bolted to the far wall and snatched up two silver cylinders. He threw one to Bart.

Pet swayed on paralyzed legs. "I will kill you for this, you pathetic mortal!" he spat.

"Be gone, evil one named Pet and you minions of Satan!" Paul yelled in response.

A shadow hand came through the wall and traced an outline over Pet. He disappeared, leaving a mist of black. The Kumrande disappeared through the floor.

Bart pulled Kat into a bear hug then he held her at arm's length. "How did you get here?"

"I was heading home and heard a sizzling sound. I turned around and saw a yellow ball of light shooting up from the ravine. It looked like it was heading toward town. I caught Paul at Grandma Bricken's." Kat took a breath a rushed on. "When I told Paul what I'd seen, he grabbed the flashlights and his bible and here we are."

"Pastor's intuition. Or, spirit-guided steps," Paul said.

"I am ever thankful for your intuition." Ken turned to Bart. "We've got to find the victim."

"What victim?" Kat asked.

"The evil thing made us watch a vision of some woman killing herself."

"Well, evil likes to deceive. It may have been only a vision to destroy your strength."

"Can't take the chance. I'm almost sure I recognized the high set windows of the cannery."

"Then, we start there. I'll take this." Bart took the second LED flashlight from Kat.

"Now you and Paul come with me." Ken grasped their elbows and gently pushed them to the chain-link gate. "Make sure she gets home okay, would you Paul?"

"Of course, I will."

Ken handed Carnelian's leash to Kat. "Take her with you. She's worn out."

"What about protection?"

"Look at her." Carnelian leaned against Ken's leg. Her eyelids drooped shut, then popped open.

"Poor thing." Kat hefted the ball of fur into her arms. "Don't forget to call."

Ken patted his pocket. "I won't."

Ken watched Kat retreat down Main Street, Carnelian's tale swishing loosely with each footstep. "She's a pretty courageous pup."

"Changing your opinion of dogs?"

"Not what I said."

"Whatever." Bart lifted his chin toward a steady stream of cars and RVs meandering through the Ravens Cove business district. "Such a normal activity. Little do they know the danger in this quaint small town."

"Never know what lies underneath the skin—or a city," Ken said. "Guess we'd better get to it."

Bart headed into the courtyard. He pointed at the brown boulder. "Dang thing looks pretty safe, except for the ugly face. Who'd have known, given the right circumstances, it can devour a living person in a heartbeat."

"If the white wolf hadn't shown up, not to mention God's holy angels, we wouldn't be having a tourist season right now." Ken referred to Benny, Bernice Tellamoot's pet who had mysteriously come to Ravens Cove at the same time as the buildings of Old Town. The tourist attraction took on a life of its own when the late Mayor unintentionally opened a portal that allowed Iconoclast and his army back into the Cove.

"Here goes." Bart yanked on the cannery door.

"Same decorator, I see," Ken said.

Red-stained walls gave way to soot-covered windows. High-edged, metal-topped tables were positioned in a U-shape in the middle of the building. Inside the horseshoe was a woman, slumped over, a knife in her chest.

"Why couldn't it have been a vision?" Ken rushed to the woman. "Oh, this just gets worse."

Bart joined Ken in front of the corpse. "It's Ivy June Coistrell."

"This corpse was breathing in the vision. What in the name of all that's good is going on here?"

"Better call Billings."

"Already on it." Bart put the phone to his ear. "Hey, Doc. We found Ivy June Coistrell. I think you need to get to the Old Town cannery building. I know this should be something the Smotherly's can take care of but there's some extenuating circumstances on this one. Thanks, Doc." Bart clipped the phone to his belt. "He's on the way."

Ken scrutinized the body in front of him. The flesh reminded him of a days' old bruise. The eyes had the vacant look of all the corpses he had examined in the past. "I can hardly wait to hear his opinion."

Bart whirled when a loud crash shattered the silence. He caught a flash of light on the second floor.

Ken and Bart drew their guns at the same time.

"Good place to hide."

"My thoughts exactly."

Ken mounted the stairs first, was struck in his gut, and stumbled backwards. A ball of mustard-yellow light darted through a doorway into a pitch-black room.

"Do you care to hazard a guess?"

"Don't know what it was, but you can bet it isn't friendly." Ken took a deep breath, jogged up the metal stairs, and into the vacant office.

Bart came up behind him. "Where'd it go?"

"Only God knows. I'm just glad it's gone. I've had enough paranormal encounters for one day—for a lifetime actually."

"Anyone here?" Doc Billings' voice echoed through the cavernous building.

"Be right down."

"Just want you to know I'm applying to the morgue in Anchorage. It has to be more normal than this. And I think I've seen almost every way a person can be killed."

"Well, until you get that job, can you do your work here?"

"Not much that I haven't already done." Doc pointed to the autopsy sutures. "Of course, the ritualistic knife is an addition since the last time I saw her."

"Sorry, Doc. I'll get it." Bart gloved a hand and withdrew the knife. A yellow-green fluid gushed from the site. A trickle of deep red followed.

"Blood?"

"Don't be silly. The corpse had no blood." Doc swabbed the area and took a sniff. "It sure smells like blood."

Ken dug into his coat pocket and pulled out a vial of clear liquid. "One way to find out."

Billings handed the swab to Ken.

Ken stuck it in the vial and shook. The liquid turned purple. "Sure enough."

"Definitely applying to Anchorage." Doc shook his head and walked into the daylight.

"Hope not. We'd miss you."

"The only good thing I can see in this is we don't have an additional victim on our hands," Ken said.

"I was sure it was Annie Scofland. I'm so glad I was wrong."

"Still, I won't feel good until we know she's safe."

"And we know the last person who saw her."

"Next stop is the antique store and some hard questions for Mandy Thomas."

"Why did you pull me out of the attic?" Pet demanded.

"The holy angels would have been dispatched in response to the man's plea, and they would have thrown your miserable hide into the depths of the earth. In hindsight, I should have let them."

"But you didn't."

"You should not have shown yourself." Atramentous spoke to the black and purple fish ball in the leathery palm of his hand. He curled his narrow, razor-clawed fingers over the pulsing sphere.

"How did I know you'd be released? The hag had to be stopped."

"You do not have an altruistic pulse in your body! Your eagerness to move up in our ranks motivated you. Then, you enlisted the Kumrande who cannot be trusted—only controlled. I hope you've learned only your fallen brothers are your friends."

I do not believe in friends—unless you are properly motivated—and you are. Pet calmed to a melancholy hum.

Atramentous looked at the pulsing orb. "Have you found Gorgon?"

"The one they call Lilith? I have found her servant."

"Where is she?"

"I had to kill her."

"Did you at least get her to tell you where the Gorgon resides before she died?"

"Well, no. I had to use her to make a point."

"You are worthless! Why Iconoclast finds you useful, I do not understand."

"I freed you! How worthless was I then?"

"You did nothing of the sort! The dark prince negotiated with the One I cannot name for our release. If anything, the repulsive half-breed Gorgon freed us because of her threat to the One's precious humans. All you did was conjure up an opening—a weak one I might add—which allowed only me to come through. It almost imploded before I was free."

"Still, you are here."

"To clean up the mess you've made! Now, where is the skull key?"

"On the table."

Atramentous pointed to the skull-shaped rock in the courtyard. "Put the key in the mouth of Dacoit to open the tunnels to the center of the earth."

"Do it yourself. I don't answer to you!"

"Since I am Iconoclast's second-in-command, and Iconoclast is not here, I disagree."

"I should be his captain. Who was shrewd enough to avoid the abyss—twice—while you and all those smarter minions of Iconoclast were imprisoned?"

"Yes, you were free. And your rash decisions and lack of control over the Kumrande has allowed them to make an alliance with a spirit who cannot be subjugated and works to destroy us all. Free Dacoit!" Atramentous unclenched his hand and turned his palm to the floor. The purple and black ball plummeted toward the ground. A gnarly foot burst from the sphere before it hit the boards.

"You tried to harm me!" He spat at Atramentous.

"Consider it a warning! Go!"

Pet dissolved into the floor and reappeared next to the beak-nosed skull in the center of Old Town. He dropped the ivory skull into the right eye socket. The hollow sizzled. Miniature lightning bolts bounced around the opening until it glowed with a crimson light.

The light danced to the left socket, setting it ablaze with color. A sparkling red tendril flowed like tears from both eyes to the earth. The base of the boulder started to glow. Pet became a mist and reappeared beside Atramentous.

"Awakening the rock is dangerous. Dacoit is a spirit of its own will and power. Are you strong enough to control him?"

Atramentous glared down at Pet. "How dare you question my abilities. I can send you to the abyss right now."

"I am only saying Iconoclast is the only demon who has been strong enough to bind Dacoit." Pet tensed and waited for the shockwave of pain which preceded being hurtled into the earth. It didn't come. He opened one eye and looked into the smirking face of Atramentous.

"Iconoclast's strength is beyond question. He has proven himself in the millennia since the downfall in the Garden and the taking of the first mortal. The corruption of Lilith was his greatest triumph— and his curse. The Gorgon has proven to be both a strong spirit and a great enemy."

"All true, my lord." Pet bowed.

"Since Iconoclast is not here, it is my duty to awaken Dacoit. I am strong enough to control him."

"And it is done."

"Where is Lilith's prison?"

"With the humans. I will have it soon."

"Without her prison, we are defenseless to stop the Gorgon."

"Why do we want to stop the Gorgon? She is only after the same thing we are—destruction of the humans."

"The Gorgon's alliance is only to herself. She is not human, and she is not a demon. This makes her dangerous. She believes if she destroys us, the enemies of the One, she will find favor with Him and be restored."

"Why does this concern you? Are we not stronger than this she-thing?"

"Strength is not my concern. Imprisoning the Gorgon is. When Lilith learns of the murder her servant, she will know we are here, and she will declare vengeance. Something we do not need!" Atramentous glared at Pet.

Pet dropped his eyes. "Agreed."

"How did you manage to trick her servant into taking human form? It was the only way to kill her."

Pet grinned. "She, like all of her kind, had an insatiable hunger. All I did was create the illusion of blood, and the smell brought her to the old building."

"You surprise me. Although it caused us great trouble, it was inspired."

Pet stood taller under the praise. "Thank you, great one."

"We can use this to our advantage. Lilith's anger will cause her to be reckless. She will come out of hiding. Then we will take her and confine her once and for all. Find the jar!"

Chapter 17
Gorgon Explained

Mandy Thomas hummed a happy tune as she dusted the antique shop's display cases. *Things are starting to turn around for me. I can feel it. My sister is going to find out just how smart I am. Then I can be free of her and all her stupid ways.*

"Enjoying the new job?"

Mandy whirled around. "You don't look so good, Detective Dayton."

"I've been better. But then, you haven't."

"What do you mean?"

"Well, I think you have a permanent job. How about you?"

"You aren't making sense. Annie's coming back tomorrow night." Mandy's cell phone chirped. She looked at the readout, pressed the mute button, and shoved it in her pants' pocket.

"Don't you want to take the call?"

"Just a friend. I can talk later. What can I do for you?"

"I need to know what you've been doing since late yesterday afternoon."

"Don't answer." Ken's flushed face belied the anger he tried to control. "What are you doing here, Dayton? You're a guest in this town, or don't they teach you protocol in the academy?"

"They do. This is a different situation. Every time a body shows up, this woman is tied to it. Now, my partner is missing. I need some answers!"

"What do you mean, your partner is missing?"

"He was supposed to call the office yesterday. No one's heard from him."

"Why do you think I know anything about his disappearance? I don't even know your partner!" Mandy wailed.

"You knew the latest victim. He knew the latest victim and lied about who she was. I think you know where he is."

"I don't!"

Dayton gripped Mandy's arm. "I don't believe you! You've been hiding something from the get-go, and I want to know where Detective Watermill is!"

"You're hurting me!"

Ken pried Dayton's fingers from Mandy's arm. "You're too close to this case. I think you'd better take a walk, and let me get to the bottom of this."

"Have it your way, *chief.*" Dayton spat. "I'm going back to Alese Bricken's house. Call me when I can talk to her."

"I could press charges!" Mandy yelled at the slamming door.

"You might want to hold up on filing a complaint for the moment. You have bigger concerns."

"Like what?"

"We identified the body from the ravine."

Mandy's upper lip started to glisten. "Who?"

"Her name was Ivy June Coistrell."

"Don't know her."

"You know her as Madame Piquant."

"I only saw her once. Why does this have anything to do with me?"

"Detective Dayton has a point. You seem to be connected to everyone who's turned up dead."

"It's just coincidence—I didn't kill anyone."

"You don't have to commit the murder to be tried for it. An accomplice to murder is just as guilty as the one who does the killing. You're connected to each and every one of the people who have died since this case began."

"It's just a twist of fate! I haven't done anything."

"Maybe you have, and maybe you haven't. But you do see why it looks suspicious for Annie Scofland to have just picked up and left without a word to anyone don't you, Mandy?

"She's away on a business trip."

"We need proof. Otherwise, I'm going to arrest you for kidnapping."

Mandy took hold of the glistening counter. "I swear she's on a business trip!"

"Not anymore." Annie Scofland dropped her bag in front of the jewelry case.

"Ms. Scofland?"

"In the flesh."

"I told you she was on a trip! Now, leave me alone." Mandy ran to the back of the store.

"My, she's upset. What's all the hubbub about, anyway?"

"I can't go into detail; just had some things happen which led me to believe you were in danger."

"Oh, I see."

"Why did you leave in such a hurry?"

"Oddest thing. I got a call. Said my sister was in the hospital in Idaho. They didn't think she'd make it. I called the number. Sure enough, the person who answered confirmed it."

"How is she?"

"That's what's odd. My sister was never in the hospital. I don't know who called or why. I was so relieved. I took the opportunity to spend some time with her and do a little buying for the shop. Hopped a plane late yesterday, and here I am." Annie searched the storefront.

"Something else missing?"

"The stray who adopted me. Mandy was supposed to take care of it."

Ken raised an eyebrow. "Kat found her in the woods. She was in a bad way."

"What? Please excuse me. Mandy told me she'd take care of the dog!" Annie headed into the office. She reappeared a few minutes later.

"Everything okay?"

"I said what I needed to. I'm just glad the dog's okay. She kind of wormed her way into my heart."

"I understand." Ken felt a like someone buried a knife in his chest. *I can't believe I'm going to miss that noisome beast.* He took a deep breath. "We'll get the dog back to you later today."

"Thanks." Annie gave Ken's hand a quick shake and walked over to greet some customers browsing the glass kiosk.

Ken headed into the back office. "I still have some questions, Ms. Thomas. Pull yourself together and come to the station. If you don't, I'll let Dayton come back and have another go at you. He's just itching to pin a murder—any murder—on you. Got it?"

Mandy wiped her wet eyes and nodded. "I'll be there in an hour."

"Don't be late."

"Wouldn't dream of it," she called after him. Mandy pulled out her cell phone, scrolled to the last incoming call, and dialed.

Wendy's head popped through the office door. "What are you doing in here? Annie Scofland just gets back and you leave her alone to deal with customers?"

Mandy sighed, pressed *end*, and smacked the phone on the desk. "I've had a bad day. I was almost accused of her murder. So, forgive me, but I was pulling myself together before I tried to greet the public!"

Wendy lowered herself into a chair. "How deep are you into this Mandy? How deep?"

"I don't know what you're talking about, *big sister.*" Mandy swept past her, then turned on her heel. "Look— oh, never mind."

"Hey, Mandy. Seen Wendy?" Kat asked.

"In the back."

"Looks like Annie made it back. You still have a job?"

"Don't know. First thing she did was accuse me of losing her stupid dog."

"You were taking care of it?"

"Yes. Dumb thing ran out the front door. I figured it would show up when it got hungry."

"You're kidding, right? You didn't go looking for it?"

"It's a stupid dog—and a horribly noisy one. It never shut up. I couldn't hear myself think. I was going to look for it in a few days. Sooner, if I'd known Annie was going to show up."

"If BC hadn't led me to her, she'd be dead right now."

Mandy shrugged. "Well, it's not."

"I wish I'd left you in Anchorage. You make me sorry I stood up for you." Kat headed through the doorway and handed Wendy a cup of coffee. "Thought it was high time I returned the favor."

Wendy gave her best friend a wan smile. "Your timing is perfect." She raised the cup and sat down.

"Why so glum?"

"I tell you, she's up to her eyeballs in this mess. I just know it! I have a bad feeling, a truly bad feeling, about where this is going."

Kat touched Wendy's hand. "I wish I could say something to make you feel better, but I know she's in it, too. I'm so sorry. We'll get to the bottom of it." Kat stood up and marched toward Mandy.

"Wait for me." Wendy ran after her.

"Now's a good time to go see Ken Melbourne."

"What do you know about it?"

"I know he's expecting you. And I know you well enough to know you're gonna try and skip town before he sees you." Kat crossed her arms. "I'm going to make sure you get to that interview."

"Aren't you going to defend me—*big, bad sister?*"

"Not this time. Get your hand off the overnight bag I see sitting beside you, and let's go."

"Oh, I don't think so, sis! I'm out of here." Mandy came around the counter rolling the small suitcase.

Kat gripped one arm, and Wendy took the other. "For once in your miserable life, you're going to do what you said you would." Wendy pinched Mandy's hand until she let go of the bag.

"I'm sure Ken will love hearing about how you abused me."

Kat eye's narrowed. "I know he would. If it were true."

"Well you're Wendy's good friend and his girl of the hour. Who'd believe you?"

"You have a point, Mandy, but you see, I saw the whole thing." Annie Scofland walked up shaking her head. "I never suspected this side of you."

"It's not me—it's them."

"I almost believe you. Except you were going to leave. I'll keep your bag here until you're finished at the police station." Annie took the overnight case and rolled it back behind the counter.

"You're just as big a loser as the rest of them," Mandy screamed.

"I am sure more naive than I ever thought," Annie said. "Consider yourself fired."

———————— •◦◦•◦•◦ ————————

"Tell me again how you came to be guardian to this shrieking banshee?" Paul yelled over Carnelian's unrelenting bark. A lull in foot traffic on the street brought quiet to the car's interior.

Josiah turned to Paul. "Well, Kat had business at the station, and she felt Carnelian was too new to her life to be left alone. What else could I do?"

Carnelian jumped over the seat like a gazelle over a small hedge and sat on the console between them, giving a lick first to Paul then to Josiah. "Can hardly stay mad, can you?"

Josiah scratched the dog behind the ears and ran a hand through her coat. "She is a beauty."

"I'll try to remember her attributes," Paul said right before Carnelian's paws landed on the dashboard and an earsplitting bark announced an older woman and man approaching the crosswalk.

The mayor's assistant rushed up to the driver's side window. "Seen Bart? We got a situation, and I can't reach him on the phone." Carnelian quieted and walked across Paul's lap.

"What a doll." Jenny patted her on the head. The dog returned to its spot between the driver and passenger.

"I think this dog just wants everyone to pet her."

"Be my guess."

"Haven't seen Bart. Wait, he and Grandma Bricken are outside the general store." Josiah pointed across Main Street.

"Thanks." Jenny took off across the street and intercepted Bart before he ducked into the general store.

"Looks like Kenneth's at the police station." Josiah pointed to the late-model SUV. "How about we drop her off so we can get to church and work on those rickety stairs?"

"I had no idea you were a carpenter, too."

"Jack of all trades. Master of none." Josiah chuckled.

The *tick-tick* of toenails echoed through the police station. "Tell me that's not who I think it is." Ken called out from the breakroom.

"Of course it's who you think it is! Hi, Carnelian." Kat launched out of her desk chair. "Thanks, Josiah."

"Not a problem. Although I'm not sure my ears feel the same way."

Kat giggled and took the leash. "How's my girl?"

Carnelian yipped, yanked the leash from Kat's hand, and trotted to the coffee room.

A metal chair screeched. "It's going to attack me!"

"Kat! Get this dog! Now!" Ken shouted.

Kat ran into the room. Carnelian was under the table, hackles up and snarling at Mandy.

"What is wrong with the stupid animal?" Mandy was standing with the chair between her and the table. "If it bites me, I'll make sure it's euthanized."

Kat dropped to all fours, crawled under the table, and yanked on the leash. "Come here, you." She pulled the halter-clad dog toward her. The low, threatening sounds continued.

"Stop it!" Kat scooped Carnelian into her arms. She tied the leash to the leg of her desk.

A crinkling sound caught Kat's attention. "What have you got?" Kat took a piece of paper out of the dog's mouth and read aloud, *Mandy, Gorgon is with you. Do not forget your instructions. Stay safe.* Kat walked back to the interrogation room.

"Found this on the floor." Kat handed the paper to Ken.

"What is it?"

"Looks like she dropped it." Kat looked at Mandy.

"What?"

"I was with Mandy the first time I saw that word." Kat pointed to Gorgon.

"Where?"

"In Grady Spawldine's house."

"Well, Mandy, you have some explaining to do. Who and what is Gorgon?"

"Why would you think I'd know?"

"Maybe because this note's addressed to you. Now give me some answers."

"I don't know if it's a code word or a person!" Her eyes pleaded for Kat to believe her.

"I don't believe you. What do you know, Mandy?"

"I don't know anything!"

"She may not, but I do." Bart called from the other side of the wall. "Gorgon is an ancient name. Means hag."

"When did you get here?"

Bart poked his head around the corner. "Just now. Had a message from Josiah waiting for me after I got free from an emergency meeting of the council. Josiah said he didn't know why, but thought you'd like to know about Gorgon."

ESP at its height again. Only in the Cove. Kat shook her head and walked back to her desk.

"Okay, so what is this Gorgon?"

"Another name for Lilith. Josiah says the last time Lilith was seen was in Russia where some aristocrat contained it and ended up dead for the trouble. She, and her jar of a prison, disappeared right afterward. Some cult formed and vowed to find Lilith. Supposedly this cult still exists and they are still looking for her. Something about great power and riches—isn't it always the way?"

Ken's eyes bored into Mandy's. "Is this some kind of get rich quick scheme?"

"No. What I understand is there is a lost artifact, and it is very important to my friend."

"And what makes you, or your friend for that matter, think this artifact is in Ravens Cove?"

"Well, my friend's friends found a Denali Native who told them a story about a guy who traveled with Bering to Nome and somehow joined the local Natives and ended up here."

"So, I need to talk to your friend."

"Not happening."

"Why?"

"Because I promised I'd keep my mouth shut. That's why."

"When you promised that, did you realize you could end going to jail for murder?"

"No. But that doesn't matter now."

"Mandy, the only way to clear your name is to give us his."

"I already told you—I won't."

"So, you are going to take the fall for this guy?"

"If I have to."

"What makes him so important?"

"He's none of your business."

"Oh, it is more than my business—it's police business. Your friend is the one person who can clear you or condemn you."

"Not telling—not now, not ever."

"Well, then you are going to get a nice stay in the town jail."

"For how long?"

"For as long as needed. You may not have committed these murders, but you are in the middle of them. Give me your phone." Ken held out his hand.

"I can't."

"I wasn't making a request. Give me the phone."

"I've got to make a call or something bad is going to happen."

"I'm willing to take the risk. There is something bad happening already. Or haven't you noticed?"

Bart walked through the door. "She means something bad's going to happen to *her* if she doesn't make a phone call. Right, Mandy?"

"Yes." Mandy hung her head, then snapped it straight. "But to you, too. If my friend doesn't get this artifact, bad things will happen to you, too."

"Meaning?"

"You will be sorry—or dead." Mandy leaned back in her chair and crossed her arms.

"I need names."

"Don't have any."

Ken stood up. "Then, let's get you into your new accommodations."

"Fine with me. I could use some sleep."

223

Ken escorted Mandy out of the breakroom.

Kat stood at the steel door leading to the jail cell. "You brought me to Anchorage and played me all along? Didn't you?"

Mandy grinned. "Think whatever you'd like."

"Tell me the truth, Mandy. You scammed me, right?"

"Yes, I did! When are you going to grow up, Kat? I did what I needed to do and you and all of this town are going to pay for what you did to me."

"You mean like Wendy who tried to raise you, or Bart who loved you in spite of how you treated him? You mean those people deserve to pay for loving you?"

"You don't know anything! Open your eyes. Wendy and Bart are just users. Well, I'm doing the using now!"

"I loved you, Mandy. I never used you," Bart said.

"Maybe not in the normal way, but you tried to use guilt to make me stay here. You wouldn't leave this place. You only cared about yourself."

"You are sick, Mandy! You've turned being loved into being used. You are really sick!"

"No. You and Bart and your stupid Grandma—not to mention my muddle headed sister—are the sick ones! Thinking you can love someone enough and everything will be okay. At what price? Then, that person is stuck in this dead town, living a dead life to please everyone else. You're sick. And Grandma Bricken is the sickest of them all!"

"I've heard enough of your mouth for now." Ken yanked the door open and led Mandy to the cell.

———•◦×◦•———

"The Gorgon must be hiding somewhere close." Homunculus scoured the base and interior of the hag tree.

"My leader, why do you think it would come back here?"

"This tree fed Lilith's spirit while it held her prisoner. If she has not feasted since the woman, she will come to it for refreshment—something comes. Hide!" Homunculus dove into a crop of alders and peeked through the branches.

Atramentous slithered up the path to the ravine, cutting a trail through the rolling fog. He shook off the last layer of mist and touched the hag tree. The sound of rustling leaves filled the air as it—then its carbon copies—quaked in response.

"Ah, old friend. I have great news! The dark lord ordains you be brought to full strength."

Gambogian floated to the ground. "It is good to be free again."

Atramentous smiled. "Dacoit is of great use at times. Now, do your work."

Gambogian pointed at the hag tree. A tendril of jaundiced fire jumped from his hand. It circled the guardian hag, bounced down the path, and lit each of the smaller harridans. The air buzzed as the yellow light strengthened.

Homunculus pushed through the alders and stood before Atramentous. "Why do you do this? They are not to be alive again!"

"The plan has changed."

"This is our home!"

"This is *Iconoclast's* home. We have been commanded to take it back."

"You promised!"

"And you gave your loyalty to the Gorgon. Contract broken. Do you want to meet the fate of Nihilist?" Atramentous's snarl shook the trees and ground.

"No."

"Then be gone to your underground dwelling. Be grateful you still live."

Gambogian touched the hag tree. "She is at full strength."

"Then, ordained guardian of this place, call to your children and break the rock at the ravine floor."

Iridescent ochre tendrils shot out from gnarled branches. The electric rope looped from one tree to the next and stopped at the last tree on the path. The ravine walls groaned when the vibrant green foliage withered and the clean rocks were enveloped in an inky sludge.

"So it is done." Atramentous winged his way down the pathway, flying higher to avoid the place of holy fire. He landed in front of the boulder on the ravine floor. An oozing crevice ran the length of the rock. He blew on it. The stone crumbled to pebbles at his feet.

Atramentous stepped into the ravine. He took flight and circled the entire gorge. Wherever he passed, the vibrant foliage and bushes withered. He stopped at the fresh-water pond and exhaled. A red mist settled into the crystal clear liquid. Tar cascaded from the waterfall and plopped into the crimson vapor.

"I do wonder, Iconoclast, what deal you made to get this back."

"Not to wonder."

Atramentous whirled to the sound of his commander's voice and bowed.

"I reminded the great one I stopped Gorgon before. He pleaded my case, and I am here." A gruesome smile broke across Iconoclast's lips, revealing pointed, dagger-like teeth.

"And the One who created the universe allowed your return?"

"I am here. So are you. Where is Pet?"

"He is at the mansion."

"Call to him, and find me food."

"Done."

"Wait!"

"I can only touch the unclean. I have been forbidden to take a human from the Cove—for now."

"Then who?"

"Find the person who brought the dead to Ravens Cove. This human is mine."

"How do we know that one is here?"

"What stops you from leaving here and luring the prize to me? I command you to do so." As they talked Iconoclast's commanders appeared one by one.

"Welcome." Atramentous gave a bow of acknowledgement to Venenose, Caitiff, Prevaricator, Bruit, Trepaner, and Profligacy.

Gambogian floated through the ravine opening. "Good you are back, old friends." He turned to Iconoclast. "I seek your permission to find the one who destroyed the tree."

"Why should I grant your request?"

"The one who murdered the tree is my enemy."

"Well, then, you find your enemy and my dinner—they are one and the same."

"It will be done."

Iconoclast turned to Atramentous. "The one Gambogian seeks is the one I have been given. I have other orders for you. First, we gather at the old house."

Impatience to exact revenge burned deep within Gambogian. He considered ignoring the order. He decided not risk Iconoclast's rage. "To the old house."

The eight took off into the sky; a deep fog over the town hid their flight. They entered Old Town and the mansion in secret.

———————

Kat picked up a pencil and drummed a steady beat on the legal pad. *I know the legend Bart talked about. Why?* She dropped the pencil. "Ken I need to go home for a bit. Would you keep an eye on Carnelian until Annie gets here?" Kat's voice took on a sad tone.

"How about I go, and you babysit the little beast?"

"Stop acting like you don't like her. You know you do."

Ken ruffled Carnelian's fur. "She was growing on me, but it doesn't matter now. She goes back to Annie."

"I'm gonna miss you, little one." Kat smiled into the intelligent brown eyes and looked back to Ken. "I don't even know what I'm looking for. So, it would be of little use for you to go."

Ken sighed and took the leash. "Fine."

Kat grazed his cheek with a kiss. "You're a good man—but I knew that. Why else would I marry you?"

"Which begs the question—when are we going to set a date?"

"Soon. Bye."

"How soon?" Ken said to Kat's back.

"As soon as I can wrap my head around being Mrs. Kenneth Melbourne," Kat whispered under her breath. She stopped at the road to Old Town. "What is going on?" She turned off Main and stood outside the chain-link fence.

The mansion twisted and turned in the setting sun. Kat closed her eyes and squinted at the old house. The unnatural dance continued. The pristine white paint gaped with each movement revealing weathered and rotting boards. Fire-red light pulsed through the attic windows.

Kat scanned the rest of the town. "Oh, no." Kat's eyes never left the boulder in the center of the square as she shoved a shaky hand in her pocket. "Pick up. Pick up!" she urged.

"Miss me already?" Ken's voice calmed the fear in Kat's stomach to a dull roar.

"As a matter of fact, I do. But it's not why I called. Something's happening to Old Town. The house is dancing and the boulder has changed color."

"Get out of there! I'm on my way."

"If you're coming by yourself, I'm staying right here."

"I'll find Bart. Get out of there now!"

"I'll be at the cabin."

"I don't want you to be alone. Call Wendy, and have her meet you there."

Kat's need to be independent gave way to the concern in Ken's voice. "Right after I hang up."

"Hello? Anyone here?" Carson Watermill called into the vacant police station. "I do love the trusting people in a small town—no matter how misplaced it is. Now where would they keep evidence here?"

Watermill spotted the half-glass door behind the reception area. "If I were a small-town cop, I'd keep the evidence close. Bet they do, too." He walked through the gate and tried the doorknob. "Not as trusting as I thought."

Watermill's eyes came to rest on a heavy brass orb on Kat's desk. "Just what I need." He picked up the ball, pulled his hand into his coat sleeve, and rammed it through the windowpane.

"Who's there?" A voice called from the back.

Watermill walked over to a steel door and peered through a narrow window. "Ivy June, couldn't you have taken care of this before you got yourself killed?" He pushed on the door. It held. "Another lock? These people don't trust anybody."

"Who's there?" Mandy called out again.

Carson Watermill leaned against the wall beside the door. "Think, think, man."

Adumbration shimmered against the wall, disguised as a tree's shadow swaying in a breeze. The fog separated to show a malevolent grin. He floated to Watermill and breathed in his ear. A thousand words turned to thoughts with one breath.

Watermill shivered and sneered. "How could I have been so blind? Ivy June gave herself for Lilith—here! Lilith never left this place. I must take her vessel." He jogged to Ken's office.

"Locked office but not evidence." Watermill picked up the jeweled jar, a book, and a snake-clad statue. "How did you get here?" he said to the figurine. He shoved it under his arm and eyed the leatherbound tome. "So you're *The Book of Fallen Angels*. My god wants you, and she will have you."

"Now, find the one you seek," Adumbration whispered.

Watermill tapped the jar. "I bet some local will be happy to give me the complete lowdown on this place." He smiled. "They always love to talk about their insignificant lives in a no-name town. Next stop. Lilith."

"Yes, next stop, the Gorgon. Then, we take her." Adumbration dove through the floor and toward the ravine.

———•❉•———

"Good to see some color in those cheeks," Grandma said to Detective Dayton.

He grinned. "Thanks to some amazing doctoring, Ms. Bricken. I was at death's door, wasn't I?"

"You still look a little weak."

"I am tired, but I think I can go back to Anchorage."

"How are you going to get there?"

"Got some great news this morning. I think it's the other reason I'm feeling so good."

"Good news helps to mend the body—and the soul. Care to share?"

Dayton sat down at the kitchen table. "I do. I don't know if you are aware of it, but my partner had become a suspect in all this mess."

"Oh, dear."

"I knew it couldn't be true. He finally returned my calls a couple of hours ago. Said he'd taken two days' leave, and just needed to get away for a while. He went to some remote fishing lodge. Said he was so burned out on police work, he drove straight through Ravens Cove to Clayton and caught a charter out."

"So, he couldn't have been a part of all this. Very good news, detective."

"I knew it! He's been my partner for five years and has always been a straight arrow—straighter than me if it's possible." Dayton sat back and smiled.

"He's coming to get you, then?"

"He is." Dayton looked at his watch. "In fact, he should be here within the hour."

"It has been a pleasure. I hope to see you again."

A loud laugh escaped Dayton. "I've been a huge pain, and you know it. Thanks for being kind to me anyway."

"You're welcome."

Dayton's eyes dropped to the coffee cup in front of him.

"Something still bothering you?"

"I just realized Carson—my partner—didn't give me an explanation about why the victim found at the ravine looks just like the girl he introduced as his cousin."

Grandma patted his hand. "I always feel like that kind of thing is better said in person. Maybe he does, too."

Dayton relaxed. "Makes sense. Well, I told him I'd meet him in town. Better get moving."

Dayton's cell phone chirped. "Sorry. They can find me anywhere when my office wants." A dark look came over his face. "I need to find Melbourne."

"What seems to be the problem?"

"The office just tried to call my partner. Says his cell is going directly to voicemail. Doesn't make any sense. He's back on duty and wouldn't turn it off."

"We don't have the best cell service here. Still using two tin cans, I'm sure." Grandma smiled.

"His phone's getting service. It's pinging a tower near Ravens Cove."

Grandma stood up and took her cane from a hanger at the kitchen door. "Let's go find your partner—or someone who can."

Chapter 18
Everyone Worships Something

Carson Watermill batted at the swarm of mosquitoes around his head and trudged deeper into the woods. "I just know you've got to be here, Lilith."

A glimmer of color caught his eye. He headed off the trail, and picked his way through the low-lying brush to an emaciated black spruce. He yanked a piece of cream and red cloth from its withered branch and examined the fabric. "I know this pattern." Ivy June Coistrell's hobo-style carpetbag streaked into his consciousness. "Why were you here, Ivy June?" Watermill stuffed the fabric into his pocket and made his way back to the animal trail he'd been following.

The tangle of black spruce and Devil's Club gave way to a dark river bank. He smiled when he spied a wooden footbridge spanning the waterway. It disappeared behind a barrier of bare and gnarled spruce trees. Watermill headed down the wet slope to the water's edge. A barbed stone fell to the ground at his feet. The object hummed to life. The detective bent forward for a closer look. Shades of purple and black pulsed in rhythm to the eerie tune.

Watermill picked up the arrowhead and placed it in his palm. "There have to be some batteries in this thing." He turned it over to look for a power source.

A stabbing pain shot into his hand and raced up his right arm. Watermill dropped the sharp stone and looked on in horror as skin gave way to white bone. Blood filled the deep wound, and poured out onto the ground. He snatched the red and cream fabric from his pocket and stuffed it in the wound.

Terror melted away and an inexplicable sense of euphoria took its place. The pain melted away when visions of power and riches filled his head. He retrieved the arrowhead and studied it with excitement. "You're what I've been looking for! It is not her but you!"

As if in agreement, the arrowhead vibrated, then hummed a seductive tune.

A dark mist formed above the muddy earth and mushroomed skyward. Gambogian stepped through the black curtain in his demon form. "Are you the one who killed the tree?" he thundered.

Watermill's eyes left the mesmerizing colors in his hand. Cold fear gripped his stomach when his eyes met Gambogian's blood-red ones.

"Answer!" Gambogian demanded.

"Yes. I chopped down the tree outside of Ravens Cove."

Gambogian smiled, revealing moss-colored fangs. His voice took on the sound of a gurgling brook. "Did you take the vessel the tree held?"

Watermill calmed. "I did."

"Did you open it?"

"Why do you ask?"

"Oh, an old friend of mine resided in the jar. I want to see her again."

Carson's eyes lit with excitement. "You worship Lilith, too?" She is wonderful, isn't she? Such power."A thrill ran through Watermill as he remembered the tales passed down through his cult—of the contentment all felt who had seen and worshipped Lilith.

"She is a rarity. Did you release her?"

"I was chosen by my brothers to seek her hiding place. I did what so many others only hoped to."

"I can see you are pleased by your accomplishment. Do you have the jar?"

"I do."

"Oh, that is very good. May I see it?"

Watermill considered the appeal. "Why not?" He held the vessel up to Gambogian.

"Commander, it is the one you seek!" Gambogian roared.

The creak of leather overpowered all other sounds of the night. A gale-force wind forced the tall grass and gnarled trees into a low bow.

The roar of the air fractured the trance Pet had thrown over Watermill. His saucer-shaped eyes watched two winged giants descend from a moonless sky.

Gambogian bowed to Iconoclast, then Atramentous. He dropped the jeweled urn into Iconoclast's open hand.

Iconoclast considered the heavy pot. "It is Lilith's prison. I am pleased, Gambogian." He focused hunger-filled eyes on Watermill. "I've been looking for you."

"Why are you looking for me? I don't know you."

"Oh, but I know you. Which is what's important." Crimson saliva trickled from Iconoclast's mouth. "Now I feast."

The intent of the dark commander's words blasted into Watermill's conscious mind. "Keep the jar." He bolted toward the muddy embankment.

"No, my friend, you will stay." Atramentous twisted into a black rope and catapulted after Watermill. He looped around the detective's waist and dragged him back.

"Open your hand." Iconoclast roared.

Watermill's fingers flew away from his blood-soaked palm.

"I'll take that." Iconoclast snatched the arrowhead.

"Can I go now?"

"Oh, no. You have brought an even greater destiny on yourself than you would have imagined, Detective Carson Watermill."

"How do you know my name?"

"I know the names of those who are mine."

"I'm not yours! No man belongs to anyone but himself."

"You are wrong. By releasing the Gorgon, you became the one puny human I have permission to devour—for now." Iconoclast rocketed forward and seized Carson Watermill.

———◆◆◆◆◆———

Wendy shook her head and stared at the groceries in Kat's arms. "You are the only person I know whose stomach overrides any crisis."

Kat laughed, then pointed in the direction of Cook Inlet. "What do you think's going on?"

Wendy squinted to the west. "All I see is haze."

"No, not the fog at the base of Mount Redoubt. It's closer to the beach and to the right. See it?"

"Now I do." Ravens and eagles blackened the sky above the slate-blue water. Several broke away, rocketed to the earth, dipped, and shot back into the crystalline sky.

"Some fisherman threw fish guts on the beach again."

"Too many carrion birds for a prize so small. Let's get to the cabin and see if we can get a better look—from inside where we're safe."

Wendy scooped the groceries from Kat's arms, popped the Subaru's trunk, and lowered them into the charcoal-gray well. "Get in."

Kat slid into the passenger seat and leaned toward the windshield to get a better look at the black mass.

Wendy parked alongside Kat's deck. "Let's get inside."

Kat got out of the car, her eyes never leaving the turmoil in the western sky. "I've never seen anything like it. It's like a gyrating storm cloud!"

"Hey, Kat."

Kat looked at Wendy. "Uh-huh?"

"There's a trail of blood here."

Kat dropped her eyes to the ground and followed the red drops and smears up the porch stairs and into the house. She streaked up the steps and through the cabin door. "BC!" she yelled.

A black and red streak dashed out from behind the couch. "Oh, my lord, BC." She scooped the feline into her arms.

Wendy sprinted into the room and scanned the blood-splattered walls.

Tears streamed from Kat's eyes. She stretched the bottom of her T-shirt into an open sling, put the feline in the pouch, and wrapped the soft material over his body.

"Hold him still." Wendy examined the cat and located an oozing slash. "Looks like it's only the back leg. But the wound is deep. He needs to get to Carl."

Kat rushed into the kitchen, grabbed two hand towels, and wrapped them around the cat's back leg. "Those answers I'm looking for are going to have to wait. Call Nyna. Tell her we have an emergency."

"I'll take him, Kat. I have a feeling whatever you came here to find is important."

"I can't leave him alone, either."

"If we don't get to the bottom of this, we are all gonna end up a lot worse off than this cat. I can't do that—you can. I promise I won't leave him."

Fresh tears filled Kat's eyes. "Thanks, Wendy." She took a forest green and black checked flannel shirt from her bedroom closet, swaddled BC, and followed Wendy to her car.

"Set him on the passenger seat."

A powerful wind followed by a loud *swoosh* sent Kat to her knees. "What the heck?" She looked up to see a bald eagle climb and level.

"It's after BC. Get him in here." Wendy threw open the passenger door and ran around the hood to the driver's side.

"Why are they after BC?" The eagle turned and dove at Kat. She covered the cat with her body, lowered BC into the passenger seat, and slammed the door. Kat jogged toward the road.

"Where are you going?"

"To the Inlet to find out what's going on," Kat yelled over her shoulder.

Wendy threw the car in reverse and spun it to a stop where the driveway intersected the street. "No, you're going to find whatever you came here to find. I'm calling Bart."

"He's busy."

"Then he can get unbusy. Now get in the house. I'm not leaving until you do."

A familiar *swoosh* sent Kat back to her knees right before a golden talon snagged her by the hair. Kat's eyes shot skyward. Several eagles and ravens circled the car. "Now what?"

"Look at your shirt."

Kat bent her head. BC's blood had stained her shirt the color of rotten cherries. "No wonder—you win." Kat ran for the small cabin and slammed the door. She peeked out the living room window. A trail of dust lingered above the dry dirt road.

"God, I know I haven't talked to you so much lately. But, if you would, please take care of Black Cat. He's so precious to me. Please. Oh, I forgot—in Jesus' name. Please."

Kat looked toward the kitchen then to the living room. *What am I here for?* She heard a small voice in her head whisper *bedroom.* "Good a place as any, I guess." She walked through the doorway and perused the celadon-green walls and the brass bed she inherited from her Gran Tovslosky. She continued to scan the room until her eyes came to rest on the birch closet doors. Kat yanked on the off-white ceramic handle and glanced at the clothes, the vacuum cleaner, and a scarred and paint splattered step stool leaning against the back wall. She looked up and spotted her box of memories. Sadness gripped her heart. *Do I have to? Yes,* the small voice answered.

She dragged the stool into the room, climbed to the top step, and tugged on the box. "Whoa!" Kat gripped the wall to steady herself and wrestled the box to the ladder's top rung with her free hand. She dropped it at the foot of her bed, sat cross-legged, and stared at the brown cardboard.

"I guess you aren't going to open yourself." Kat peeled back the creased flaps and stuck her hand into the contents. She pulled out a photograph. A pre-adolescent Bart smiled, his arm around a dark-haired, green-eyed child of six or seven, and a younger version of Grandma Bricken. Jagged mountains in shades of gray and white jutted up in the distance. Three log cabins, one with a sagging roof, sat in a horseshoe-shape around the trio.

"What's in the background?" she said. A long shadow was the only clue of the photographer's identity. "I don't remember anyone else being with us." She put the picture aside to ask Grandma later. She stuck her hand back into the box and came up with a chain made up of light red, brown, and lime-green construction paper links. An elbow macaroni and pinto bean turkey came next, then her book of Russian tales.

She flipped through the book's brightly colored illustrations, and turned to the inside cover to see the date it had been published. An inscription jumped out at her. "I never saw this!"

Remember your roots. Always remember your roots, Katrina Agnes Tovslosky. When I'm not there to remind you, these tales will. They are of our people. After you read them, go and look at the quilt I made when you were but a small button on this tapestry they call life. I'll love you always. Grandmama Tovslosky.

Kat hugged the hardcover book to her chest. She looked around the room. *Stupid. BC is not here.* She longed to pull him into her lap and cry into his thick, black fur. She buried her head in her hands and sobbed. A soft muzzle pushed through her hands until a wet snout touched her nose. Kat threw her arms around Carnelian. "How'd you get here? Why aren't you with Annie?"

"My fault," Paul answered from the doorway.

"Pastor Paul!" Kat swatted at the tears and stood up.

"Ken asked I bring her to you. Old Town is not the best place for her right now."

"Annie Scofland was supposed to come by the station and get her. What happened?"

"Ken didn't get a chance to call you?"

"No. Why?"

"He should be the one to talk to you." Paul looked at Carnelian, then to Kat. "Guess he won't mind. Seems Annie got her back to the store, and Carnelian slipped out the door as soon as a customer came in. Then, she ran to the police station and made a huge ruckus until some Good Samaritan let her in. To make a long story short, Annie said she wants what's best for the dog, and it seems to be Ken."

"He is a great guy," Kat said to Carnelian.

The dog swished her tail.

"You are a sweet one. I sure could use another hug." Carnelian leaned against Kat's arm.

Kat's warm laugh filled the air. "Where did you learn such a thing?"

Carnelian tilted her head and held Kat's eyes with her steady gaze. *I've always known how. God taught me,* the look said.

A white blur dashed past Paul.

"Benny, the girl doesn't need to wrestle right now." Mrs. Tellamoot shuffled into the bedroom.

Kat lay sprawled beside the foot of the bed. "Do you have to tackle me every time, dog?" She pushed him to the floor. "Mrs. Tellamoot? Why are you here?"

"My fault, again. She caught me outside the police station, saw this one," Paul pointed at Carnelian, "and asked if I happened to be coming here. Seems Wendy ran into her at the vet's office and told her you shouldn't be alone right now."

Kat shook her head. "Well, for once her gossip is welcome."

"I can't help but notice you were crying. Maybe I should leave you and Bernice to talk?"

Kat smiled at him. "This isn't a girl thing, Paul. Just a trip down memory lane with my Grandmamma Tovslosky."

"Those are hard trips to make. But she died in Christ, am I right?"

"Oh, yes. She loved God as much as Grandma Bricken—hard to imagine I had such great role models and ran as far as I could for as long as I could, huh?"

"Not hard to imagine. But the good news is you'll see her again. She's with Christ now. No better place to be."

"True. And we seem to be living in the true hell on earth. Glad she isn't here."

"And, again, we fight."

Kat nodded and looked at the book of Russian tales. "I don't know why, but this is why I'm here." She held the old book up for Paul.

"Is it in English?"

"Some is. My Russian is very rusty." Kat smiled remembering her grandmother's patient instruction in her native tongue. "But I had a great teacher, so maybe I can muddle through."

"If you tell me where to find it, I'll put on some coffee, and we can go over the book together," Mrs. Tellamoot said. "As I told you a few days ago, we need to talk."

"I'll take my leave. You're in good hands now." Paul patted Carnelian, then Benny. "Very good hands."

Kat's glanced up from the book of fairytales when Mrs. Tellamoot returned. "Thank you." Kat took the coffee cup and set it beside her on the floor.

Mrs. Tellamoot grinned. "Well, now there's a sight to behold."

Carnelian was on her side. Her feet hidden under the bed; her head resting an inch from Kat's right elbow. Benny was sound asleep at Kat's feet.

"Here it is!" Kat shouted.

Carnelian's eyes flew open. She jumped to her feet and barked.

"It's okay. Just me getting excited." Kat ran a slow hand down Carnelian's back. The sheltie vibrated beneath Kat's touch as she continued to emit low growls.

"So, what did you find?"

"The tale of Gorgon—a trapped spirit in a tree."

"Oh, I'm so glad you found it! Your Grandmother Tovslosky was a wise woman—a prophet some liked to say. The reason I'm here is because one day right before she passed from the earth, she came to me and said, 'Bernice, I'm going home soon.' I told her she was being silly, and she was healthier than I was. She shook her head and said, 'I know what I know.' Then, she asked me to share something with you but not until the tree at the head of the ravine was destroyed. Then, I was to give you a message."

Goosebumps covered Kat's arms and neck. "What did she want you to tell me?"

"An angel of God came to her and told her you were put on this earth to fight. Not to fight man but to fight evil. She burst into tears and begged Almighty God to take this from you. The angel said it was your destiny and could not be undone. The Almighty One wanted her to know, and her to tell you, you do not fight alone. His angels are with you, even now."

Kat's eyes misted over again. "Thanks, Bernice." Kat looked to the ceiling. "Thanks, Gran. I miss you so much."

Bernice patted Kat's hand. "Now, tell me what you've found."

"Oh, right. This is almost the same story of Lilith in the book Josiah got from his priest friend. Except, this story mentions other details, too."

"What does it say?"

"It says Gorgon and the fallen angels are arch enemies. They fight for the same prize."

"Why do two evils fight? It's counterproductive."

"She isn't like the demons. She was a human who became so evil, humans called her a demon. They had no other term for it. The legend talks about a jar." Kat's eyes widened when she read the description. "I know this jar!"

"You've seen it?"

"One like it—right down to 'the color-changing gems melted into the stone' as it says here."

"I see."

"It also talks about a matching casket—like for a dead person?" Kat looked up at Bernice Tellamoot.

Bernice laughed. "No. That is an ancient description of a box used to hold trinkets or jewelry."

"This illustration reminds me of the missing box."

"How does this container come into this?"

"Well, it seems it was made first as a way to imprison this spirit, but the box could not hold Gorgon. It didn't have enough magic." Kat wrinkled her nose. "Magic?"

"We've had crazier things going on here."

"True. Anyway, the jar had stronger magic and it held the spirit—as long as the seal of death was on it. What is a seal of death?"

"Don't know."

"The story says the jar is the only thing which can contain Gorgon's spirit. And Ken has the jar." She picked up her phone.

"What's up?" Ken said.

"The jar is Lilith's prison."

"How do you know?"

"I found it in an old book of Russian legends from Gran Tovslosky."

"A book of fairytales?"

"Guess not all fairytales. It's a prison. You still have it?"

"It was in my office last I checked."

"This book says it's the only way to contain Lilith."

"I'll be finished here shortly. Then, I'll go get the urn. Stay home. Wendy still there?"

"No. She had to take BC to the vet. He's injured, Ken. I'm waiting to hear from Doc Douglas."

"What happened?"

"I think an eagle tried to take him. They were swarming the house earlier.

"I don't want you alone."

"I'm not. Mrs. Tellamoot's here.

"Thank goodness. Talk soon."

Kat looked at Bernice. "Ken has the jar. If this thing is here maybe we can catch…"

"Hello? What's Doc Douglas say?"

"Deep wound but not life-threatening. Says it has all the markings of an eagle talon. The cuts are from BC working himself loose. He said BC would have been a goner if the talons hadn't missed the vital parts."

Thank you, God, Kat thought.

"He's keeping BC overnight."

Kat's elation turned to sadness. "Is it necessary?"

"He's the doctor."

"If he thinks it's the best."

"He also wanted me to tell you to be careful."

"Him, too?"

"Something about when eagles start a feeding frenzy, for lack of a better term, they get fierce. You could end up as collateral damage if you get in the way."

"Got it."

"Hey, Kat, are those eagles still outside?"

Kat walked to the living room window and looked at the sky. "There may be fewer of them now."

"How about we take a drive to the Inlet?"

"I told Ken I'd stay put. Plus Mrs. Tellamoot's here."

"Don't you want to know what has the birds in such a state?"

"I do."

"Well?"

Kat looked at Bernice. "Can you stay for a bit?"

"If you have something to do, I'll be happy to stay and keep an eye on these clowns," Bernice answered.

Kat looked down to see Carnelian mouthing Benny's front paws. Benny had an ear in his jaws and looked up at Kat. "They do seem to be enjoying themselves. Still, I don't want to impose."

"You're not."

"Okay, then. Come and get me, Winsome."

"So where are they?" Wendy looked left, then right.

Kat pointed ahead. "They're up closer to the mouth of the river."

Wendy inched the car over the wet sand. "Glad for all-wheel drive. At least I won't end up like some of our unsuspecting travelers looking for a cheap place to camp."

Ravens and eagles circled high above the river, reminding Kat of a black whirlpool. "People are so thoughtless. Whoever caused this surely didn't care about the danger to others."

"You know we get lots of visitors this time of year, Kat. Most of them don't even know we have bears, much less the hazards associated with a bunch of excited eagles."

Kat jumped out of the car and strode down the beach. "Ignorance is not an excuse. I wish I could get my hands on the no-good jerk who almost killed BC," she yelled into the wind.

Wendy inched alongside. "Get back in. We can drive there."

Kat looked at the myriad of birds. "Good idea."

Wendy rolled forward, avoiding a flock of ravens swooping in to pick at a piece of the prize—a chalky white substance tinged in red.

Kat leaned out the window. "What's blowing in the wind?" she asked Wendy.

"Oh my Lord! It looks like the leg of a pair of jeans, and I think the leg's still in it."

"I've seen more of this phone than I want to see for the next year." Kat hit speed dial.

"Hey, Bart. We got another body," Ken yelled.

Bart took his eyes off a forest-green algae he had been watching creep up the side of the pine log cabin in Old Town. "Who found it?"

"Kat and Wendy."

"Where?"

"The beach."

Bart took the phone. "We'll be right there. Stay put, and DON'T touch anything."

"Hope there's enough left to touch. The birds have done a job," Kat said.

"Just what I wanted to hear."

Kat put the phone on the dashboard. "We wait."

———— ◆•◆◆•◆ ————

Grandma Bricken looped her cane over its hook in the kitchen. "I wish we could have had more luck."

"Melbourne's still not answering his phone." Detective Dayton glared at Grandma Bricken. "Is there anyone who'd know where to find him?"

"I do." Kat breezed through the door and kissed her grandmother on the cheek.

"Where?"

"Last I talked to him, he was on his way to the beach." She turned to Alese Bricken. "I have something I need to ask you."

"Where's the beach?"

"About a fifteen-minute walk from here. Go to Main, take the ravine path until it branches to the west. Take a right, and you're on the beach." Kat took a breath. "Gram, who took the picture in this photo?"

Alese Bricken smiled. "Your Grandmother Tovslosky. Don't you remember?"

Kat shook her head. "I don't."

"What a wonderful day it was! We took you and Bart to the bay. We walked through those abandoned cabins your great-grandfather built, then picnicked on cold chicken and rice that your Gran Tovslosky cooked up just for that trip. The Inlet sparkled in the sun—like someone had thrown a million tiny diamonds onto its waves. We talked all day about the legends and tales of Grandmother Tovslosky's people."

"Wait! Grandmamma didn't want the Russian legends to be overshadowed by the Native ones."

"Correct. Do you remember any of them?"

"Bits and pieces. I dug out a book of Russian fairytales she gave me when I was little. There's a story in the book that I think is the key to this whole mess."

"Excuse me. Are you sure Melbourne's still at the beach?"

"Why the need to talk to Ken?" Kat asked.

"My partner's missing. I need his help."

"I'll find out." Kat dialed. "Ken? Detective Dayton's looking for his partner. He'd like to talk to you. Are you still at the beach?"

"Yes. I'm going to be here for a while. Tell him I'll come by when I'm done."

"Will do."

"Kat, you still there?"

Kat put the phone back to her ear. "I'm here."

Ken scrutinized the shining gold and engraved lettering of the badge Bart had just handed him. "Let me talk to the detective."

Kat put the phone in Dayton's hand. "It's for you."

"Sounds like one of ours, alright. I'll be right there." He turned to Kat. "How do I get to the beach again?"

"Tell you what, I'll walk with you. It'll be faster."

Ken met them before they reached the river's mouth. "I found this." He handed the detective a plastic bag containing a brass-colored medallion.

Dayton's face turned crimson. He shoved the evidence bag back at Ken. "I want to see the corpse." He climbed up a soft hill of sand in the direction of a large white bag.

Ken jogged up to the detective. "It's unrecognizable. The birds did a job on it before we got here."

"I'm a homicide detective, remember?" Dayton marched toward the oversized duffle bag.

"Detective Dayton you shouldn't be here." Doc Billings looked at Ken.

"It's okay, Doc. What'd you find?"

"Male. Liver temperature indicates he's been dead a couple of hours—if that. There is no throat, no heart, and well, the eyes…"

Ken guided Billings away from Dayton. "What about the eyes?"

"In laymen's terms? Purple and black goo."

"How can it be? The holy angels of God threw Iconoclast into the abyss last time!"

Doc raised his eyebrows. "Can't tell you, but I'm sure it's what we are looking at."

"Who is Iconoclast?" Dayton spoke from behind Ken's right shoulder.

"Dayton, this is a private conversation."

"And that may be my partner over there! Who is Iconoclast?"

"You wouldn't believe me if I told you."

"You listen here. If that's my partner and this Iconoclast had something to do with his death, I want him in custody—now."

"Know how you feel. But believe me when I say, traditional police work will not bring this killer to justice."

"Good police work will bring any killer to justice!"

"Detective Dayton, he is not being rude. He's telling the truth," Kat said. "Iconoclast is not human."

Ken's eyes widened. The look said, *You didn't say that to him, did you, Kat?*

"Someone has to say it, Ken. This guy's involved whether we wanted him to be or not. The truth is the truth."

Bart joined the group, peeling a latex glove from his right hand.

Dayton looked at Kat, Ken, then Bart. "They have just confirmed that almost everyone I've met in this town is crazy."

"I overheard. Kat's right. Iconoclast isn't human."

"You, too?"

"Here's what you need to know. There's a body over there oozing purple and black stuff from its eyes. I guarantee you the body's missing a brain. There will be pinpricks at the back of the eyes, once they can get past the purple slime to confirm it. The Anchorage ME will verify this substance is not from Southcentral Alaska—probably not from Alaska at all."

"How can you be so sure?"

"Because Iconoclast has visited Ravens Cove twice in my lifetime. Each time, bodies showed up just like this one. It was not a human who caused it. It was a demon."

Okay, it's official. My career is now finished —in Anchorage and with the FBI. Ken hung his head.

"Had to be said, brother."

"Had to be?"

Doc Billings quietly witnessed the all-too-familiar interchange between Ken and Bart. "Gentlemen, we need to get the body identified. There was nothing other than a badge on him—and a tattoo."

"A tattoo in four inch black letters which says, 'Everybody Worships Something?'" Dayton asked.

"As a matter of fact, yes."

"It was Carson's favorite saying. I think the identity's 100 percent."

"Detective, there's nothing more you can do here. How about you join us at the station?" Ken's voice was full of compassion.

Dayton nodded. "I'd like that. What I'd really like is to have a go at Mandy Thomas. I think she may know why my partner's dead."

"Shouldn't be hard to arrange a meeting—she's occupying our only jail cell in the city."

Chapter 19
True Colors

Mandy jumped off the only piece of furniture in her cell—a steel cot covered by a blue and white mattress. She trotted to the bars. "I told you something bad would happen. But you wouldn't let me make a call."

"Something bad happened alright, little girl, and if you weren't in police custody, I'd arrest you for murder." The vein in Dayton's neck bulged, and his mouth went tight.

"You can see Detective Dayton thinks you killed his partner."

"His partner? I didn't kill any..." A light dawned in Mandy's eyes. "The guy at Grady's house with you?"

"That is correct."

Mandy ran to the toilet and threw up. She rinsed her mouth under the faucet in the stainless steel basin. "Sorry, I'm better now."

"You seem a little too upset to have only seen him once. Who was he to you, Mandy?" Ken asked.

"He was my contact. The one I needed to call last night."

Dayton yanked on the cell door. "You lying little witch." He whirled on Ken.

"Give me the key."

"No. You'll do something we'll both regret."

"Why do you think I didn't tell you before? Who'd have believed me?"

"Carson Watermill wouldn't have done anything to break the law!"

Mandy gripped the bars. "Let me tell you about your partner. He was one of Grady Spawldine's favorite clients! And I was one of Carson's favorite tricks!"

Mandy skittered out of reach right before Dayton seized her fingers. "You're gonna wish you'd never been born."

"If you can't take the truth, you should leave." Mandy breezed toward the wall and plopped onto the cot.

"You are a real piece of work, Mandy. I didn't know anyone could disgust me as much as you do right now. Thank heavens Wendy isn't here." Kat turned her back to the bars.

"Go get her, would you? I'm just itching to tell Miss Know-It-All what I think of her. Maybe then she'll finally keep her big nose out of my life! In fact, you can just tell her I wish she were dead! My life was great until she dug her claws back into me."

"You call being in prison a great life, Amanda?" Bart's voice broke with emotion.

"You are such a sap. You think I ever cared about you? No. Once you were of no use to me, I was gone. Or didn't you notice?"

"I noticed."

Ken broke in. "Mandy, let me see if I can help you understand what's happening here. You've been used. There are forces at work which cannot be explained in rational terms. Believe me when I say, you've helped orchestrate the release of a living nightmare. No one is safe. Not even you. These things walk through walls just like you and I do through air. Save your own miserable hide, and give us some information."

Kat walked up to the bars. "The man died in a gruesome way, Mandy. If you have any humanity left in you, help us."

"There's nothing you could do or say to make me help you."

"If you won't help us. Maybe you'll give us the information to help yourself. How about a little show and tell?" Ken held an eight-by-ten photo to the bars. "You want to end up like this?"

Mandy's cold eyes swept the photo. She turned her head to the wall. "The shock factor doesn't work on me. If it didn't work after I looked at my dead boyfriend, why do you think I'd care about another gruesome picture? Dead is dead."

"This one's different. Look closer. Then tell me dead is dead."

Mandy smirked and pulled the picture through the bars. "What happened to his eyes?" She focused on the mouth frozen in an eternal scream. She threw her hands over her ears.

"Dead isn't always just dead," Ken said.

"Who is he?"

Dayton's eyes narrowed to threatening slits. "A good man until you got your claws into him."

"Carson?"

"What's left of him," Ken said. "But, I'm sure he's still around. The souls of victims like him seem to hang comfortably in the Cove."

"And they like to visit old friends." Kat remembered Josiah being in this same jail cell and visited by a couple of twins who had been a scourge of the Cove until they lost their lives to Iconoclast.

Mandy paled. "Why would he want to visit me?"

"Well, I don't have a clue. But I'm sure he has something to say. So how about letting me know what he wanted you to get here."

"A box and the key that locked it."

"A key like the one on the dog's collar?"

"The nasty thing. It almost bit me when I tried to get its collar off. That's when I threw it into the street—right in front of an oncoming truck. Stupid sap hit the brakes and the dog took off toward the ravine. I should have drowned it when I had a chance."

"I'd like to take a chunk out of your hide myself. You're the most evil person I've ever met." Kat strode to the wall across from the cell.

"Whatever. Anyway, Carson found out the woman here had brought a Russian-style box with her. He told me the box was a family heirloom and they'd been looking for it for hundreds of years. He contacted her and asked if she'd send a picture of it to him online. She did. He told me to come back to the Cove and get it."

"And how did Spawldine figure into this?"

"Carson had some kind of a cult thing going—worshipped some woman. He was one of Carson's 'followers.' And he had the statue, of course. Still, he started asking too many questions and, well, became a liability. So, Carson turned him into an asset, and he was my way to the Cove. You're all saps." She spat.

"Mandy, you played into the hands of a murderer. Who's the sap?"

Mandy stared into space, as if a daydream had just taken control of her mind. Her eyes darted from left to right, then she let out a shrieking giggle. "I can't change what's happened. Don't know if I'd want to, either. Bye." She crawled backwards on the bunk and turned to the wall.

Kat shook her head and said to Ken, "she wasn't always like this."

"What happened to her?"

"Don't know."

"Pastor Paul's the closest thing we have to a counselor. Maybe he can help her."

"I don't think she wants to be helped."

Ken cupped Kat's chin in his hand. "No one is beyond hope."

"I've seen more of this woman's personality than I ever cared to," Dayton said. "I know it's hard for you to believe because she was your friend. Still, Amanda Thomas is like all the other sociopaths I've seen. No conscience, no love for anyone but herself, and will do anything to get what she wants."

"You are probably right, detective. No matter what her personality type, this is going to break her big sister's heart."

Bart took Kat's arms and turned her to face him. "You can't share any of this with Wendy. It's still an investigation."

"She needs to know, Bart."

"She does, but not until we can get this settled."

"I don't know how to avoid the conversation."

"Yes, you do. You can tell her we are holding Mandy for now, and she can visit her in jail. That's all."

"Okay."

The ting-a-ling of the station's door announced a visitor. Kat pushed through the metal door.

Horace Stoddard raced through the reception gate. "Every building in Old Town is bleeding."

Ken strolled to Kat's desk. "Say again?"

"I said those buildings are bleeding. Amos Thralling was walking back home from the river and saw balls of light hanging over Old Town, and told me all the buildings were covered in a dark red paint. I didn't believe him, so I went and looked myself. It's dark red alright, but it's not paint. There's a thick red liquid oozing from the roof and running down the walls. If that's not enough, there's ochre-yellow balls of fire hanging over every building."

Dayton shook his head. "I'll say it again. This town is under some kind of mass hallucination."

"You can call it what you like, Dayton. We just call it another day in the Cove."

"Where is Pet?" Iconoclast's roar shook the mansion's attic.

"I am not his keeper," Atramentous replied.

"If you want to stay in this world, you'll find him, and find him now!"

"I'm right here." A birch-bark snowshoe, with purple and black sinews dissolved into a black mist. The small demon walked through the veil and stood facing Iconoclast.

"Why do you test me so?"

Pet rolled himself into a black and purple ball. "Because I can," he hummed.

Iconoclast grasped the small ornament and turned to his captains. "Pet has done more in my absence to prepare for battle than any of you. Explain it to me."

Pet buzzed with pride. "Yes, explain it to him."

"He has proven himself worthy." Atramentous growled.

A misty cyclone blew into the attic. Bruitt bowed, "The girl was easy. A few whispers and her hatred peaked. She is alone and vulnerable."

"Then why are you here? Take her completely."

Bruit bowed again and shot through the roof.

"Find the Gorgon," Iconoclast spat at Atramentous.

"The rest of you bring me that troublesome clan of Kumrande."
Hurricane force winds from the demons' wings forced the crimson
drips on the attic walls to the ceiling.

Iconoclast uncurled his fist. "While they find the Kumrande, you
and I will scour the deep forest and find the old hag."

"Oh, a hag hunt! How fun!"

"It is not all about fun and mischief, Pet. Will you ever learn?"

"I hope not. Why else would I cause the mayhem I do?"

"If you did not serve the purpose you do, I would send you to the
abyss myself and chain you there."

Pet hummed a mean tune. "How are the great ones?"

"Other than me?"

"Of course, you are the second greatest in our realm. But the others?"

"They are tormented and gnaw for release. It is what we are doing here."

"You are here only to contain Gorgon!"

"I am here to contain Gorgon, and I will. Then I will take what is
mine and release my brothers." Iconoclast soared to the small cabin
and walked through the wall. A circular ball floated in the fireplace.
"Show yourself now."

"I am Madame Piquant." The ball of light danced to the floor beside
a hollowed-out bowl of birch wood and a cane topped by a silver wolf's
head. The shining orb dissolved. A young blonde stood before Iconoclast.

"Who commands me to show myself?" She picked up the cane and
leveled it at Iconoclast. Red light shot from the wolf's eyes.

Iconoclast caught the scarlet light and rolled it into a ball. He
hurled the sphere back at the spirit.

Ivy June Coistrell burst into flames.

"I am your master! Bow before me."

The ghost crumpled to the ground.

"Much better." Iconoclast pushed the cane into the fireplace.

"What do you want of me?" she seethed into the floorboards.

"I want to know where Gorgon resides."

"She does not tell me her living place. She only commands I follow
her. And I follow *her* willingly."

Iconoclast pushed his foot into Ivy June's back and forced her face against the floor. A red bolt of lightning arched above the spirit and then plummeted into her core.

The hag writhed in the unearthly flames. "I hate you," she spat.

"As you should." Iconoclast pressed the razor-sharp toenail into her spine.

The spirit screamed, "Forgive me!"

"Now, who do you serve?"

"You. You are my master," she answered.

Iconoclast lifted his foot. "If I could take your pain and feed on it I would, you putrid spirit. But it has already been done. Now where is Gorgon?"

"She resides in a place no one can find her. She has forbidden any of her followers to look for her. I tell the truth!"

"Call the others to you. Now."

A deathly shriek escaped the spirit's lips. Grady Spawldine dropped through the ceiling, a jagged-edged dagger in his hand.

"Do not attack him. He is from the one over all hell."

"I don't care who you are, I answer to Gorgon." Grady lunged. The knife pulled free from Grady's hand, spun in the air, and blasted through his semitransparent body. Spawldine fell to the ground.

"If you do not do as I say, I can make sure you relive this pain throughout eternity."

"You are the one about whom Gorgon speaks!" Grady said.

"I am also the one who took your grandmother's soul and sent her to your side while you lay dying."

Grady trembled at the memory of his last moments as a human. His grandmother appeared to him and pressed her hand into his chest, smiling the evil smile she had been so famous for in her lifetime. "You are dead, Graduate Spawldine," she had said before he drifted into blackness.

He had awoken sometime later, hungry. An insatiable hunger which could not be satisfied.

"If eternal pain doesn't concern you, then I can bring your grandmother here to feast on your measly energy. Tell me where Gorgon resides."

"I do not know."

"I do not believe you." Light jumped from Iconoclast's fingers and surrounded the man. It became small daggers of red and dug into the silhouette from all directions. His shrieks filled the air.

Carson Watermill shot downward through the roof.

"Glad you could join us. Bind them." Pet threw purple and black tendrils outward and caught them in the sticky ropes.

Spawldine shrieked curses at Iconoclast. Iconoclast moved a hand. A black and red web sewed itself to his lips.

Iconoclast whirled on Carson Watermill. "You released the Gorgon."

"She was part of my heritage."

"She was part of your curse, you fool! Now you are mine forever. Because you have been given to me, you obey me. Where is she?"

"I am only yours for now. She will destroy you."

"She will try."

"Where is she?"

"At the bridge—a few feet from where you took my life."

"Okay, so Amos and Horace weren't exaggerating." Ken took in the buildings of Old Town. A sticky brown liquid streamed down the walls of the mansion, cannery, and cabin. Once on the ground, it inched into quartz courtyard.

"I could have gone a lifetime without seeing those things glowing again." Bart pointed to the shimmering eyes of the rusty-brown skull.

"I accept it. We are never destined for a normal life." Ken said aloud—to God more than those around him.

"What do you consider normal?" Josiah asked.

"Some are called to fight the good fight, Kenneth. Why do you think you were so drawn to law enforcement?" Grandma Bricken asked.

"You do not need to be here—I do not need you here. Go home," Bart scolded.

"We are called here."

"Me too." Paul joined them.

"What's going on? How did all of you get here so fast?" Detective Dayton asked.

"Funny thing about Ravens Cove. When it's under attack, certain people become psychic—for lack of a better term."

"Psychic?" Dayton replied.

"Only seems to happen when we are in a spiritual battle. Most of the time, the town's pretty normal—and quiet."

"A spiritual battle?"

"I know I sound crazy. If you have the gumption, stick around. It's going to get interesting and possibly deadly before this is over."

"It's already been deadly."

"You haven't seen anything yet." Bart thought back on the bodies he had seen at Old Town before they were taken by God's angels and buried.

"The battle is not to be here," Josiah said. "There is an old bridge. It is close to the mouth of the river."

"You're kidding right? It won't hold a mosquito, much less a person."

Alese Bricken smacked her cane into the sidewalk. "We both received a vision of a battle at the footbridge."

"So did I," Paul added.

Bart brought his hands to his face. *Make this stop. Old people and battles. Why my town?*

"What better place than your town?" Josiah responded.

"You have got to stop doing that." It shook Bart to his core when Josiah answered unspoken thoughts.

Kat jogged up to Bart. "Thank God I found you! Mandy's lost it! She's in the corner of the cell babbling and pulling out clumps of her hair." Kat looked at the bleeding buildings. "Oh, not good."

"Understatement," Dayton said.

"No kidding." She turned back to Bart and Ken. "She's spewing obscenities and calling God's Holy Spirit horrible things."

Paul looked Kat in the eye. "She's what?"

"You heard me. I don't want to repeat her exact words."

"And you should never. I'm going to the station." Paul turned and walked off.

"He shouldn't be alone," Ken said.

Bart sighed, "Guess we are all going to the station."

Paul heard the shrieking and name calling from the street. He yanked open the door, and took long steps toward the jail cell.

"Whoa, Pastor. This could get messy. It's not for you to handle."

"Who is it for—you Bart—or Ken?" He gave them a hard, fire-filled look.

"It is for you, Pastor. And I'm coming with you." Josiah came up beside him.

"You may want to stay here, Detective Dayton." Kat looked at him with concern. "This is where it can get dangerous—for your soul as much as your body."

"I'm here for the ride, and I mean all of it."

"So be it." Alese Bricken took his arm. "Come, open your heart and mind to the world of the unseen."

Mandy Thomas sat cross-legged under the cell's lone window. The room was black.

"What happened to the lights?"

"I don't like them." Mandy answered. She turned on Kat. "Have you come to hear more of the truth, putrid woman?"

"I've brought help."

Mandy roared like a lion. "You've brought food?" She looked at Paul. "Get him out of here."

"I will not be leaving."

The dark metal cot strained against the rods that held it to the floor. The bolts groaned and released the bed's legs. It levitated to the ceiling and flew into the bars. "Get out!" Mandy yelled.

"I will do no such thing. Whoever you are, in the name of Jesus show yourself."

"I do not have to obey you." It was Mandy's voice. "I have another master now."

Mandy stood up, walked to the toilet, yanked the lid from the porcelain, and threw it at the bars.

Paul glimpsed a black mass hovering at Mandy's right hand. "Dark spirit, what is your name?"

Mandy faced the pastor. She moved her mouth but the words came from behind her. "You do not command me."

"I serve the One who does. In the name of Jesus, give me your name, and tell me why you are here!"

An inky silhouette stepped out from behind Mandy. "I am called Bruit. I was sent to take this mortal. It is done!"

"I call on the name of Jesus again. Be gone from here!"

"She is still mine." The mist evaporated.

Mandy glided to front of the cell. "Why are you here, and why did you banish my friend?"

"He was not your friend."

Dayton leaned over to Bart. "Did you just see a shadow talk?"

"I did. You aren't crazy."

"But good luck trying to get your superiors to believe you," Ken chimed in.

"I see why you are having so much trouble in the Bureau."

"Glad to know someone in my realm does."

"You drove my friend from here! I want him back! GET OUT!" Mandy bellowed a string of obscenities at Paul.

Kat covered her ears. "I've never heard anything like this. Mandy, stop!"

"Can't take the truth, goody two-shoes? Well it's time you learned the truth about your God." Mandy launched into a horrifying tirade.

Tears poured down Paul's face. "You have blasphemed against the Spirit of God, Amanda Thomas. There is no redemption for you." He broke into sobs.

"What do you mean?" Wendy ran up to the cubicle.

"You shouldn't be here," Bart said.

"Kat said I could visit. That's what I'm here to do. Now, what do you mean no redemp …."

"Oh, Wendy, thank the stars you are here." Mandy hurried to the cell bars. "They are treating me terribly. Look." She pulled her hair back and showed Wendy a large bruise on the side of her head.

Wendy turned to Kat. "What happened here?" she demanded.

"No one has touched her," Kat took Wendy's arm.

Wendy jerked free. "Then how did the bruise get there?"

"And look at my arm." An angry red scratch coursed from her elbow to the wrist. "They held me down and hit me when I asked to see a lawyer."

"Liar!" Alese Bricken's voice boomed in the darkness.

"I'm the liar? No, you are the liars. They can't be trusted, Wendy. Please get me out of here."

"Kat?" Wendy turned confused eyes to her friend.

"No one touched her, Wendy. Look at her eyes. Tell me she's the Mandy we used to know."

Wendy walked to the bars. Mandy turned her back.

"Turn around, Mandy."

"No."

"Turn around so I can see your eyes."

"I'm your sister—you should believe me and not them!"

"I'm trying to."

"You'd believe me without proof if you really were my sister." Mandy strode to the cell door, vaulted to the ceiling, took hold of the bars, and yanked. The steel rod creaked and bent to the rear.

"Does your sister normally have such strength?" Josiah asked Wendy.

Wendy shook her head. Tears streamed down her cheeks. "No. I need to get her to a hospital. She's obviously had a nervous breakdown."

Alese put her arm around Wendy's shoulder. "You make the call, sweet one. It would be best if she is made as comfortable as possible."

"She's so sick." Wendy walked over to the wall phone. She said a few things into the receiver then hung up. "Doc Billings is coming right over."

"A good idea," Paul said, shaking his head in defeat. "There is nothing I can do to help her now. She'll live her life on earth crazed and tormented."

"Why?"

"There is only one sin God does not forgive. Blasphemy against the Holy Spirit."

At the mention of God's Spirit, Mandy shook the cell door and screamed obscenities at the small troop.

Doc Billings arrived and observed Mandy's behavior for several minutes. He left and returned with a syringe. "I'll give her a tranquilizer. It's all I can do for her until we can transport her to Clayton for evaluation." He held the syringe in the air and headed to the jail cell.

Mandy ran for the wall. "Don't touch me!"

Billings looked at Ken and Bart. "I'll need you to hold her."

They went into the cell, and she lunged at them. She almost made it through the door before Kat yanked it shut. "Man, she's fast."

"What's happened to her? She was fine earlier," Wendy cried.

Kat shook her head. "I don't know, Wendy. Maybe the hospital can get us some answers."

Paul opened the cell door and walked through before Kat could stop him. "No!"

Mandy skittered backward, pointing at the bible in Paul's hand. "Get away from me with your book!"

"In the mighty name of Jesus, you are bound, Amanda Thomas." Paul's somber tone sent shockwaves of sadness through the group of witnesses.

Mandy's body went limp.

"You should have no more trouble." Paul walked out of the cell.

Billings took tentative steps forward. He stuck the needle in her arm. Mandy's eyes closed, and she fell into a troubled sleep.

"I'll call Clayton and get the transport here as fast as I can. Sorry shame. She used to be a bright, happy girl." Billings walked to the front office.

"I'm going with her, Doc."

"I'll come, too," Kat said.

"No, Kat. I need to do this alone—just me and my sister."

Kat dropped her head. "I'm so sorry, Wendy. I shouldn't have left her alone."

Wendy threw her arms around Kat. "I don't blame you! I just want to do this alone."

"Are you sure?"

A wistful grin crossed Wendy's lips. "Really sure."

"Ambulance is here," Doc Billings called out.

"I'll call you later, KittyKat." Wendy blew Kat a kiss and took Mandy's hand.

"I still should have been here," Kat whispered.

"You were there for her, Kat. No one can stop a friend or loved one from making frightful decisions," Paul said.

"I know. I sure wish I could, though."

"She was another casualty in this horrible war for our souls," Josiah whispered.

"At the risk of sounding insensitive—and I have been accused of that—there's still a bunch of buildings covered in weird stuff that should be dealt with. Don't you think?" Dayton said.

"The town is only a symptom of a bigger problem. Whatever waits at the bridge is the answer," Grandma said.

"Now that's a new look for this pile of wood." Bart surveyed the bridge's strong mahogany-brown boards arched across the fast-moving river.

"It looks like someone just built it." Dayton remarked.

"Looks are deceiving in the Cove. I wouldn't try crossing it," Bart answered.

The sun dipped behind the western mountains. A blanket of darkness floated over the bridge.

"Somebody bring a flashlight?" Bart quipped.

The water under the bridge started to glow.

"Not exactly what I had in mind, but it works."

Kat pointed at a chrome orange beam beneath the rippling liquid. "What's causing the lightshow? Did someone throw some searchlights in the river?"

"Not sure." Ken moved forward to get a closer look.

The glowing light drifted up and floated above the fast-moving water.

"That thing is defying gravity," Dayton said.

"Yes, it is," Kat answered.

"Who comes to worship me?" A melodic voice called out. "Come, I will make you immortal."

"I have to get a closer look." Ken walked forward.

"Me, too," Bart said.

Kat watched the pale orange beam. It puffed up like an overfilled balloon and burst, sending tiny light shards into the waters below. A mummified body with lifeless eyes floated into the middle of the river.

Kat yelled, "Ken, Bart! Come back. It's Lilith."

Ken bumped Grandma with an elbow and kept moving.

Alese caught Ken's hand. Paul took hold of his shirt.

"Bart, no!" Josiah grasped Bart's utility belt. Bart unsnapped the clasp and continued on.

Kat ran forward and planted her feet in front of Bart. "Stop, cousin."

"Don't you see how beautiful she is? She has to be an angel," he whispered and pushed her to the side.

"Tell me what you see?" Paul asked Ken.

"She looks just like the statue except more beautiful. Let me go. I want to go talk to her." Ken yanked free.

"Ken, Bart, please stop!" Kat screamed.

"I'll be right back. Just want to talk to her. Can't you see she's an angel?" Ken answered.

"What is wrong with those men?" Dayton said.

"Dayton? Don't you want to go down and see the lady in the water?"

"Why would I want to go down and see that ugly thing? I'm thinking we should all run away from here as fast as we can."

"I agree. But why isn't it having any effect on you?" Kat asked again.

"Lucky, I guess."

"What are you holding?"

Dayton opened his hand. A gold chain was laced through a miniature vial filled with blue-green fluid. It glowed with a light of its own.

"A necklace?"

"A gift from my crazy aunt when I moved to Alaska. She made me promise to wear it. Said it would keep me safe. I promised. Had it in my pocket because of this stupid wound on my neck."

"Some kind of magic amulet?"

"A trinket she picked up on one of her trips around the world. Said it was blessed by a priest. She's a staunch Catholic."

263

"Maybe your aunt wasn't so crazy. You're immune to Lilith."

"Ken, stop!"

Kat's head snapped toward Josiah's voice. She looked on in despair as Ken walked trancelike into the water.

Josiah followed him to the rocks lining the riverbank.

A cream-toned box with glowing gems of indigo blue bumped Ken's ankle. He scooped it out of the river.

"I'll take that." The sound of creaking leather closed in on Ken. The trance broke, and he ducked. A clawed hand jerked the box from Ken's hand. The heavy wings whooshed skyward. The dark giant hovered above the trees. "I will settle my score with you at a later time. Atramentous, come!"

A strong wind bent the trees like grass. Atramentous hovered next to Iconoclast.

A small brass key appeared in Iconoclast's hand. He pushed it into the keyhole of the box. The blazing jewels sparked and turned coal-black. Iconoclast thrust the rectangle into Atramentous's distorted hand. "Take this, and bury it where it cannot be found."

Atramentous rocketed into the sky.

The Gorgon dissolved into a ball of light and floated toward the dark woods.

"You're freedom is forbidden," Iconoclast's voice thundered after the sphere. A jeweled urn appeared in Iconoclast's left hand. His wings snapped to his side, and he plummeted toward the light.

"You will not contain me again!" Lilith screeched.

"Your followers have been given to me. So it ends! You go back to your prison, Gorgon who was once called Lilith.

The entity shrieked and rushed to meet Iconoclast in the air. She took her human form right before she plunged sharp fangs into the sinews of Iconoclast's neck.

Iconoclast seized the stringy tendrils of hair and yanked the hag's head backwards. The hag went limp.

The jar's lid levitated away from the base. Iconoclast raised Gorgon above his head and swung her in a circle. She moved faster and faster until she turned into a dark mist.

"By the power of hell, you are bound." An invisible vacuum sucked the mist into the jar. The lid settled over the base. A blood-red seal formed in the air and snaked around the edge of the jar. Iconoclast winged into the night sky. The flap of hundreds of wings faded until there was only silence.

"What happened? My head is killing me." Ken looked at Kat.

Kat threw her arms around him and held on tight. "I thought I'd lost you for sure!"

"Does anyone know why I'm here when Old Town's bleeding?" Bart joined the group rubbing the back of his head.

Kat laughed and dragged Bart into a hug. "You two almost became Lilith's significant others."

Bart pulled back. "Not in a million years."

Dayton slapped him on the back. "She's telling you the truth. I saw it with my own eyes. You'd be another body in the morgue if some giant with wings hadn't stepped in."

Bart turned to Kat. "Iconoclast?"

"The very same."

"If he's on the loose, our troubles are far from over," Ken said.

"I'm ready to finish this." Kat jogged ahead.

"Hey, wait! This is not the time to be without me," Ken yelled after her.

Kat stopped to catch her breath and wait for the others.

"Katrina Tovslosky?"

Kat turned and faced a tall, bronze-skinned man. She searched the man's golden eyes. "Do I know you?"

The man smiled."Do you?"

"You look familiar. Besides, how else would you know my name?"

"It is a mystery which will become clear. I have been asked to give you a message."

Kat backed up. "From who?"

"Do not be afraid. I will not harm you."

"I've had enough mysterious communications for a lifetime! So, if you don't mind, I'm in a hurry. Whatever you need to say to me can just wait." Kat waved him to the side.

The man stepped off the path and called after Kat. "You are favored. You have seen how the Holy One can use all things for His good and the good of those who love Him. He wants you to be a witness at the old town—nothing more."

"I'll keep it in mind." She gave the stranger a salute and walked toward Ravens Cove.

Ken jogged up beside her. "Who were you talking to?"

"Didn't you see him?" She turned and pointed to the path behind her. "Where'd he go?"

"Who?"

"Some guy who said he was delivering a message from God."

"Well, at least he was a part of the good-guy team. Let's get to Old Town."

Gray mist gave way to deep fog at the edge of Old Town. The buildings peeked out from the parting mist and were swallowed again.

"Well, those orbs of light are gone. That's a good thing," Bart said. "I'd feel great if the rest of this place were normal."

The log cabin was enveloped in black and green algae. The windows were completely obscured. The mansion sagged at the roofline, its five spires leaning into the dip—like laser guns from some old science fiction movie.

"That does not do anything for my security level." Bart pointed out a group of Kumrande gathered around the rust-brown skull rock. Three semi-transparent people—one woman and two men—joined the Kumrande.

Ken squinted through the chain-link fence. "Isn't that Ivy June Coistrell?"

"I think it is," Kat said.

"What do you think that means?" Bart pointed to the five spires on the mansion's roof. The points had turned and bent toward the roof's center.

Ken rubbed his face and watched the five spires wind around each other until they became a chain. The bulk of wood moved itself until its point lined up with the skull-rock.

"I think we should back up." Ken yanked Kat away from the chain-link fence.

"Who's over there?" Kat pointed to someone standing between the rock and the mansion.

Bart's eyes followed Kat's finger. "I've never seen him, but we need to get him out of there before he becomes the Kumrande's main course." He ran for the fence.

Ken sprinted to Bart's side and shook the gate. "How did this get locked?"

"Look down. There is no lock." Bart laced his fingers through the fence and yanked it hard. The gate creaked and held its position.

The Kumrande stopped moving and looked at the gate, then in the direction of the mansion. They trotted toward the man.

Bart jerked the gate back and forth in a rapid motion. "GET OUT OF THERE!" Bart yelled.

The man smiled. When he spoke, his voice reminded Kat of rolling thunder. It carried high above the *clippity-clops* of the Kumrande's hoof beats against the quartz courtyard. "Watch, Katrina Tovslosky. You are a witness."

"It's the guy I met on the path. You got to get him out of there," Kat yelled.

Ken yanked harder on the gate. "Hey, whoever you are, get out of there now!"

The giant of a man waved, then lifted his hands above his head, then threw them toward the ground. The old wood groaned. Two spires broke away from the main trunk and took the shape of a cross.

An electric tendril jumped out of the center of the cross. The blue light strengthened and blasted into the skull-rock. Crystalline light filled the boulder and poured out from the eyes and beak. It shook violently, then exploded. Jagged blue stones showered down on Old Town. The stones transformed into thousands of comets with fiery white tails.

The Kumrande shouted and turned to the forest. The fire targeted the cloven-hoofed beings. They burst into flames as the blazing stones hit their mark. Piles of ashes lay where the Kumrande had just stood. More fiery missiles landed on the ghosts of Ivy June Coistrell, Grady Spawldine, and Carson Watermill. The pebbles of fire showered down on the buildings of Old Town. The ancient buildings went up like the dry tender they were. The blue flames blazed against the night sky. The fire engulfed Old Town—then died out as quickly as it had started. A westerly wind blew the puffs of white smoke away from the town. Ashes and a quartz courtyard covered in soot were the only sign it had ever existed.

"Where'd he go?" Kat searched the ashes. Her eyes stopped on a bronze-toned being standing in the courtyard. She watched it streak into the heavens like a shooting star.

"I did know you," she breathed, remembering the kind voice of the angel who stepped into her path so long ago at the ravine. "You saved me then, too." She smiled and waved at the sky.

Bart walked up beside Kat. "Who was that masked man?"

"My guardian angel."

"Sure seemed awful normal for an angel," Dayton said. "Where'd he go anyway?"

Kat pointed to the sky.

Dayton let out a heavy sigh. "Of course he did."

The rest of the group broke into loud laughter.

"Where's Iconoclast?" Ken asked.

"I wish we could leave the question unanswered," Bart responded.

"He's free, so why didn't he come after us instead of the apparition?"

"Just as good has many aspects, so does evil. Like the threads of a tapestry only God can bring together," Dayton murmured.

All eyes turned on the detective.

"Just something my mother used to tell me."

"My guess is Iconoclast vacated before the town was destroyed. But where are they?"

"I think he left for another of his earthly dwellings. If so, we are free of him for the time being."

"Goodbye, and good riddance is what I say."

"And if he returns, we will be ready for him," Grandma Bricken said.

"We will?"

"Has God ever failed us?"

"No."

"Then, we will be ready for him and any attack he plans—if he returns. He is no fool. Since he can no longer deceive us, why would he come back?" Kat said.

"We shall see, child of my heart."

Ken felt a small tug on his pant leg. "Where'd you come from?" He bent over and picked up Carnelian. She gave him a lick on the face and looked at the ruins of Old Town.

BC wound around Kat's legs. "How'd you get away from Doctor Douglas?" She scooped him into her arms.

"That'd be on the vet's orders," Doc Douglas said. "The leg's healing nicely. No need to keep him any longer."

Douglas pointed at Kat's arm. "Glad to see your arm's about well, too."

"We Tovslosky's have always been fast healers."

Carnelian barked up at Kat. "What?"

Carnelian sat down and stared at BC.

"Just for a minute." She leaned over. BC pushed his head into Carnelian's and purred.

"Well, I'd say you definitely are a blended family." Grandma smiled at Kat and Ken, then the animals who had such peace with each other.

"The only thing left to do is make it legal." Ken looked at Kat.

Kat smiled. "And I'm ready."

Ken leaned closer. "Say it again."

"Name the time, name the place. I'm ready—are you?"

"You bet I am!"

"I'm available anytime." Paul smiled at the two of them.

"And the party can be at my house." Grandma chimed in.

"Nope. Wendy has the reception planned, and I'm going to make sure she does it." Kat thought of her friend and the horror she must be feeling right now because of Mandy's illness.

She pulled out her phone and dialed. "How you doing, Winsome?"

"Not so good. Mandy died on the way to the hospital."

"What? How?"

"Seems she had a brain hemorrhage. They think it's why she acted so badly before she died. It was a small bleed at first."

"I should have helped her!" Kat lamented.

"No, they said no one could. When she started acting oddly, the thing had started bleeding. No one could have helped her."

"Are you coming home?"

"Turn around."

Kat turned. Wendy walked to her, tears streaming down her face.

Kat did what her grandmother had done so many times. She gathered her friend into her arms and let her sob until she couldn't anymore.

"I know she wasn't my sister for a long time, but I had always hoped."

"As well you should have. How about we find Bernice? She always knows what to say to you."

Wendy smiled. "She does have a way with me. Besides, I could use petting the Benny dog."

BC growled.

"Sorry I said the B word. It's a good thing the meeting will take place without BC present."

"Definitely."

Epilogue
When the Cove Calls

Bernice Tellamoot arrived and whisked Wendy away. Benny had jumped out of the car and run to Doc Douglas for a pet.

"No treats in the pocket, golden eyes." Doc patted him on the head. Benny trotted back to Mrs. Tellamoot.

"She'll be fine. Bernice will listen just like her momma used to." Grandma Bricken told Kat.

"Yes. She will."

"So, about the wedding?" Ken asked Kat.

"What about it? You staying in the Cove long enough to plan one?"

"I'm staying."

"What about your boss?"

Ken turned to Bart. "What do you think?"

Kat slapped Ken on the arm. "I meant your real boss—FBI guy Binnings."

"I resigned. Just didn't get a chance to tell you with everything going on."

Kat locked eyes with Ken. "No kidding."

"No kidding." Ken put a hand around Kat's waist and pulled her close. "So about the wedding?"

She grinned. "Told you. Just name the day and time, FBI. I'll be there."

Carnelian yipped at Ken and wagged her tail. "We've got a built-in flower girl."

"So, I have to put up with your meddlesome body in the Cove all the time?" Kat asked.

"You bet you do."

"Don't mean to interrupt a good time, but is there a way to get me back to Anchorage?"

"Our police chief would be happy to escort you to Anchorage," Bart said.

"So much for staying in the Cove." Kat crossed her arms and glared at Bart.

"I'll be back in a day."

"You better be."

Ken pulled Kat into his arms and kissed her head. "We've got a date to set. I'm not letting anything get in the way."

"How about you go with him? Keep him out of trouble, child," Grandma said.

"Who's going to take care of the children?" Kat smiled down at Carnelian and BC.

"Douglas boards for a minimal fee," Bart answered.

"Then, I'm gone."

"I hope to never see this place again," Dayton commented.

Ken slapped Dayton on the back. "This place grows on you, Detective. You'll be back."

"Not in a month of Sundays."

"Let's get you to Anchorage and see how long it takes to see you again."

Alese Bricken watched as Kat, Ken and Dayton walked down Main.

"He will be back won't he?" Josiah said.

"Oh, yes. And I can hardly wait to see how he's going to react when he does." Alese smiled. "I've seen so many come to Ravens Cove and leave. Then there were those who came to the Cove, and it wouldn't let them leave."

"And you think this place has called to Dayton?"

"Oh, yes. He doesn't know it, but the Cove is beckoning him home. He'll answer." Alese took Josiah's hand. "Let's get you some of the coffee you like so much."

The End

www.ingramcontent.com/pod-product-compliance
Lightning Source LLC
Chambersburg PA
CBHW051541260626
47170CB00003B/1038

* 9 7 8 1 5 9 4 3 3 4 1 9 1 *